MARIANNA BAER

frost

BALZER + BRAY
An Imprint of HarperCollins*Publishers*

For my mother, with love

Balzer + Bray is an imprint of HarperCollins Publishers.

Frost
Copyright © 2011 by Marianna Baer
All rights reserved. Printed in the United States of America.
No part of this book may be used or reproduced in any manner whatso-
ever without written permission except in the case of brief quotations
embodied in critical articles and reviews. For information address
HarperCollins Children's Books, a division of HarperCollins Publishers,
10 East 53rd Street, New York, NY 10022.
www.epicreads.com

Library of Congress Cataloging-in-Publication Data is available.
ISBN 978-0-06-179949-5

Typography by Sarah Hoy
11 12 13 14 15 LP/RRDB 10 9 8 7 6 5 4 3 2 1
❖
First Edition

part one

1

BEFORE I LIVED THERE, before any of this happened, I imagined
Frost House as a sanctuary. It crouches on the northern edge
of Barcroft Academy in a tangle of lilac and evergreen bushes,
shadowed by oaks and sugar maples. Hidden enough that I
didn't even know it existed until junior year, when I chased a
field hockey ball through the underbrush into its backyard. I
assumed the white-clapboard cottage was a faculty member's
house. Most Barcroft dorms are three-story brick buildings;
this was a weathered old Victorian, small and squat, with a
wraparound porch and a mansard roof hugging the second
floor. The kind of place a family would live. The first time I
saw it, I could almost hear a whispered call mingling with the
soft rattle of leaves: *Come inside, come inside. . . .*

When I realized that the house was actually a tiny dorm, that my friends and I could *be* that family for our final semesters, I knew I'd discovered our school's very own Shangri-La. I couldn't escape the reality of senior year at ultracompetitive Barcroft, but at least my home life could be a fantasy.

Over the summer I kept thinking what good luck it was I'd stumbled upon Frost House that day. If I'd believed in anything more mystical than textbook facts back then, I might have wondered if it had been fate. I have no idea, now, if fate exists. But I do know one thing about the day I found Frost House:

Good luck had nothing to do with it.

The afternoon we moved in, a late-August storm turned the surrounding leaves into a rain-whipped, electric-green frenzy. Frost House waited in their midst. A little old lady.

"Isn't she sweet?" I said to Abby as I eased my car up the narrow driveway, branches scraping the windows on either side of us.

"Sweet?" Abby said. "Maybe a couple hundred years ago."

"Haven't you ever heard of shabby chic?" I turned off the engine of my equally ancient Volvo station wagon. The windshield wipers died; Frost House melted into a blur. Abby and I glanced back at the carful of stuff we had to unload.

"Let's register first," I said. "I'll just check if Viv is here, in case she wants to ride over with us." I also couldn't wait to see my room. I'd been picturing how to decorate it for weeks—my nightly fall-asleep ritual on the pullout couch at my dad's.

Shielding myself with an armload of cotton tapestries, I splashed up a brick path to the side door. Unlocked, luckily. I stood in the snug entryway, smelled the fresh paint fumes, and wiped the rain off my glasses. Music—The Black Keys—pulsed in the humid air. I called Viv's name up the staircase in front of me, then realized the bass vibrations were coming from a suite of rooms on the ground floor, tucked in the rear. Strange. Abby's and Viv's bedrooms were upstairs. I was the only one living back there for the next few months.

I passed through the common room—pausing to appreciate the glistening, milk-white walls; the comfortable couch and armchair; the mini-fridge and microwave—and down a short hall, music getting louder with every step: *Let me be your everlasting light*. . . . On the right, my bedroom door gaped wide. Cardboard boxes, duffels, and garbage bags littered the floor. Piles of colorful clothes covered one of the beds, which was made up with a silky violet quilt and sunshine yellow pillows.

Classic Viv. She'd obviously mixed up our room assignments.

Sensing movement on the other side of an open closet door, I laid my tapestries on the second, unmade bed. The pounding bass line camouflaged my footsteps as I crept around boxes and bags toward my unsuspecting housemate. I waited for a moment in a spot where we still couldn't see each other, only the thickness of the door between us now, and then sprang—

"Boo!"

"Jesus!" A guy spun around. Something fell from his raised hands. I reached out, caught it. *Owww.* A sharp corner of the poster-sized frame had stabbed my palm.

"What the hell?" The guy—dark hair; olive, freckled skin; about my age—took the frame from me and set it on the floor. "Are you crazy?"

"Sorry," I said, my palm throbbing but not cut. "I thought you were—"

"Wait a minute." He edged past me and turned off the speakers. The air took a second to recover. "Thought I was what?" he said. "In need of a heart attack?"

For a moment, I couldn't tell if he was kidding or not. Then he smiled, brows raised above his heavy-lidded, intensely blue eyes. Whoever he was, he didn't go to school here. I'd have noticed.

"No," I said. "Thought you were someone else." *Duh, Leena.*

Now he laughed and rested his hands on his hips. "I figured. I'm Celeste's brother. David. I transferred to Barcroft this year."

Celeste. I knew only one—Celeste Lazar, the eccentric art star of our senior class. After he said it, I recognized the delicate lines of her face mirrored more roughly in his: wide forehead, curved cheekbones, firm chin. His nose was more prominent than hers—high-bridged, Roman.

"Oh. Cool," I said as if he'd explained anything pertinent. "I'm Leena. And, unless I *am* crazy, this is my room."

David's smile faltered.

"Don't feel bad," I said quickly. "The campus is confusing. I can drive your stuff to the right dorm."

"They didn't tell you?" he said.

"Tell me what?"

"Man, I can't believe they didn't tell you." He ran his hand through his short hair and shifted his weight to his other foot. "Celeste broke her leg."

"Oh? That sucks." A cold tingle began in my fingertips. There could be no happy reason I needed to know this.

"Yeah, her room was supposed to be on the third floor of some other dorm. So they decided that since your roommate is away for the semester, and your room is on the ground floor . . ."

The blood drained to my feet. "So Celeste is living here?" I said, sitting on the closest bed.

"Well, yeah. For one semester. But it's not like they're kicking you out."

I nodded and concentrated on an acid-green, zebra-striped silk dress lying next to me. How could I have thought this stuff belonged to Viv? Or to a guy?

"Try to contain your excitement," David said.

"I'm just surprised." I forced myself to look at him and attempted a smile. "Where is she?"

"She had a thing at the hospital today. She'll be here tomorrow. It's a bad break. Really messed up the bone."

"What happened?"

He hesitated. "She fell off the roof."

"God." An image of Celeste crumpled on the ground flashed in my mind.

"Trying to get one of these birds' nests she's been collecting," David explained, answering my unspoken question. He didn't sound quite sure about it, though, and I wondered if there was more to the story. Knowing Celeste, there probably was.

A muffled ringtone came from over by the door. "Speak of the devil," he said. "She can always tell when I'm talking about her." He pulled a cell out of a backpack and disappeared into the hallway. "Hey. Everything okay?" was the only thing I heard before his footsteps receded into the common room.

I stared out a window. Branches drooped and swayed under the heavy rain.

Celeste Lazar. Living here.

A vise squeezed my chest. The same feeling I'd gotten before every chem lab last year, only tighter.

We'd been partners. The mood of the period depended entirely on what was going on in Celeste's life that week—always a new, convoluted drama: a fight, a hookup, trouble with a teacher. . . . I'd spend the seventy-five minutes listening to her stories while trying to keep her distraction from causing some sort of fiery accident with the Bunsen burner and chemicals. To make it worse, I was never sure what Celeste actually thought of me. One day, she brought me a gift to thank me for advice I'd given her: a chocolate-chili cupcake from the best bakery downtown. As we walked out of class, me happily holding the box with my exotic treat inside, I asked about her plans for the weekend. "None of your damn business," she'd snapped. Just like that, I'd become some random, nosy stranger.

And now we were roommates? I'd chosen Frost House to *escape* any drama.

Leaves swam together in my watery vision, melding into a solid plane.

A crash shook the silence.

I turned. The print David had leaned next to the closet had tipped over. I moved from the bed and picked it up. It was framed with Plexiglas, so hadn't broken. I studied the image for the first time: a close-up of Celeste's face—a self-portrait, I assumed. She was lying in dirt, eyes glassy, lips slightly parted, hair fanned out. A beetle—a big beetle—wrapped in and trailing a thin white satin ribbon walked across her forehead. The ribbon wound its way down and into Celeste's mouth.

Ugh. I rested the frame back on the floor, leaning it so the image faced the wall.

Before I could move away, though, a chill reached out from the mostly empty walk-in closet. It felt good on my hot cheeks. Not harsh and spiky, like air-conditioning, but soft, as if the door led to a deep, cool basement. I took a step inside the shadowy space, lifted my hair and let the chill skim the back of my neck, closed my eyes and breathed in. A fragrant scent—woody, musky, fermented—filled my lungs. In a strange way, the scent appealed to me, warmed me inside as the cool air stroked my skin. I imagined stepping further into the darkness and closing the door, leaving behind this unexpected new reality.

"Did something break?" David said.

I let my hair fall. "No." I faced him and placed a hand on the closet's doorframe. "This is mine."

"What?"

"This closet. It's mine. Not your sister's." The words shot out, sharp and unplanned.

David frowned slightly. "The other closet's across the hall. With Celeste's leg, I figured she should have this one."

I scanned the room, even though I knew he was right. "Oh. Sorry," I said, taking my hand off. "I forgot this was the only one in here."

What had possessed me to be so rude? "Of course she should have it," I added.

As I said it, though, a word echoed in my head. *Mine*.

2

I HURRIED TO THE CAR and slid into the driver's seat, rainwater beading around me on the crackled pleather upholstery. Abby had turned the rearview mirror to face her. She stared up at it and flicked a mascara brush across her lashes. Her warped copy of the play *Buried Child* lay spread-eagled on the dash.

"What took you so long?" she asked, glancing over at me. "I ran through all of my lines while you were in there."

"Can you grab an ibuprofen from the glove compartment?" I massaged the bridge of my nose.

"What? More shabby than chic?"

"No." I waited until she handed me the orange tablet, washed it down with a swig of flat soda followed by a cherry

Life Saver, and told her about the addition to our Frost House family.

"Hold on," she said. "Celeste is Green Beret Girl, right?"

I nodded.

"Isn't she completely nuts? She's the one who burned all José's clothes last year!"

"Not all his clothes," I said, remembering the story that had been the talk of campus for a few days. "Just his boxers."

"Whatever." Abby waved her hand dismissively. "And, you know, it doesn't even matter if she's crazy. They can't just give you a random roommate senior year. It's not right."

I turned on the engine. As the windshield wipers brought Frost House back into focus, an elongated shape moved past a downstairs window. David, I assumed. I rubbed the almost invisible mark on my palm. He probably thought I was a selfish jerk after that closet incident. But I couldn't help having been unnerved by his news. The administration shouldn't just go around changing rooming assignments.

Like Abby said, it wasn't right.

Before backing into the road, I readjusted the rearview mirror. I met my own gaze, and my eyes stared back with a controlled confidence the rest of my body didn't feel.

"I'll talk to Dean Shepherd," I said. Then, in a stronger voice, "I'm sure she'll understand."

The registration room in Grove Hall swarmed with people. I hugged, kissed, and how-was-your-summered my way to the

R–Z line at the check-in table. "Our last first-day-of-Barcroft ever," Whip Windham said as we waited for our information packets, echoing the predictable, clichéd thought I'd been having ever since I woke up that morning.

"I know," I said. "I'm trying not to be maudlin. We still have a whole year."

"Dude." Whip raised one eyebrow—his signature look. "I meant it as a good thing. A friggin' awesome thing."

Oh. Of course.

Sometimes I forgot that most people were actually anxious to graduate. I understood the feeling in general, but didn't quite get their "good riddance" fervor. While there were things about Barcroft I was sure none of us would miss—curfew, off-campus restrictions, tofu schnitzel at the dining hall—most of us would go to college, so it's not like we'd be free of classes or teachers or Sisyphean mountains of homework.

Maybe, I thought as I stared at the sunburned back of Whip's neck, maybe the difference between me and him was how ingrained I felt here. My parents had just gotten a divorce when I arrived in ninth grade. And although they liked to say it was amicable—neither of them had cheated and they'd used a mediator instead of lawyers—it had hit our lives like a wrecking ball. I'd had to build a new life; Barcroft was the foundation. Of course I was worried about leaving.

"Leena Thomas," I said when I reached the guy handing

out manila envelopes. I took mine and slid out the multi-colored sheets of paper. My housing assignment form had a note in familiar, flowing handwriting: *Hello, L! Please call or stop by and see me ASAP. Looking forward, NS.*

NS—Nancy Shepherd: Dean of Students, faculty advisor to the peer-counseling program I'd started, my mentor. I'd been looking forward to seeing her, too. I wanted to hear about her summer camping trip, which had involved an encounter with a "feroshus beer," according to my postcard from her seven-year-old daughter, who I babysat during the school year.

Now, though, instead of asking about that (Budweiser? Corona?), I had to start the semester by bothering her about Celeste.

Shaking off the thought, I slipped my registration papers back in the envelope, stood up straighter, and searched the crowd for Abby's walnut-brown curls. A shriek rattled my eardrums.

"Leena-bo-beena!" Vivian Parker-White loped toward me, all long limbs and flowery skirt and skin tanned from weeks in Greece.

"I've missed you!" I said, my smile buried in a rain-wet mass of coconut shampoo smell as we hugged.

"No," she said, "*I've* missed *you!*" I squeezed even tighter, trying to make up for months of only virtual communication. Boarding school had spoiled me—I was used to having my friends around me all the time.

14

As Viv and I broke away from our hug, Abby material-ized next to us. She bounced up and down. "Can we show now, since we're all together? We don't have to wait till we're back at the dorm, do we?"

"I almost forgot," I said. "Here, though?" A couple of sophomore boys stood right next to us. One of them grinned when our eyes met, as if he knew I was considering unbut-toning my cutoffs.

"No chance," Viv said. "Mine's not for public viewing."

"Come on." Abby grabbed our hands. She pulled us through the registration room, into a black granite hallway, and down a set of polished concrete stairs, chattering about her horrible class schedule and the "Green Beret disaster."

"It's not a disaster," I said, wishing she hadn't mentioned it. I'd go see the dean in a bit. Now, I just wanted to enjoy this moment, wanted to see if my guesses were right—an Aries symbol for Viv, and a butterfly for Abby. At the end of last semester, we'd made a pact to get tattoos over the sum-mer and had forbidden further discussion about it until the moment of revelation.

Abby pushed open the door to the girls' bathroom.

"Who goes first?" Viv asked.

"Me," Abby said.

Doing a mock striptease move, she lowered the right strap of her tank top. Two hollow-eyed faces stared up from her shoulder blade. A comedy/tragedy drama-mask thing. One face smiling, one frowning, the expressions exaggerated almost to the point of dementia.

"Ooh, I love it," I said. "Really well drawn."

"Exdese," Viv agreed, using the dorky word for excellent we'd made up freshman year. "And very appropriate, of course."

"It'll be even more appropriate if you become bipolar," I pointed out.

"Ha, ha." Abby flicked me on the arm. "Who's next?"

Viv turned around and lifted up her skirt. Smack in the middle of the left cheek of her thong-clad butt was a heraldic crest: black and red, with fleur-de-lis designs around a knight's helmet and a stag's head.

"Wow," I said. "That's . . . amazing. It's so elaborate."

"Oh my God," Abby said. "It's the Parker family crest! Isn't it? The one you showed me online?"

Viv turned back around. "Yup. Isn't it funky? It's thanks to Orin."

"Your astrologer—sorry, your *advisor*," I corrected myself, "told you to get your family crest tattooed on your butt?"

"No, of course not," Viv said. "He told me I should incorporate my family history into my identity."

Abby covered her mouth; a snort escaped her nose.

"It's an important part of my being," Viv added.

I made the mistake of looking into Abby's glimmering brown eyes, and we lost it.

I shook with laughter until my cheek muscles ached. It was perfect. The Parker-Whites are a bizarre hybrid of old money aristocracy (Parker) and new-age bohemianism (White). Their psychic "advisor" is practically a full-time employee.

Eventually, the bathroom filled with wheezes and deep breaths as Abby and I struggled to compose ourselves. Viv waited, arms crossed.

She leaned back against a sink. "Laugh all you want. But Orin said something else, too. Something not so good."

"What?" I said, bracing myself for another absurdity.

Before she could continue, the bathroom door swished open and three of our dorm-mates from junior year bustled in.

"I heard about your new roommate, Leena," Jessica Liu said as the other two went into stalls. "That should be entertaining."

"You heard? How?" I didn't like that. Other people knowing made it seem more like a done deal.

"My brother went to school with her brother. They were on the phone yesterday and her brother asked to talk to me. He wanted to make sure she wasn't rooming with some psycho."

"Hah!" Abby said. "That's rich."

"What did you tell him?" I asked Jess.

"The truth. That Celeste was in serious danger."

"Thanks." I gave her a sarcastic smile. "Anyway, I'm not sure if it's going to work out for her to live with us. Dean Shepherd wants to meet. Speaking of which . . ." I checked my watch. "She won't be in her office much longer. I should get going."

"Leen, we're not done!" Abby said.

"We'll finish later, okay?" I gripped the chilly metal door handle. "I need to deal with this."

3

ALTHOUGH THE RAIN HAD STOPPED, the humid air still clung to me like a full-body sweater as I hurried past the stately brick buildings of the main quad on my way to Irving Hall. Barcroft is one of the oldest boarding schools in the country, and while the newer buildings are flashy and modern, the central campus is quintessential New England prep school.

Marcia, the dean's assistant, said I'd have to wait a few minutes. I sat on a leather chair and rearranged the legs of my cutoffs to separate my clammy skin from the slick surface, then took out my packet and thumbed through my registration materials. Black type floated into abstract designs as I silently rehearsed my conversation with the dean.

Until now, I hadn't given much thought to the fact that it would have been her decision to move Celeste to Frost House. But sitting here, I couldn't understand it, given how well Dean Shepherd knew the situation. How well she knew *me*.

After answering a posting on the job board freshman year, I'd started babysitting her daughter on Sunday afternoons while the dean was with her husband, who was in hospice with terminal cancer. We kept the arrangement after he died, as well. Sometimes I stayed to help with dinner and ended up eating with her and Anya. I think she was happy to have someone to distract her from stuff with her husband, and I loved listening to her talk about books and music and places she'd lived and traveled. Growing up as an only child, I'd spent a lot of time with my parents and their friends; she reminded me of one of them.

Probably some kids at Barcroft thought I was a suck-up, hanging out with the Dean of Students. But I didn't ask her for any special treatment. Until Frost House, of course.

I called her the day I discovered it last fall. "I saw the most amazing house all hidden in the bushes," I said, words rushing out. "And I peeked in the windows and I think it might be a dorm. Is it? Because it would be the most perfect place to live for senior year. All quiet and separate, kind of like living off campus, away from the frenzy. And if it is a dorm, how many—"

"Slow down," she'd said. "Describe it for me."

20

"Off Highland Street, by the playing fields. White clap-board, Victorian."

I could have described it down to the fish-scale pattern of the shingles on the roof. My father restores old houses and my mother is a realtor, so I grew up learning all about colonials and Victorians, gables and lintels and cornices. From the moment I saw the little house, I'd felt a weirdly intense desire to live there. As if it was the answer to a question I didn't even know I'd been asking. I'd wandered around all four sides, appreciating its architectural quirks and fantasizing: *warm evenings hanging out on the porch; reading, curled up in a window seat.* . . .

"Off Highland Street?" the dean had said. "That's Frost House. A four-student dorm. Reserved for senior boys."

"Boys?" I hadn't considered that possibility.

My reluctant acceptance of this news lasted less than twenty-four hours, during which I kept going back to Frost House in my mind. The next day, I couldn't resist an urge—a pull—to visit again in person. As I stood there, staring up like I was lovesick for one of the guys inside, I struggled with what to do. I wanted to call the dean back, wanted to see if there was any chance it might be switched to a girls' dorm for the next year. But it seemed like such a big favor. While I debated, a slender column of smoke rose from the chimney and curled into the blue sky. A working fireplace? In a dorm? I took my phone out of my bag and called.

I told her honestly how worried I was about the stress of

senior year, and how much difference living in a small dorm would make. I told her that boys didn't appreciate window seats and wraparound porches. She laughed.

"Even if we could switch it to a girls' dorm," the dean said, "you'd still have to go through the housing lottery. There's no guarantee you'd be the girls who get to live there."

"I know," I said, watching the smoke from the chimney dance away. "But if it's a boys' dorm, we won't even have a chance."

"Well," she said after a moment. "It *is* only a matter of four students. Let's see what we can do."

And now she'd moved Celeste in, without even telling me?

I took a deep breath and tried to concentrate on the blue paper that listed my class schedule: Molecular Biology, Gender Relations in America, Calculus—

"Leena?" The dean's voice made me look up. She was standing in the door to her office, smiling warmly.

"Welcome back," she said, beckoning me to her. "Come on in."

Dean Shepherd closed the office door behind us and drew me into a hug. "It's wonderful to see you," she said. "You look healthy, rested, all those good things."

"Thanks. You too." Her ash-blond hair had been cut pixie-short, bringing out her bright hazel irises.

She patted the chair next to her desk. "How was your

summer? You survived the twins?"

"Barely," I said, sitting. I was indescribably thankful my stint at all-day babysitting for five-year-old twin boys was over. "But it paid really well. So thanks again for recommending me. How's Anya?"

"Great. She can't wait to see you." The dean's smile lingered, but not in her eyes. "I want to talk more about everything later, Leena. There's another reason I wanted to see you now. Not to catch up."

"I know."

"Oh." She nodded once. "I'm so sorry you didn't hear it from me first. I left a message with your father for you to call me yesterday, when we made the decision."

"He must have forgotten," I said, unsurprised. It did make me feel a little better to know she'd tried to get in touch with me, though.

"It's my fault," she said. "I should have called again. Celeste is just one of the crises I've had to deal with this week."

"I feel bad for her, of course," I said. "But, the thing is, it's only me, Viv, and Abby in Frost House, and I'm wondering if she might feel uncomfortable, living with a group of friends. Not that we wouldn't be nice to her. Just . . . it might be awkward. Do you know if . . . if there might be another first-floor room open somewhere?"

From the slightest intake of her lips, I could tell this wasn't what the dean wanted to hear. A pang of guilt twitched in my gut. "Maybe one of the dorms in the middle of campus," I added. "More convenient."

"There were a couple of other rooms we could have moved her to," she said. "But I talked it over with faculty who know Celeste, and we all felt that Frost House was the best option."

"Really? Can I ask why?" There were other rooms—that was good news.

She placed her palms together and interlocked her fingers. "Between us, there's been some difficulty with Celeste's family over the past year. We think it's best if she's in a small, quiet dorm. More like a home."

With Celeste there, it wasn't a home anymore. Homes are for families, not strangers. And our family was set—Viv, the caretaking mother; me, the problem-solving, fix-it father; Abby, the impatient, excitable kid. Where would Celeste fit in?

"I just don't picture the two of us as roommates," I said.

"I know, Leena. But Ed Roper told me you got along beautifully as lab partners in his class last year. One of the things we all appreciate about you is your ability to get along with different people. Frankly, I didn't feel comfortable with the other possible roommate matchups."

Her eyes held mine. I saw admiration in them, but also expectation. The vise tightened around my chest again.

A knock came at the door.

"Yes?" Dean Shepherd said.

While the dean had a conversation with Marcia, I

scanned the paper-strewn surface of her desk. Two thick manila files sat by a Lymphoma Society mug. Handwritten tabs read *Celeste P. Lazar* and *David M. Lazar.*

I never wanted to be a thick file.

"Of course," Dean Shepherd said, once we were alone again, "if you have any serious objections, I'll rethink the other options. The last thing I want is to make you unhappy. And I know how much you've been looking forward to Frost House."

Even though she knew that, she was counting on me to agree to this. For some reason, she thought Celeste needed Frost House, and I trusted Dean Shepherd. Could I do this for her?

"Just this one semester, right?" I said. "When Kate comes back from Moscow, she'll be able to move in?"

"Definitely. Kate will be your roommate this spring, as planned. Celeste's cast will be off by then."

"What if it's not? Or what if she wants to stay?"

"Leena." The dean smiled. "You have my word that Kate will be your roommate in Frost House next semester. No matter what happens with Celeste."

I looked down at my hands, pale and veiny. White and blue. Like porcelain, I'd been told. I curled them into fists.

"Okay," I said. "I'm sure it will be fine."

Sometimes I wonder what would have happened if I'd taken that resolve and told Dean Shepherd I wanted Celeste moved somewhere else. Would things have turned out differently in the end?

For Celeste, yes, of course. But for me?

I still would have lived in Frost House, after all.

4

WITH ONLY TWENTY MINUTES before dinner, I couldn't bring myself to put on all my clothes after cold-showering. I stood in front of a fan, wearing boy shorts and a bra, trying to figure out the best furniture arrangement for my side of the bedroom.

The room extends off the back of Frost House—almost more of a sunporch. Three of the walls have windows that look out on the postcard-size backyard bordered by thick foliage. Even on a gray day like this the room glowed with natural light. Along with the original moldings around the windows and the worn wooden floorboards, the light made the space especially cozy and cheerful. Welcoming.

It was even nicer than I'd remembered over the summer. But, of course, the furniture setup and decorations I'd planned weren't possible now that it was a double. *Look on the bright side,* I told myself. Celeste's bedspread and pillows were pretty, and her hat collection looked funky lined up on a bookcase. It could have been worse. She could have been a fan of cliché posters like *Starry Night* and *The Kiss.*

David had placed a bunch of persimmon-orange tulips in a painted ceramic vase on top of her dresser. He'd also put three tulips on *my* dresser, in a water bottle. I couldn't believe he'd thought of that, considering everything else he had to do. And considering how rude I'd been to him.

A framed snapshot sat next to Celeste's vase. I stepped over and picked it up. David stood between Celeste and a stocky man I assumed must be their father, an arm around each of them, on a white-sand-turquoise-ocean beach. Celeste was laughing—beautiful, as usual; David had a goofy look—eyebrows raised and mouth in an O, like he was faking surprise. He was shirtless. My gaze momentarily got stuck on the muscles that led from his hips into his low-slung trunks. Other than his average height, I hadn't noticed much about his body during our disastrous meeting. Looking at the picture, I could tell he was built like the soccer guys—slim and cut.

On David's left, Mr. Lazar was much rounder and his face appeared to be in motion. The slight blur kept me from recognizing any features he shared with his kids. What sort of "difficulties" had the family had this past year? Mrs. Lazar wasn't in the photo. Maybe they'd gotten divorced. I'd spent enough time with Celeste that I would have known if one of her parents had died.

I set the photo back down. Next to the dresser, the closet door stood open just enough to show the Mardi Gras effect of Celeste's wardrobe.

Out of curiosity, I opened the door wider. The closet air—still cooler than the rest of the room, despite all the clothes—reached out and brushed across my skin again, bringing with it that same pungent scent. A pleasant shiver ran through me. Probably the smell was from the door having been sealed tight during the heat of the summer. Or maybe a liquid—wine, cologne—spilled in there once, permanently soaking into the wood. It reminded me of something . . . or somewhere. I held the scent in my mind and tried to remember, but couldn't come up with anything more concrete than a vague emotion. One you feel in your chest, not your gut. Contentment, maybe.

As it had earlier, the combination of the cool air and the smell made me wish that I could close myself up in there. Avoid this altogether.

I ran my fingers over the clothing crowded together on the hanging bar: a poufy red satin skirt, a geometric-patterned wrap dress, a lapis-blue sari—the antithesis of my own unofficial prep-school uniform of various jeans (straight leg, cutoffs, and minis), T-shirts, and hoodies. My hand came to rest on a familiar fuchsia-and-gold, gauzy fabric. I recognized the skirt Celeste had worn the first day of chemistry class last year.

She had sashayed into the lab wearing this long, narrow skirt with extra fabric gathered at the rear, like a bustle from the 1880s made modern. I'd guessed that it was either some very expensive designer thing, or that she'd made it herself. She hadn't gotten it at J.Crew. On top, she wore a plain white undershirt. No bra. She didn't need one, but still.

When we were put together as lab partners, I told her how cool the skirt was.

"It hides my nonexistent ass," Celeste had said. Her wide, disconcerting eyes scanned me up and down before she added, "You're lucky. You don't have that problem."

"Thanks," I'd murmured, not sure whether "screw off" would have been a more appropriate response.

Now, I took the skirt out of the closet, searched along the waistband, and couldn't find a label. Maybe it *was* hand-made. On a whim, I undid the hidden zipper on the side, then stepped in, wondering what it felt like to wear it. I wriggled the fabric up until it hesitated at my thighs. I was much curvier than Celeste, but the material had some stretch in it. I wriggled some more.

The skirt squeezed over my hips. I didn't bother with the zipper. Soft fabric hugged my bare legs as I took tiny steps toward my full-length mirror. How had Celeste managed to sashay in this?

"Leen?" Abby's voice called. The *thwak-thwak* of her flip-flops sounded from the hall. "Ready for dinner?"

"Not quite," I called back.

She appeared in the doorway. "Whoa, Nelly."

"What do you think?" I did an awkward 360-degree turn.

"I think you better be careful living with her doesn't drag you over to the dark side."

"I lived with you for a year and emerged unscathed."

"Touché." She sat on my bed, amidst the bags I hadn't unpacked yet. "Viv and I are starving. Are you wearing that to Commons?"

"Yeah, right." I eased the skirt back down. "Let me just—" A tiny ripping sound froze my movements.

"Oops," Abby said.

I slid it the rest of the way off and double-checked the fabric all over, holding my breath. "Seems fine. Thank God," I said. I started to walk toward the closet, anxious to get the skirt out of my hands.

"Hey," Abby said. "Your tattoo!"

I stopped and twisted around to look at my low back. A geometric flower grew there, a little larger than a silver dollar. Thick black lines surrounded ruby, sapphire, and emerald petals. I got a shock every time I saw it, like I'd inhabited someone else's body.

"It's like stained glass," she continued. "Really pretty."

"Thanks. It's of this window in my bedroom in Cambridge."

"At your dad's?"

"No. My old room. Before we moved."

I turned my attention back to the skirt, clipping it onto

the hanger and hanging it up in the exact spot it had been before. I felt an immediate sense of relief.

"I shouldn't have done that," I said, shutting the closet behind me and leaning against the door.

"What?"

"Tried on her skirt. Or looked through her stuff at all. Here I am, worried about what kind of roommate she'll be, and I'm totally invading her privacy."

"It's not a big deal," Abby said. "And if Celeste thinks you're a bad roommate, maybe she'll move out." She raised her eyebrows.

No—I didn't want it to be like that. I'd agreed to the arrangement, after all. Being a bitch wouldn't help anything. And, despite my fleeting urges, neither would disappearing into the depths of the closet. I wasn't Lucy Pevensie and this wasn't a magic wardrobe.

"Give me two minutes to get dressed," I said. "I'll meet you out front."

I rummaged through my bags until I found a denim mini and my favorite navy-and-white-striped tee, quickly put them on, and sat on my bed to do the buckles on my sandals.

Across the room, I noticed that the closet hadn't stayed shut. The latch must not have caught, even though I'd leaned against the door. It had eased open to show a strip of inviting darkness.

As if it was telling me I could always change my mind.

5

"I'm going to find Cam," Viv called. She headed out of the food-service area into upper left, our favorite of the four dining rooms in Commons, where Cameron, her boyfriend, was saving us a table.

"Behind you," Abby called back.

I took a minute to pick a Granny Smith apple from the fruit bowl and followed in their direction.

At the entrance to the dining room, a lone guy with dark hair and a soccer player's build stood holding a tray, his back to me. David Lazar. Damn. Could I slip past unnoticed? Did I want to? He turned his head, side to side, shifted his weight from foot to foot, the way he had when he'd told me about Celeste. Of course, the view in front of him was a sea of unknown faces.

"Need a place to sit?" I asked, stepping up beside him.

He glanced over. "Leena, hey," he said. "Thanks, but I'm pretty wiped. Probably wouldn't be great company."

So why hadn't he just taken an empty seat? Maybe, despite the tulip gesture, he didn't want to eat with *me*.

"Sorry I was rude at the dorm," I said, adjusting the dishes on my tray so it was more balanced. "If you want to sit alone, that's cool. But I'm with the rest of Frost House, if you're curious to meet them."

He tilted his head slightly. "They're not going to hide under the table and jump out at me, are they?" he said.

I laughed. "No. I think you're safe."

We started into the room. I scanned it quickly until I spotted Viv and Abby at a table by the tea-and-coffee station.

Commons is one of Barcroft's older buildings. It has a grand, Gothic feel—high, arched windows, paneled walls, massive chandeliers, and dangerously slippery marble floors. It took serious concentration to walk, hold my tray, and say hi to everyone I passed whom I hadn't seen yet since being back at school, especially since I was conscious of David watching me from behind.

As we neared the table, Abby's eyes were round, like I was bringing a gift-wrapped box with her name on it. The neckline of her tank top had dipped mysteriously lower.

"So," she said to David, after he and I had sat down and I'd introduced everyone, "your first meal here and you

34

already found the best dining room."

"Did I?" he said. "Celeste mentioned this is the one she usually eats in."

"Yeah, she would," Abby said.

"Why's that?" David asked. I thought I heard an edge in his voice.

"Upper left tends to have more artsy types." Abby gestured at students around us, as if they were all splattered with oil paint. "Although, Leena and Viv aren't artsy, so it's not a given. Jocks and more conservative types tend toward upper right. But some of the football guys are in *here* tonight, so that's not a given either. The lower halls tend to have underclassmen and more nondescripts. Kind of a mishmash. Anyway, this is where you should look for us first. We're usually here. Except when we're not." She grinned.

"Valuable information," he said, smiling back.

A tall, auburn-haired girl I recognized but didn't know stopped at the table. "David, right?" she said. "We met earlier? At registration? I just wanted to say that if you're interested in the Ride Club, you should totally come talk to me about it. My name's Cora."

"Thanks so much," David said. "I will."

After Cora floated away, Abby pointed a carrot stick in her direction and said to David, "*That's* why you're going to want to find us at meals."

"Uh, why?" he said.

"You're such a rarity," she explained. "A new guy who's

not fourteen years old. You're going to need our protection from the swarming hoards."

"Should I carry a Taser or something?" he said, pretending to be alarmed.

"Oh, definitely." More grinning.

I took a bite of thick, buttered bread and swallowed past my immature jealousy of the obvious spark between Abby and David. Also, I hoped Abby was just flirting, that she wasn't considering him as a possibility. Gorgeous as he was, we were living with his sister. It could get messy if one of us hooked up with him and it didn't go well. Although maybe I didn't have to worry about that with Abby. She didn't have the fiascos I did when it came to guys.

"Cam?" I said. "You go on Ride Club trips sometimes, don't you?"

"Yep," Cameron said, peeling a banana. "Usually the overnights." He and Viv had been together since freshman year. They were noticeable around campus since, after a late growth spurt, Viv towered five inches taller than him. They hated when people called them cute; but, well, they *were*. "You bike for fun?" he asked David. "Or are you trying out for the team?"

"For fun," David said, "and transportation."

"Are you an artist, like your sister?" Abby asked.

He shook his head and took a sip of lemonade.

"I bet you're a . . ." She rested her fingertips on her temples, pretending to be psychic. "A musician. You play guitar."

"Nope," he said. "Tone-deaf."

There was a brief silence. I think we were all expecting David to say what he *did* do, what activity/talent/passion he'd be emphasizing on his college apps. He didn't say anything, though, just ate a couple of black olives off his salad.

"Will you guys help me with my peer-counseling presentation for the new students tonight?" I asked Viv and Abby. "I'm already nervous."

"You'll be amazing," Viv said. She looked at David. "Leena started this whole program where students are trained to counsel other students about stuff, for kids who'd rather not go to psych services. It's been really successful." She said this so proudly. I squirmed in my seat, embarrassed.

"Other schools have similar programs," I said. "It's not that big a deal."

"Celeste told me about it," David said. "And I noticed your thing on the orientation schedule."

"We're excited to have her in the dorm," Abby said. David didn't respond so she added, "Your sister."

"Oh," he said. "Uh-huh."

"Are you guys twins?" she asked. "Or are you a junior?"

"A senior, but I'm a year older." He paused. "I took last year off."

"Ahh—an older man . . ." Abby's voice was kiddingly suggestive. "What'd you do?"

David pushed his rigatoni marinara around his plate. "Different things." His energy had shifted. Maybe he really was tired, like he'd said, and not in the mood to be grilled.

"Abby?" I said. "Can you pass the salt? And the pepper, too?"

She pulled a Plastic Man to reach the shakers but didn't switch her focus. "Did you travel?" she asked him.

"Not really. A week in Costa Rica."

"If you did anything interesting, you should be on Viv's show."

"Definitely," Viv said. "Cam and I host a WBAR show on Tuesday nights. We play music, but we also have guests on to talk about whatever. You could talk about what you did last year, why you're at Barcroft now, what sign you are . . . you know, stuff. It's fun."

David laid a napkin over his pasta, as if covering a corpse. Blots of red seeped through the thin, white paper. "How's this?" he said. "I had to leave school—Pembroke— because they busted me for cheating. At the same time, my dad's mental illness got really bad and I didn't want him to have to live in a group facility, so I moved home to help my mother take care of him. But I guess I didn't do a very good job because he decided the government had sent me there to poison him. Barcroft took into account the extenuating circumstances, and the fact that I got really good grades at Pembroke, and let me in. Any questions?"

The sounds of other diners' conversations, laughter, and utensils clanking against their plates seemed to swell around us as we sat there staring at our food. I struggled to come up with the right words. A schizophrenic father. God.

Unfortunately, Abby spoke first. "You might want to put a different spin on that for the radio show," she said.

I knew she was hoping to lighten the moment, but she just sounded harsh.

David didn't look up.

The meal ended quickly. On my way out of the dining hall, I stopped to put my tray—minus silverware and uneaten apple—on the kitchen conveyor belt. David placed his after mine.

"Sorry," he said. "Long day. I should have sat alone."

"It wasn't you." I plunked my utensils in the designated bin of murky dishwater, trying not to let any splash on us. "They meant well, though."

We followed the flow of students into the hallway and down marble stairs that were smoothed unevenly by years of footsteps. I let Viv and Abby go on ahead, instead keeping pace with David.

Outside, he said, "I have my ride," and gestured to the bike rack at the north end of Commons. I was walking the same general direction, so I drifted next to him.

"Is, um, is your father okay?" I asked as he squatted by a blue road bike. He'd obviously gotten sick of answering questions. Still, I couldn't leave it hanging like that.

"Depends what you mean by okay," he said, undoing the chunky padlock. "He's alive. Living in a facility, for now."

"I think it's amazing that you took care of him," I said. "Schizophrenia must be so . . . scary."

"He's actually not schizophrenic. Something similar."

"Oh. The one . . . what's it called . . . with mood-disorder symptoms?" I asked.

David stood up, massively thick chain in his hands, brows drawing together. "Schizoaffective," he said. "Yeah. Do you know someone—?"

"No, no. I took Intro Psych last year."

"Oh." He wrapped and fastened the chain around his waist. I couldn't believe he could bike with it on. "Well, yeah. It's scary. In lots of ways."

I watched the late sun stream orange through plum-colored clouds. Probably one of the reasons it was scary was because it has a genetic component. The things I didn't want to inherit from my parents—selfishness, undependability— were things that were under my control, not predetermined, but I still worried about them. This was a whole different story.

"When is Celeste getting here tomorrow?" I asked as David backed his bike away from the rack.

"Not sure yet. You know . . . what Abby said in there . . ." He stopped and met my eyes. "You guys don't have to pretend you're happy to live with her. I know you're not, and I don't blame you. You had this nice, private thing going on."

Even though he didn't sound defensive or judgmental, my first instinct was to lie, to tell him that we really were happy to live with Celeste. Then I wondered what the point was.

"It's not that I dislike her," I said, twisting the stem of my apple. "I mean, I love how creative and . . . passionate she is. But she makes me nervous. Sometimes, I think she might not even like me."

"Really?" he said. "I know she can be a pain in the ass, but she definitely likes you. She said . . . What was it?" He thought for a minute and then smiled. "Oh, yeah. You remind her of an angel."

"An angel?" I said. "Hardly."

His gaze traced a path from my chin to my hair. "Maybe she meant you look like one."

My hand flew to the top of my head. "Frizz. Not a halo," I said, hoping my suddenly hot cheeks hadn't pinked. "And if you knew she liked me, why did you have to talk to Jessica Liu?"

"Jess—? Oh. Right." He sounded a bit sheepish. "It's just, Celeste doesn't always have the best judgment about people and . . . I tend to be pretty protective of her."

We held eyes for a minute. Something had shifted; the connection between us had changed. We'd stripped some things away, like when you strip away layers of lumpy paint and get down to the smooth, original wood.

I gestured in the direction of Frost House. "I have to go prepare my presentation."

David nodded and swung a leg over the frame. "Guess

I'll see you there, if not before."

I'd turned the corner toward home when I heard, "Leena?" He biked toward me. "One other thing."

"What?" I said.

"Spoons."

"What?"

He rode around me in a circle. "Abby wanted to know what I do. That's it."

"Spoons?" I said, turning to follow his path.

He smiled, wide, with full-on dimples. In this light, the blue of his eyes reminded me of raspberry slushies. "See you, Leena," he said. And rode away.

I decided to finish unpacking and arranging my room before working on my presentation, and as I filled drawers and shifted furniture and hung pictures, I kept wondering what David had meant. People played spoons as instruments, but he'd said he wasn't a musician. There was a card game called Spoons; I found that hard to imagine. So, what . . . ?

I hadn't come up with any feasible possibilities when I joined Viv and Abby upstairs. I didn't ask for their input, though. Not that I thought it was a big secret. Just that something about the way he hadn't said anything at dinner made me keep it to myself.

I did want to talk about something else.

"You guys?" I said after they'd declared my speech ready for the tender ears of the newbies. "I know that having

Celeste here wasn't the plan, but I think we should make an effort to be welcoming. Not fakey-fake nicey-nice. Friendly."

"Seriously?" Abby had been sprawled on Viv's shaggy white rug, eating a brownie. Now she sat up. "You realize you're asking me to go against my true nature? Like asking a vampire to be a phlebotomist and not drink from the vials."

"I know," I said, placing my hand on hers in faux sympathy. "You're truly a mean, mean person. But this won't change who you are. No one outside of the dorm has to know."

She sighed. "In that case, I suppose I can do it."

"Viv?" I said.

"I'm always nice," she answered from her cross-legged position on the cushioned window seat. "And I don't even care she's living with us. I love it here already. This room is so damn cozy. Orin must've read it wrong." Rain tapped the glass behind her. Another storm had started.

"What does Orin have to do with anything?" I asked.

Viv paused, a mug of tea halfway to her mouth. Her eyes darted to Abby, who shrugged, and then back to me. "Oh, nothing."

"You obviously told Abby," I said. "Come on, you know I won't take it seriously."

"We decided not to tell you because you're the one who picked Frost House," Viv said, resting her mug next to her knee. "I guess, though, if you won't believe it anyway . . . He didn't want me to live here. There's some sort of . . . darkness connected to it."

Heat spread up the back of my neck. "You're right. That's stupid."

"Then again . . ." Abby waved her brownie. "He could be talking about Green Beret."

I loved Abby, but that was the last straw. "That's it," I announced, pointing at her. "Let it all out now. Purge. Every nasty thing you have to say about Celeste."

"What?" she said.

"Pretend Celeste is here with us. Let her have it. So when she gets here you don't have all this snark built up."

Viv laughed. "Abby has an endless reserve of snark."

"Just try," I said.

Abby shrugged. "Okay." She took a bite of brownie, closed her eyes, and thought for a minute while chewing, then began. "What are you wearing you look like a crazy person and why are you so dramatic and your brother seems nuts too and why are you living here we don't even know you and why do you wear that green beret all the time or ever la la la I can't think of anything else oh yeah if you're going to go schizo like your dad please don't do it here and stay away from matches." She opened her eyes.

"Is that it?" I asked.

Abby nodded.

"Okay," I said. "Let's have a toast." We all picked up our tea and scootched closer together. "To Frost House," I said.

"To Frost House," they echoed.

We clunked mugs and drank, to the applause of a deep rumble of thunder.

The first night in a new place usually gives me a tinny, homesick feeling that makes it hard to sleep. Not homesick for anywhere in particular. Just a general feeling of uprootedness. Loneliness. Even if people I love are sleeping nearby.

To help me that night in Frost House, I put on my favorite mellow-girl-singers playlist; made up my bed with my oldest, softest sheets; and set Cubby—a hollow wooden owl my dad carved for me—on the windowsill near my pillow. Cubby's spot has always been next to my bed. When I was little and scared of the dark, I kept a small flashlight inside her. Now, I just liked the familiarity of having her watching over me with her round, yellow glass eyes.

Even with Cubby here, I was expecting to toss and turn.

And, at first, moments from the strange day cluttered my head—so different from what I'd anticipated when I woke up this morning. Not *all* bad—there was David's smile as he rode away . . . Soon, though, thoughts of the day faded and I was just *here*, in my new room. I concentrated on the breezes that slipped through the slightly open windows and fluttered across my skin. The air was cooler now, because of the second storm. I listened to the sounds that mingled with Rachael Yamagata's low, breathy voice: rain pattering on leaves, windowpanes rattling softly, a door creaking.

I imagined the house was saying it was happy I'd finally arrived.

The feel of the bed underneath me, the shape of the room around me, the woody smell of the air: it was all so familiar. I didn't feel homesick or lonely at all. In fact, just the opposite. I was so comfortable—so at home—that Viv probably would have said I'd lived in Frost House in a past life.

Viv. The darkness. I smiled at the ridiculousness.

Before I knew it, I was asleep.

6

THE NEXT MORNING, I was sitting on my bed reading an online article about schizoaffective disorder and its effect on families while supposedly reaping the soothing benefits of a chamomile-jasmine aromatherapy facial mask. I breathed in deeply through my nose. If the aromatherapy was bull, at least the extra oxygen would relax me.

The side door to Frost House squeaked open and the thud of uneven footsteps sounded in the common area.

"Hello, hello?" Celeste's voice called.

I shut my laptop and rushed to the bathroom. For some reason, I hadn't expected her to arrive this early.

I rinsed and dried my face, put my glasses on, checked my reflection in the mirror, tightened my ponytail. Celeste was just another person. No need to be nervous.

She and David stood in the middle of the bedroom. A chunky cast on her left leg peeked out of a full-skirted white dress with Mexican-style embroidery and a turquoise sash. The cast was painted gold, her toenails neon orange. Her thick, dark brown hair was longer than I'd ever seen it, half-way down her back. Despite a tan, her face seemed drawn, emphasizing the bone structure she shared with David.

He was wearing a thin, white T-shirt and faded black jeans, cut off at the knee. I had a sudden realization that he'd been in my dream last night. The details were fuzzy. Still, I couldn't meet his eyes.

"Hey, Celeste," I said. "I'm really sorry about your accident."

"Yeah, it sucks. For you, too. Right?" She hopped over and gave me a wiry-arm hug. "David told me you didn't even know until you got here. What assholes."

"It's not a big deal. It'll be fun."

She let out a little snort. "You say that now."

I didn't know how to respond.

"Much as I like hearing you charm people," David said to his sister, "I'm gonna get going. Once you thank me for setting up your stuff, that is."

Celeste glanced around distractedly. "Oh, crap," she said. "Did I forget to pack the beetle photo?"

"No," David said. "It's in the closet. I thought Leena might not appreciate having it hanging."

"Leena doesn't care," Celeste said as if she could possibly know this. "The RISD admissions woman loved it."

"Fine." David sounded exasperated. "I'll hang it later. Now, are you going to thank me? Or what?"

"Thank you. You did a very nice job. Sure you aren't gay?"

He turned to me. "If she acts up, I'll loan you my Taser." He smiled and I couldn't help but smile back way too widely, both because David was so cute and because as Celeste's lab partner, I'd definitely have taken him up on his offer a few times.

"Call if you need anything," he said to Celeste. "And don't make Leena regret letting you live here."

He held out a fist. Celeste bumped it twice, then they pressed their palms together, hers tiny next to his. A small hollow opened in my chest, the place where a sibling would fit.

David left. As I listened to his receding footsteps, I had an irrational impulse to call after him, to tell him not to leave me alone with his sister.

"Pretty room," Celeste said, sitting down on her bed. "Too many windows, though. Like being in a fishbowl." She sucked in her cheeks and made fishy lips.

"Oh, well . . ." I said. "No one's ever in the backyard. Did you see the smaller room with our desks across the hall? And we've got our own bathroom. The fixtures are old and funky, but the water pressure is good." I caught myself before droning on. "Sorry, I sound like my mother, the realtor."

"Anyone else on the first floor?"

"Just Ms. Martin, our house counselor. Her apartment takes up the whole front."

"I had her for history freshman year. She's kind of a twat. Who's upstairs?"

"Abby Brenner and Vivian Parker-White."

"Not sure if I know them. I'm terrible with names. What did I always call you in chem?"

"Lisa."

"Oh, right. Leena's much better." Celeste reached back and began twisting her hair into a knot. "I like your glasses," she said. "They counteract the dumb-blond thing."

"Excuse me?"

"Not that you're dumb. Just that with your big boobs and blondie-blond hair you could look it. Black glasses help."

I refrained from saying thank you, the way I should have when she made the comment about my butt that first day of chem. Anyway, my hair isn't that blond—sort of a caramel color. And as for my boobs, they're only a C— hardly enormous.

"David's noticed you," Celeste continued. "I can tell. Do you like him? Or do you already have a fuck-buddy?"

Fuck-buddy?

"Uh, no."

"You don't think he's hot? I was kidding about that gay thing."

She talked this way about her own brother?

"I meant, no, I don't have a boyfriend."

And didn't want one this semester, for numerous reasons, even if he wasn't related to my nutty roommate. Not that I would have minded if Celeste was right and David *had* noticed me. No objections there.

"Me neither, at the moment," she said, pushing herself up to stand. "I had a thing with this amazing guy over the summer. The bassist for Wishmaker. Do you know them? Anyway, I was completely in love, but he ended up being all obsessed and stalkerish, so I had to go through this big mess to get out of it. Really sucked. Maybe there's a guy here who has a cast fetish."

"I have to run the peer-counseling orientation for new students in a little bit," I said, grateful I had an excuse to leave. "Do you need to use the bathroom, or anything, before I shower?"

"Nope." Celeste's back was to me as she looked through her closet. "Something stinks over here," she muttered, shutting the door. I grabbed Cubby off the windowsill and hid her in the towel I was carrying. I didn't want to have to explain why I was taking a wooden owl with me to the bathroom.

On my way out, Celeste picked up the family snapshot off her dresser.

"That's a nice picture," I said. "I was so sorry to hear—"

"Look." She turned to face me. "I don't know what big-mouth David told you, but let's get something straight. I do not discuss my father. Got it? Do. Not. Discuss. My. Father."

"Okay. But if you ever want to talk—"

"I won't," she said. "Ever." She shoved the photo into her top drawer, all the way at the back. "David doesn't know when to keep his mouth shut. I hope you do."

"I guess, yeah. I mean, I do."

"And speaking of David's big mouth, I want you to know I didn't do it on purpose." She tapped one of her crutches against her cast. "I know he thinks I did."

"He told me it was an accident," I said.

"I'm just telling you. Don't believe everything he says. He thinks I'm some sort of delicate creature. I'm not. Okay?"

"Okay." Although I'd known Celeste for longer than I'd known her brother, if I'd had to trust one of them, I would have picked David.

In any case, I didn't need to worry about it right now. I had a presentation in front of two hundred students to get through. I went to the bathroom and turned on the shower in the claw-foot tub. While waiting for the water to heat up, I lifted off Cubby's head. My first semester at Barcroft, I was embarrassed about a prescription I was taking for a urinary tract infection, so I'd hidden the pills in here. Since then, Cubby had become my quirky portable medicine cabinet.

I took out the folded piece of paper that lay on top: a list I'd made of the pills' usage and dosage information. I didn't keep them in their boxes or bottles, but in tiny plastic

baggies, labeled with a Sharpie—*Tylenol PM, Sudafed Sinus &*
Cold, Ativan. . . .

All I needed this morning was one of the round, white
antianxiety pills. That should do it. My body's nervous,
physical reactions got in the way when I made presentations.
The antianxiety medicine was for emergencies. Not spazz-
ing out in front of the new students definitely qualified.

After showering and brushing my teeth, I went back in
the bedroom.

Celeste stood holding her vase of orange tulips. "What
was David thinking?" she asked me. The flowers hung
limply, leaves a sickly yellow, petals shriveled. The last
time I'd noticed, they hadn't even opened the whole way—
nowhere near dying. Across the room, my three were still in
the flush of early bloom. They were from the same bunch.
How could only hers have died?

"Maybe they ran out of water?" I suggested.

She shook the vase a little, then dumped it in the trash.
A stream of water poured out along with the flowers. "Oh,
well," she said. "An untimely frost, I guess."

"What?" I thought I'd misunderstood.

"*Romeo and Juliet*?" she said. "Juliet's death. It's compared
to an 'untimely frost' that kills flowers in their prime." She
stared at me as if this was supposed to make sense. "This is
Frost House, right?" she continued. "Must be in the air."

"*Frost?*" I repeated.

Celeste's gaze shifted to my tulips. "On this side of the

53

room, at least," she said.

A chill prickled across my neck, even though I didn't understand what she was trying to say. Obviously, frost wasn't what had killed those flowers. With anyone else, I would have assumed they were completely kidding.

But something in her expression told me she didn't quite think it was funny.

An hour and a half later, I turned over my last page of notes on the podium in front of me. Finally, the end was in sight.

"So, to sum up," I said, looking out at the rows of faces, "the peer-counseling program is all about students supporting one another. We know how hard it is to make the transition, to deal with the pressures of school. Don't feel bad asking for help. And, I promise, we have an amazing group of students working with us. You'd be lucky to talk to any of them.

"Are there any questions before my cohead, Toby, tells you about the training program?"

I hoped my speech hadn't been too boring. Despite taking the pill, I'd felt too nervous to make eye contact while speaking, so I hadn't noticed how many of the new students had been surreptitiously (or unsurreptitiously) texting or playing video games.

"Yes?" I said to a small girl in the front.

"Uh, so . . . I . . ." Her voice was shaky. "No, never mind. Forget it."

"Sure?" I said. "There are no dumb questions."

She nodded, and I made a mental note to ask her privately, after the meeting. Maybe it was something she didn't want to say in front of a room of strangers.

"Anyone else?"

I searched the audience for hands. Then I saw David. He sat in the last row, out of place in the room of mostly freshmen. Our eyes met. *Fuck-buddy.* The word flashed like a neon sign over his head.

"Okay, so . . ." I ruffled through my speech notes and willed my blush to go away. "I guess that's it then. Here's Toby."

I shielded my face from the strong sun as I stood talking to Dean Shepherd on the path leading from the auditorium to the main quad, keenly aware of the fact that David hadn't passed by us yet.

"You haven't mentioned your college visits," Dean Shepherd said. "How did they go?"

"Okay," I said. "I don't have a first choice, yet. Maybe Wesleyan, or Columbia. But they're both super long shots." Whenever I talked about colleges, the air I was breathing felt a little thinner. It seemed impossible that I'd choose the right place, even more impossible that the right place would choose me. And most of the money in my college fund had been spent on Barcroft.

"It's worth a try," the dean said. "Michael used to teach at

Wesleyan. You'll have to come to dinner soon and meet him."

"You're still seeing him?" I said. "That's great."

At the edge of my vision, I sensed people approaching. I snuck a look—it was David and some girl—then kept my eyes on the dean as she told me about her boyfriend.

"Hi, David," she said when he reached us, alone. "Settling in okay?"

I made my mind a blank slate, ignored that neon sign over his head. Or at least I tried.

"Pretty much, thanks," he said, then turned to me. "Actually, I just wondered if you were going back to the dorm now?"

I moistened my lips. "After lunch, I am." Was he looking at me with more than friendly interest? It was hard to tell; his eyes had such a natural intensity. In the end, probably better if he wasn't. I might not be strong enough to resist.

"Could you give this to my sister?" he said. "I'd bring it myself, but I have another orientation thing and I know I'll just end up forgetting." He handed me a small white envelope, then added, "Assuming you haven't kicked her out already, that is."

An image of her holding the dead tulips flashed in my mind. "Not yet," I joked back. Folding the envelope into my bag, I could tell it contained a key.

"David," the dean said. "I spoke to Harry Weintraub and he's ready to meet with you whenever. You have his number and email?"

"I do," David said. "Thanks."

"Seems like a nice young man," Dean Shepherd said as he walked away.

I watched his retreating figure—the broad shoulders, the defined calf muscles—and noticed he had a bounce in his walk, not the usual too-cool saunter of a good-looking guy. "Nice young man. Is that a euphemism for hot as hell?" I asked the dean.

She laughed.

"And what was that about Dr. Weintraub?" I said. He was a teacher and well-known mathematician. I'd wanted him for Calculus, but he was taking a couple of years off. "Isn't he still on leave?"

"Officially, yes. But he agreed to work with David on an independent study."

So math was David's thing? He must have been pretty brilliant for Dr. Weintraub to make a special point of working with him. I wondered what spoons had to do with it. . . .

"David told me," I said. "You know, about their father."

The dean nodded. "It wasn't my place. But I'm glad he did. And Celeste arrived this morning?"

"Yup."

"How was that?" she asked, putting an arm around my shoulders.

"Well," I said, "it's going to be an interesting semester."

"You know what Edith Wharton said?" the dean replied. "She said, 'I don't know if I should care for a man who made

life easy; I should want someone who made life interesting.'
Maybe the same applies for roommates."

I supposed that was the best way to look at it. If I anticipated an interesting—if odd—semester with Celeste,
someone so different from me and my friends, and saw it as
a chance to get to know her better, then I wouldn't be disappointed. Still, I held on to the hope that didn't necessarily
mean it wouldn't also be easy.

7

My mother called when I was on my way back to Frost House after lunch. I wasn't in the mood for a long conversation, but picked up anyway because I knew she'd keep calling until she reached me. I hadn't talked to her since arriving at school, had only sent her and my father brief messages saying I'd gotten here safely. My father had written back: "Remember to get car inspected. Visit soon. Dad." My mother was higher maintenance.

I walked down Highland Street, giving her a brief summary of the weekend.

"What kind of interesting?" she said when I used the word to describe Celeste again. "Medieval castle? Skyscraper?"

Matching up people with architecture: our family

version of "If you were an animal, what kind of animal would you be?"

The perfect answer came as I turned into the Frost House driveway.

"Casa Batlló," I said. Casa Batlló—an outrageous apartment building in Barcelona with colorful, mosaic walls that seem to ripple, balconies that look like enormous skulls, a ceiling that swirls like a whirlpool. Disconcerting, but beautiful.

"You were scared to death of Casa Batlló," my mother said. "Do you need me to call that Dean of Students woman, honey? I don't want you living with some girl you're scared—"

"Mom," I interrupted. "I was only six when we went to Barcelona." Gravel pressed into the thin soles of my sandals. "Everything is fine here. I have to go, okay?" It bothered me when she tried to get involved in things about my life she didn't understand, things I could take care of myself.

If she wanted to be a part of it all, she shouldn't have moved across the country.

Ignoring my comment about needing to go, she began to tell me about an article on a new kind of yoga that she was going to email me. "Apparently, it's much better for managing stress than the kind I've been doing," she said. "If there's a studio near Barcroft that offers it, I'd be happy to pay for you to take classes."

"Uh-huh," I said, heading down the hall to my room. "Sounds great."

As I set my bag on the floor in the bedroom, I registered something strange on my bed. My mother's voice chirped on as I moved closer. Sheets of newspaper covered with rows of small, dark . . . what? I moved closer. Bugs?

"Sorry, have to go," I said. I hung up without waiting for her response and stared.

Cockroaches. Dead. At least a hundred. Shiny brown with spindly legs. On my bed.

A roar filled my ears.

"Celeste!"

There were dead cockroaches.

On my *bed*.

I couldn't take my eyes off the carcasses. Some as big as two inches long. Legs and antennae and slippery-looking abdomens. A battlefield. I shivered violently, as if all those tiny legs were crawling on my skin, scrabbling up my arms and my spine and my neck.

This was not interesting. It was repulsive.

"Celeste!" I yelled again.

I heard the flush of the toilet. Celeste came thumping in.

"I know, I know. Sorry," she said in a blasé voice. "I needed to see if they all arrived okay."

"Take them off," I said. The angry roar in my ears was so loud I was sure she could hear it, too. "Take them off my bed. Now!"

"Okay. Let me just get their box." She hopped over and grabbed a shoe box off her dresser.

"Why do you even . . . why do you even have them? This is so disgusting."

"For a photo project. It's taken me a really long time to get enough of them. You can't just buy them anywhere."

"Really, really disgusting," I said. "And why didn't you put them on *your* bed?"

She gave me a look as if I were the crazy person. "No room."

I glanced over. Celeste's bed was covered with ten or so small birds' nests and what appeared to be an assortment of little bones. God, I wished Dean Shepherd were here to see this—what she was asking of me. David, too, for that matter.

"I'm going to go out for a little while," I said, not knowing where I'd go, just knowing that I couldn't be here with her. "When I get back, there will be no dead things in the bedroom. I don't care what you do with them. I just don't want them in my bedroom."

"Fine. Sorry, I didn't know you had a phobia."

"It's not a phobia!" I said. "It's perfectly normal! This is not the sort of stuff that should be in my bedroom! Especially not on my bed!"

Celeste's eyes narrowed. "Okay," she said. "I get the point. But it's not like you haven't touched my stuff, too."

I looked at her blankly.

"Unless David tried on my skirt," she said.

Her skirt? My heart started thumping. How could she . . . ?

"Did you think I wouldn't notice?" She put the shoe box

down again and hopped over to the closet. She tugged at the doorknob, jiggled it, pulled. "This stupid door won't let me in. It keeps sticking."

"The wood's probably swollen." I went over and turned the knob. The door opened easily.

As Celeste reached inside, I had the irrational hope that she was going to bring out a skirt I'd never seen before, a skirt I *hadn't* touched. But her hand emerged with the pink, bustled one. She held it out so I could see that down one side, on the seam, was a long rip—three or so inches.

I stared at it, momentarily speechless. That rip had not been there after I tried it on. I was sure. And it didn't even look like it could have happened accidentally. Still, a guilty feeling wrapped around me, as tight as the skirt had been.

"Celeste," I finally said, "I didn't rip your skirt. I mean, I did try it on for a minute, but—"

"You could have at least hung it back up."

"Hung it . . . ? I did hang it up."

"Funny. I found it on the floor."

"But I did hang it up. I promise." I had hung it up well, hadn't I? And I'd checked the fabric so thoroughly.

"I can fix the rip," she said, putting the skirt back in the closet. "That's not a big deal. But is this how it's going to be? You punishing me for living here? Because if it is, we should forget about it right now. I can tell the dean this isn't going to work, that I need a room somewhere else."

63

I imagined the scene. "No," I said. "No, you don't have to do that."

"Are you sure?"

"I'm positive. Why don't we . . . start fresh?"

"Like, forget this stuff happened?" She gestured at the skirt and the bed.

I nodded.

Celeste seemed to consider this for a moment. She hopped over, delicately picked up one of the roaches, and held it up to her face. "What do you think, little guy?" she said. "Forgive and forget?"

She turned the roach so his head faced me, turned him back, and wiggled him so he appeared to be nodding at her.

"Okay," she said. Then she smiled. "Leena! I'm so happy to be living with you."

When I reached the end of the driveway—still not knowing where I was headed, or what exactly had happened back there, only knowing that there was a great big lump of unpleasantness in my throat—I ran into Abby and Viv, carrying grocery bags.

"Thomas!" Abby called as she bounded up to me. "Check it out!"

Her bags were filled with microwave popcorn, ice cream, pretzels, Diet Coke, protein bars, trail mix. . . .

"Wow," I said. "That should keep us going."

"What's wrong, Leen?" Viv said, clearly picking up on my

lack of enthusiasm. "Was your presentation okay?"

"Fine," I said. "It's just . . ." And then, even though I knew I shouldn't give Abby ammunition against Celeste, I couldn't help telling them what had happened.

Abby's mouth dropped open as I spoke. "That's the foulest thing I've ever heard," she said. "I can't believe she'd do that to you."

"She must have been clueless that you'd mind," Viv said.

"But, also, isn't it so strange about the skirt?" I turned to Abby. "You were there when I tried it on. Wouldn't we have been able to tell, if it ripped that bad?"

Abby shrugged.

"You didn't go back and try it on, did you?" I asked.

"And left it on the floor, ripped?" she said in a tone of disbelief. "Are you serious?"

I immediately realized how offensive the question had been. "Of course you didn't," I backtracked. "Forget I said it. It must have been me."

8

THAT NIGHT AFTER SIGN-IN, we all gathered in the common room for a beginning-of-school dorm meeting. Ms. Martin, our house counselor, was late. Abby, Viv, and I sat on the couch, which I'd spruced up with one of my tapestries. The cushions were so old and squishy that the three of us had sunk together in the middle, like we were in a hammock. Celeste sat in the armchair, her cast propped up on the coffee table. She wore a black silk camisole, green satin pajama pants, and an orange turban-type hat with a rhinestone pin on the side. Hopefully, Abby wouldn't make a comment about the outfit. I'd asked her and Viv not to say anything about the roaches, and as far as I knew, they hadn't.

When I'd returned to the dorm this afternoon, the bugs

were nowhere to be seen. In their place on my bed lay a vintage sleeveless top, light pink with tiny black beads in a fireworks pattern.

"I don't know why I bought it," Celeste had said. "It's too big for me. I know you're not into clothes, but I think it would look hot on you. Keep it, if you want."

"Thanks," I said. "It's really pretty." I'd never have chosen it for myself, but I'd have liked it on someone else. Maybe it would look good. I handed Celeste my own peace offering—a bouquet of dried Chinese lantern flowers I'd bought for her in town.

"Dead already. Good thinking," she joked as she reached for her vase. "Look, David told me it was a total bitch move to put those roaches on your bed. I suck at this roommate thing. I want to try to be better, though. You have to tell me when I'm screwing up." After arranging the flowers, she set the vase back on her dresser. "Perfect. This was my granny's. She had a superstition about never letting it sit empty."

I'd felt better about the vibe between us after that, but the thing that still nagged at me—even now, as I waited for the dorm meeting to start—was the rip in her skirt. Like I'd said to Abby, I just didn't see how I could have missed it. Not to mention that I'd definitely hung the skirt back up. I was sure of it. So if it wasn't me . . . ? Had someone else been in our room, when neither of us was there?

I was trying to stop worrying when Ms. Martin arrived.

Traditionally, at the first dorm meeting of the year, the

faculty house counselor lies about how thrilled she is to be living with a bunch of teenagers.

Nothing happened the way I expected that semester.

"I'm on deadline to finish a book," Ms. Martin said after briefly introducing herself. "So if the sign on my apartment door is turned to 'privacy please,' which it will be often, only knock for emergencies. You're all seniors; I'm assuming you're responsible enough not to need much supervision."

Her most attractive quality seemed to be her cat, a big-bellied, saucer-eyed Russian Blue named Leo. When he trotted by, I scooped him up onto my lap and ran my hand through his thick, soft coat. He turned in a circle as if he was going to settle down, but when his face brushed against my T-shirt, he let out a sharp yowl, leapt off, and darted out of the room, hackles raised, tail puffed up like a billy club.

"Sorry," I said to Ms. Martin. "Most cats really like me."

"He's not usually going to be allowed out of my apartment," she said. "So you won't have to worry about him."

One of his claws had left a tiny pull in the fabric of my shorts. "Was he out earlier today?" I asked. "In our room, maybe?"

"Definitely not," Ms. Martin said. "He was at my ex-husband's. We share custody."

They shared custody of their *cat*? Viv and Abby nudged me simultaneously; Celeste made a noise that began as a snort but turned into a cough. I bit down on my lips to keep from laughing.

Oblivious, Ms. Martin began going over all of the dorm rules: sign-in at ten during the week; eleven thirty, face-to-face sign-in on Friday and Saturday; no drinking, smoking, drugs; parietals—permission to have a guy in your room—granted any time before sign-in, as long as Ms. Martin was home to give approval; same for permission to go outside the town of Barcroft, except for overnight, which required a chaperone letter. Then she asked if anyone had an issue to discuss.

"Last year," I said, "I organized a dorm dinner one Sunday of every month. We switched off cooking. It was really fun. I'd like to do it again this year, if you don't mind loaning us your kitchen. It'll be easier with so few people. We could even invite guests from outside the dorm."

"Sounds fine," Ms. Martin said. "Just give me the dates well in advance. Anything else?" She checked her watch.

Celeste spoke up. "A couple things. First, I don't know if they didn't clean in here, or what, but my closet smells like something died in it. Also, we need new shades for the windows back there. Most are broken, and I swear to God, it felt like someone was looking in at me when I changed today."

"Are we talking about stuff that needs to be fixed?" Abby chimed in. "Because there are a ton of things maintenance could do upstairs."

"It's as if they haven't touched this place in a million years," Celeste said.

"Totally," Abby agreed.

"That's not true," I said. "They painted."

"You all know that I have nothing to do with this," Ms. Martin said. "Put in work orders with maintenance. And, Celeste, the house was fully cleaned. I assume the smell is just from years of being a boys' dorm." She stood up and gave us a tight smile, said, "My research calls, girls," and left the room.

As soon as her apartment door shut, we all burst out laughing.

"She's a charmer," Abby said.

"What the hell did she mean, it smells because boys lived here?" Celeste said. "They rubbed their jocks on the walls?"

"Ew," Abby said. "And that poor cat!"

After we laughed a little longer, Viv asked if we wanted to go upstairs. "We still have brownies that Abby's mom made," she said to Celeste. "Not to mention popcorn, pretzels, candy . . ."

"Thanks, but I've got stuff to do," Celeste said. She began maneuvering herself out of the chair.

"You sure?" I said. "The brownies are amazing."

"AP portfolio class tomorrow. Have to figure out what I'm showing Ms. Spatz. I have a million things to choose from."

"Okay," I said, happy that we'd made the offer, and, truthfully, relieved that Celeste had refused.

* * *

Every year, there was one room in the dorm that became our default hangout; this year it seemed like it was going to be Viv's. When we got upstairs, Abby went to get polish to paint our nails, and Viv resumed working on a giant wall calendar to help her keep track of where she was supposed to be and what assignments were due when. I hooked up my iPod to her dock and chose a playlist, an upbeat one Abby and I listened to on road trips. I was feeling giddy with beginning-of-semester excitement again. I'd survived my presentation, the dorm meeting had gone fine, and classes started tomorrow. I loved seeing who else was in them, meeting new teachers, inaugurating fresh, unblemished notebooks. . . . Dorky, I know.

Abby returned with three different polish colors and gestured that she'd do my nails first. I picked a dark metallic blue called "Nuit de la Coeur," remembering for a moment how whenever my dad took me to the hardware store, I used to pore over the colors and names on the paint chips. He and my mom had let me choose the paint for our front door when I was seven or so, and I'd picked "Razzlematazzle," mostly for the name. Years later, I'd still said it under my breath when I opened the door.

Abby shook the bottle and started on my right hand. For a few minutes, we listened to music and concentrated on our separate thoughts. Eventually, Viv looked over from where she was drawing a half circle on September 9. Probably noting the stage of the moon. "So," she said, "Cam gave me some good news. It turns out Jake and Eliza broke up."

I flinched, causing Abby to get polish on my skin. "Why is that good news?"

"You guys left stuff in limbo," Viv said. "Maybe you can see where it goes again."

Was she kidding? "It wasn't left in limbo. He ditched me for Eliza."

"Not because he didn't like you," Viv said. "He didn't know how into him you were."

"The hooking up didn't clue him in?" I snapped, more harshly than I meant.

Viv began fiddling with one of her dangly earrings. "Sorry," she said. "I thought . . . I don't know. I guess I got excited because he's friends with Cam and it would be so perfect. I wasn't thinking. Sorry."

I bit my cheeks and stared down at the rhythmic movement of the brush. "It's not just about Jake," I said. "I've told you, the last thing I need this semester is a relationship drama. I don't want to have anything to do with anyone until after my applications are in and I've kept my grades up. Do you know how crazy my schedule is?"

"You always make some excuse, Leen," Viv said gently.

"Yeah," Abby said. "Last year you found the stupidest reasons not to get together with anyone."

"I didn't like anyone last year," I said. "Spare me the lecture, okay?"

"Fine," Abby sighed, and then went on to talk about Ponytail Guy, her new crush.

It annoyed me when she and Viv made it seem like my reluctance to get involved was a problem. They were the ones who'd had to scrape me off the floor at the end of sophomore year, after Jake McCormick, and freshman year, after Theo Fletcher.

With both Jake and Theo, I'd assumed that hooking up meant something *more* was happening between us—maybe not the first time we got together, but after that, definitely. I got all stupid excited: going totally out of my way to run into them at Commons or between classes, doodling our entwined initials, and writing the boy's name in fancy letters on the side of my class notes. But both times, the old saying about the danger of assumptions had proved true. Jake moved on to Eliza without even thinking he needed to tell me, and Theo moved on to the rest of the freshman class.

Looking back on it now, I knew that I'd been partly to blame. I hadn't said what I wanted, or asked what they wanted, just skipped along in my own little bubble of deluded happiness. But I still felt the burn of humiliation when I remembered how easily and thoroughly I'd been devastated back then. I wished I were the type of person who could casually hook up. I wasn't, though, no matter how much I loved kissing and fooling around. (At least what I'd tried—free rein for my hands; boys' hands just up top.) And this semester, with my tough classes and college applications, I couldn't afford any emotional turmoil. Friendship, flirting—that was fine. It's not like I wanted to live in a convent. But that was as far as I'd go. I had the rest of my life for kissing.

Abby finished my nails and moved onto Viv's, and as the night went on, the pauses between our comments got longer and my eyelids grew heavier. I kept thinking about my bed and how well I'd slept last night. Eventually, I struggled to my feet. I had to face Molecular Biology at eight a.m. That was what I needed to concentrate on this semester—my classes.

I kept my steps on the stairs and down the hall careful and quiet, assuming Celeste was long asleep. I found her in bed with the covers pulled all the way over her face. It was a warm, late summer night. Was she one of those really skinny people who are always cold? I hoped I wasn't going to discover she had an eating disorder. One of the things that had stressed me out about the bigger dorms was sharing the bathroom with bulimics. Because of the peer-counseling thing, I usually got roped into confronting them. There's an unspoken agreement at Barcroft: whenever possible, don't involve faculty.

With all of the windows, our bedroom wasn't ink dark, so much as grainy, charcoal gray. I could see Celeste's closet door gaping open again, which made me think of her comment at the dorm meeting—her insistence about the horrible smell. I tiptoed over and breathed in through my nose. It still smelled good to me. I waited a few minutes, letting the scent bring me that feeling I'd had earlier. Warmth, comfort. Definitely a memory. What was it? My old cedar chest? No. I leaned farther in, inhaled once more, and shivered slightly. If the scent had been more perfume-like, I would have guessed that it reminded me of the way my mother smelled when I was a baby. The feeling was that essential.

Something made me turn my head. Celeste was propped up on her elbows, staring at me.

"Oh." I snatched my hand off the door. "I didn't know you were awake."

"They won't let me sleep."

They, meaning us? "I'm so sorry. We tried to be quiet." She couldn't have heard what we were saying, could she? I walked quickly over to my bed.

"Not you guys," she said. "Them." She flailed a skinny arm at the windows. "The trees, the moonlight. I told you, there are too many windows here. And there's this, like, constant breeze prickling my skin, touching me. It's creepy. You slept here last night. Didn't it bother you?"

"Actually, I fell asleep right away. Should I shut the windows a bit, so it's not as breezy?"

"No. That nasty smell from the closet took over the whole room. It was making me gag."

"Do you want some Tylenol PM?"

"I don't take drugs." She said it like I'd offered her crack.

"Okay. Well, I'll get some new shades, if that'll help. If we put in a work order, they won't get around to it until graduation."

"Can you do something about the closet, too?" she said. "You must have noticed the smell, standing over there."

"I think it's just the wood," I said, turning on the small lamp by my bed and finding my basket of toiletries. "Smells kind of old and musty. I don't mind it at all, but I grew up in an old house."

"There's old, and then there's dead."

I glanced back at the closet. She couldn't be talking about the same smell I was. "Did you store all your bugs and bones and stuff in there? Maybe it's them."

"Those do not smell. Anyway, you said you didn't want them in the bedroom. I put them across the hall. I'm telling you, Leena, there's something in here. Something weird and gross. And unless the boys who lived here left behind a corpse, it has nothing to do with them."

With that, she lay down and pulled the sheet back over her head. In a case of utterly perfect timing, a breeze swept through the room at the same time and the closet door slammed shut with a bang.

Celeste sat up straight. "Why did you do that?" she asked me, alarmed.

"I didn't," I said. "It blew shut."

"Blew shut?"

She stared at the closet as if she couldn't quite grasp the concept. Then lay back down, not taking her eyes off it, making sure it didn't startle her with another sudden noise. Finally, she drew the sheet over her head again.

"'Night," I said to her covered figure as I turned off the light and headed to the bathroom.

"I doubt it," she said. "Not in here."

9

I steadied my feet on the chair as I reached up, drill in hand, and repeated, "Many prokaryotes are able to take up non-viral DNA molecules," in an accent like the Terminator's.

It was Saturday morning after our first week of classes, and I was multitasking: switching the old, broken shades for new ones I'd bought at the mall, while listening to my recording of Friday's unnervingly complicated lecture by my bio teacher, Mr. Baumschlager.

Not exactly how I wanted to spend a day without classes, but it needed to be done. Celeste had had insomnia all week, and continued to be paranoid that someone could be watching her through the windows. I wasn't sure why I didn't share her caution—it was true that a person in the backyard could have seen everything we were doing. To me, though, the garden felt like an extension of my space.

As for the bio lecture, after struggling in a couple of subjects at Barcroft, I'd figured out that the more a subject daunted me, the more trouble I had paying attention in class. Apparently, my brain left the room when it was confused. Ritalin hadn't worked, so—at the suggestion of a tutor—I'd started recording and re-listening to classes last year, and had made honor roll for the first time.

"The genomes of eubacteria, archaea, and eukaryotes—"

A knock came at the door behind me. I turned. David stood in the doorway, hands in the pockets of his low-riding jeans, wearing an orange tee that said I LIKE PI on it.

"I expected you to be more muscular," he said, smiling. "And male."

"Herr Baumschlager." I stepped down from the chair and moved over to my laptop to pause it. "Yesterday's bio lecture. I enjoyed it so much the first time I had to listen again." I figured I didn't need to be embarrassed about my nerdiness in front of a guy with math humor on his shirt.

"My sister around?" he said. "She called me to help you guys do something. Hang these blinds, I guess?" He picked one up off the floor, still rolled and wrapped in plastic.

"Really?" This was my project. I hadn't asked her to call him. "She's not even here. Her wireless connection wasn't working so she went to the library."

"God, she's such a twerp sometimes." David shook his

head, like he was sort of annoyed, sort of amused. "Well, since I'm here, at least let me help. She asked me to hang that photo of hers, too."

Usually, I preferred to do projects alone. But I did have a ton of homework this weekend and was supposed to take Anya to the park tomorrow. "Okay," I said. "Thanks."

We headed down the hall to get parietals.

Over the past week, I'd run into David around campus and here in the dorm a few times. Always happily. Aside from the gorgeous thing, he was friendly and easygoing, and knowing he was around made me feel like if I ever had a major problem with Celeste, there was someone sane who could mediate. It was pretty obvious he was an equal-opportunity flirter, so I wasn't convinced that, like Celeste had said, he'd noticed me in particular. But since it didn't matter either way, I just enjoyed the buzz I got from his attention.

Back in the room after getting parietals from Ms. Martin, I assigned David the duty of measuring for the new brackets, while I finished up removing the old ones.

When the drill stopped screeching, he asked, "Where'd you learn how to use power tools?"

"My dad," I said. "He's a carpenter, old-house restorer guy. Big into DIY."

"My dad's smart as hell," David said. "But the only thing he can hit with a hammer is his thumb."

"It takes practice." I wondered if his dad was a

mathematician, like David. Like the man in the movie *A Beautiful Mind*. "I've been using tools since I was a kid," I said. "I made that bookshelf this summer."

I turned to point and noticed not only the muscles in David's back when he raised his hands, but also what he was doing. "Are you measuring the front of the molding?" I asked.

"Yeah," he said. "Why?"

"With this type of molding and these brackets, it has to go inside the frame. See?" I held one up and demonstrated.

"Oh. Right." He smiled. "Maybe I'll hang the photo first."

I took down the last of the old brackets as he got the frame from her closet. "So, you inherited your dad's," I coughed, "*talent* with this stuff. Is he where you got your brain for spoon math, too?"

"My what?" David said.

"Well, I know that you're a math whiz. And you made that comment about spoons. So I figure you were talking about some type of equation or theory, or something." I was kind of kidding, but also a little serious. I didn't know anything about superadvanced math, and I hadn't come up with any more plausible idea.

"Like, physicists have string theory, and mathematicians have spoon theory?" he said, standing there holding the photo.

"Yeah, exactly."

David laughed. Hard. "Spoon theory. That's great."

81

"So if that's not it," I said, enjoying the goofy heh-hehs of his laughter, "are you going to tell me what you really meant?"

"I don't think so," he said, still smiling really wide. "It's going to sound lame in comparison."

"The more you delay, the more you're building it up," I teased.

"Okay, okay." He rested the photo on the floor and hooked his thumbs in his pockets. "I took a metalwork class last year and developed a bit of an obsession with spoons."

Metalwork. "Wait," I said. "So you actually *make* spoons?"

He shrugged, as if to say, "See? Lame."

"Spoons have always annoyed me," he said. "I could never find the right one for the right job." He went on to describe how he made them for specific uses. One had a built-in rest, so that it didn't touch the table after you used it to stir your coffee. One had a small hole in the basin, so you didn't get a whole lot of milk with your bite of cereal.

"You realize this is kind of weird, right?" I said. I couldn't decide if it was cool-quirky weird, or just plain strange.

"I guess," he said. "It was something . . . concrete to do. You know?"

That I understood. Making something useful, something you could touch, that solved a problem. Like the bookshelves I make to fit in weird-shaped spaces. I'd made the one for this room low and wide, to fit under a section of the windows. Seeing it in its place was incredibly satisfying.

"Is this still an obsession?" I asked. "Are you going to write your college essays about how you want to bring better spoonage to the masses?"

"No," he said, turning his attention back to hanging the photo.

He didn't say anything else, so I got my pencil and tape measure and had just begun correcting his measurements on one window when he asked, "Is this a good spot?" He was holding the frame up in the only free wall space, at the end of Celeste's bed. "And do you mind if I hang it? I wouldn't want it on my wall if I were you."

"Go ahead," I said. "That's perfect." Perfect because it wouldn't be very visible from my side of the room. I didn't feel so strongly that I'd tell David not to hang it, but I definitely didn't need "Dead Celeste the Bug Charmer" to be the last thing I saw before falling asleep at night.

"Can you mark the spot for the nail?" he said.

I stepped off the chair and crossed to where he stood, then had to lean next to him—just touching—to make a dot at the center of the top of the frame. His smell of coffee and warm boy skin filled my lungs and melted through my limbs.

David suddenly shifted to look behind us.

"What?" I said, stepping back, looking, too.

"Thought I heard someone," he said. "I think I know why Celeste feels like she's being watched in here." He gestured over at my bed, where Cubby sat with her wide owl eyes directed right at us.

"Oh," I said, smiling. "Yeah. You've got to watch what you do in front of her. She's all-knowing."

We went back to our respective tasks. I drilled holes in the first window frame, then got my screwdriver and one of the new brackets.

"Is all this—making bookshelves, carpentry stuff," David said after finishing hammering, "something you'd do? Like your dad?"

"Not professionally." I twisted a screw around, around, around. . . . "I love buildings because of him, though. I was always convinced I wanted to be an architect."

"But?"

"Now I'm thinking I might want to do something that's more people-oriented. Social work, maybe. Or teaching. Or . . . I got really into my psych class last year, so maybe psychiatry."

"You'd be a great teacher."

I looked over at him. The photo was hanging and he'd started measuring windows again. "How would you know?"

"Both my parents are teachers," he said. "My mom's a professor. My dad taught middle school. I can spot a good one a mile away. And I saw you give that presentation, remember?"

"Oh, right." I brushed a loose section of hair behind my ear, almost stabbing myself in the eye with the screwdriver. "Well, the good thing about teaching is that I feel like I can major in lots of things and go into it. But if I want to be an architect or a psychiatrist, it's more . . . complicated. I feel like I'd have to decide soon."

"You'd want to go to med school?" he said.

"So I could write prescriptions. I know therapy helps, too. Obviously, it's hugely important. But so much of everything is chemical."

I began turning the next the screw into the window frame. "Like schizoaffective disorder. Therapy can only do so much, right? It's all about neuroscience and"—I almost said genetics—"and biology." The wood splintered, the bracket broke off and clattered to the floor. "Damn."

"It's not like science has done anything great for my dad," he said as I stepped off the chair and scanned the floor for hardware. "Jesus. I don't know if he's better when he's on or off his meds. Well, no. That's not true. But he's bad in different ways."

"But new drugs are coming out all the time." I bent over to grab the bracket and screw, then stood and faced David. "Eventually, you know, in the future, mental illness won't even exist. Not in our lifetime, I guess. But eventually."

"I think we'll just make new problems as we fix the ones we have."

"You and Celeste aren't big on medication, are you?" I still couldn't understand why she'd choose insomnia over Tylenol PM.

"I guess we're kind of cynical." David said. "We've gotten

our hopes up too many times. But, I mean, of course if something happened to her, or to me, I'd be happy there were options."

"Do you . . . is that . . . is it something you guys talk about? You know, the possibility . . . ?"

He nodded. "We have a pact."

"A pact?"

"Sometimes, when people first get sick, they know something's wrong but are scared to talk about it. Celeste and I have a pact so if one of us ever starts . . . I don't know, *worrying* about thoughts we're having, we'll tell the other one."

He sounded sweet, but kind of naïve, until he added, "Of course, there's not much I could do to help her, at that point. But at least I could keep her from doing something, you know, desperate." He paused. "My dad has. A couple times."

"I don't blame him." After I said it, I realized how awful it must have sounded. "I mean, stuff must be so difficult for him."

"Not everything," David said in a flat voice.

"I tried, in eighth grade," I said. "And I'm sure my life wasn't nearly as hard."

The words hit the air before I could stop them.

"I didn't *really* try," I added quickly. Had I just compared my immature stupidity with his father's serious mental illness? "I took a bunch of pills," I said, "but I threw them up. I didn't almost die, or anything. I'm sorry. I shouldn't have made that connection. It wasn't that big a deal."

86

"Sounds like a big deal," he said. "What happened?"

"Well," I started, my heart suddenly pounding. Why had I mentioned this? "Like I said, I think stuff can be really . . . physically based. My body was going through hormonal changes, my chemistry was all screwed up, and my parents were getting a divorce and I just kind of lost it."

"The divorce was messy?"

"No," I said. "They didn't even use lawyers."

"So—"

"They were making me decide if I wanted to stay in Cambridge with my dad or move to LA with my mom."

"As a thirteen-year-old?" he said. "Of course you were upset. Nothing to do with hormones."

"People's parents get divorced every day," I said, "and it doesn't make them want to kill themselves. I mean, my parents both *wanted* me. I got much better after I was on anti-depressants for a bit."

"Who did you pick?"

I wiped my forehead and rested my hands on my hips. "Neither. I was close to both of them and didn't want to . . . you know, choose one over the other. So in ninth grade, I came here. Some vacations I go to LA, some I go to Cambridge. Sometimes I go to Abby's family."

"That's kind of sad," David said.

"It's not," I said. "It was the perfect solution. During the school year, my friends are my family."

"There's a big difference between friends and family."

"Thank God," I said. "Friends you can *choose*."

I smiled, but instead of smiling back, David's expression hardened like cement. So did his voice. "I'd choose my dad and Celeste," he said. "Over anyone. And I always will."

"Oh. Of course." Blood rushed up my neck and flooded my cheeks. "I didn't mean that. I was talking about myself, about my own family. Not about yours."

It took a couple of seconds for his face to soften. "Sorry," he said. "I just assumed."

"That's okay." I stepped back up on the chair and refocused on hanging the shades, something I knew how to do. My hands trembled.

We worked for a while in unsettled silence. I couldn't believe how many stupid things I'd said. I wasn't usually so tactless. After a few minutes, I asked, "Would you mind if we listened to my bio lecture?"

David didn't answer right away. "It's not you," he finally said, keeping his eyes on what he was doing. "I'm just so used to being defensive about my family. But you've been so cool about Celeste moving in here, hanging these blinds for her, and you're not all freaked out about my dad, like people get. I appreciate it."

I could tell that this was a major thing for him, protecting his family. I guessed maybe he'd had to take his dad's place, in some ways.

"Thanks," I said. "I appreciate . . . your appreciation."

Really? That's the best you could do?

Now he looked at me and smiled. "And I appreciate your appreciation of my appreciation."

"That's so sweet." I put a hand on my heart. "I appreciate your appreciation of my appreciation of your appreciation."

We laughed—holding eyes. As I stared, something moved behind him. I looked just in time to see the photo he'd hung fall right off the wall, onto the bed. It landed with a clatter as the Plexiglas jostled in the frame.

David turned. "Oops," he said.

Because we'd smoothed over the tension between us, I allowed myself a little dig. "I think, maybe, it's better if you leave the home-improvement projects to me."

After David left, I couldn't settle down to homework quite yet—the conversation had been too intense and now I had too much on my mind. I decided to see if there was anything I could do to fix Celeste's closet door. She kept having trouble opening it, and I didn't know if it was a problem with the knob, or if the wood was swelling.

I tried the handle and the door opened smoothly. I turned the knob back and forth, looked at the movement of the latch. It seemed fine. I shut the door and opened it again, seeing if the wood stuck. It didn't. I couldn't tell what the problem was. I leaned my back against the doorframe, shut my eyes, and breathed in. My skin tingled. Then the emotion—that sense of contentment, safety—penetrated my cells. It's weird, how scents can be so powerful. My mother once told me that smells are key to selling a house. Freshly baked bread, cinnamon, and coffee are best, she'd said.

The day I came home from school in eighth grade and our own house smelled of baking bread, I wanted to vomit. Instead, I ran upstairs, to the one place the smell couldn't reach.

Wait a minute.

I breathed in again.

The attic.

That was it, wasn't it? My attic fort in our house in Cambridge. That's what the closet smell reminded me of. I slid down to the floor and folded my legs into my body. I couldn't believe it had taken me this long to make the connection.

Our house was a fixer-upper; my parents had always planned on turning the spacious attic into a living space. But, in the meantime, it had been a curious kid's heaven—full of my parents' and even my grandparents' histories in junk and paper: love letters, old school report cards, yearbooks, clothing, toys. . . .

If the whole attic was my kingdom, my fort was my castle. It was hidden behind a rusty file cabinet and a coatrack where someone's ancient furs hung in plastic bags, just a simple pine frame, covered by an old sheet, with pillows and a few stuffed animals inside. An older cousin had helped me build it, and I'd sworn her to secrecy. What was the point in having somewhere to disappear to if other people knew where I went?

I squeezed my knees closer to my chest now, remembering the day the Dumpster had arrived, the week we'd moved out. "Okay if I trash the wood from your old playhouse, Bean?" my dad had said. Turned out, my parents had known about it the whole time. One of the many things I'd become disillusioned about.

"We've grown apart," my mother said when she'd told me they were splitting up. "All we have in common are you and the house, Leenie."

Well, yes. Wasn't that their *life*?

We were a trio, after all. A unit. Whenever we played the "what building would you be?" game, I'd tell them that Mom was the downstairs floor of our house, I was the middle floor, and Dad was the top, not separate buildings at all. They let me believe I was right.

It was obvious why I'd thought that. I'd lived in that house from the time I was born, and fixing it up was my parents' passion. Why had they bothered if they knew we were just going to sell it to strangers?

After the divorce, they both moved to condos: my mother to an all-glass, modern monstrosity in LA, where she was originally from, and my dad to a supposedly "luxury" one-bedroom on the outskirts of Cambridge with hear-through walls and hollow doors. I was reading *Catcher in the Rye* the first time I saw my dad's place. I decided his condo was the architectural equivalent of Holden's phonies. I couldn't believe my dad, of all people, was living there. He said it was temporary; that was three years ago.

Now, I ran my hand lightly across Celeste's clothes. Was David trying to bring his sister back to a less messy time, by being so protective of her? Maybe they'd had an idyllic childhood, with a father who wasn't sick yet. Maybe David's vigilance was an attempt at keeping Celeste safe from the ugliness of reality.

Maybe he was trying to build her a fort.

When I emerged from my closet reverie, I took a moment to rehang Celeste's photo. I wasn't quite sure why it had fallen to begin with—there was actually nothing wrong with the way David had installed the nail. To be safe, I took the nail out and hammered it in again, at a bit of a steeper angle. After resting the frame on it, I studied the image for a moment. Even though it was disturbing, there was something compelling about it. Still, I didn't understand how Celeste could want to look at a picture of herself in which she appeared dead. I hoped—for both of their sakes—that David was just a worrier. That he didn't need to protect his sister from anything.

Later, after dinner, I was in the bedroom going over my notes for my first, short English paper when Celeste appeared in the doorway. "I've never been so over-caffeinated in my life," she announced, then hopped in and collapsed next to me on my bed, letting her crutches fall on the floor.

"Where've you been?" I asked.

"The Mean Bean. The guy there is madly in love with me." She handed me a crumpled, white paper bag. "He gave me two free iced latte refills and three of those dark chocolate biscotti. Now I'm supposed to meet people at open mic at Graham House and I'm all juiced up. And I'm going to have to pee every five minutes. You want to come? I might sing. If they're lucky."

"You sing?" I opened the bag and broke off a piece of cookie.

"No. But I pretend I can."

"Tempting," I said, smiling. "I think I'll stay here, though." I was about to turn back to my notes when I remembered. "Hey. Don't you notice anything?"

It took her a moment. "The shades, you mean?"

"Yeah. What do you think?"

"They look okay," she said. "But can't people see right through them? They're just paper."

"No," I said. "Maybe at *most* someone could see fuzzy silhouettes."

I went back to studying as Celeste got up and began putting together an outfit to wear to the open-mic thing. When she'd finally settled on a dark red dress with black net tights, I noticed her looking around at the windows. I thought I saw her shiver slightly, before she grabbed her crutches and her clothes and headed to change in the bathroom.

That night was only one week into the semester. I don't think I ever saw her undress in the bedroom again.

10

THE SHADES DIDN'T DO A VERY GOOD job of helping Celeste sleep, either. With the windows open, they flapped and crackled in the wind. Or so she said. With the windows closed, the air in the room was stagnant and stifling. Also, moonlight filtered in through the rice paper. So, despite my best efforts, after three or so weeks at school, Celeste hadn't gotten a good night of sleep yet, and I heard about it. Often.

Every time someone came to me for peer counseling and had complaints about their roommate—which was a lot of what us counselors dealt with at the beginning of the year—I wished I could offer my own stories, so we could commiserate.

During one of my sessions, a redheaded freshman was especially upset. She sat in the chair across from mine, crying, trying to explain to me all of the ways in which she was unhappy.

"Is the roommate situation what's bothering you the most?" I asked when she seemed to have finished her initial, somewhat rambling explanation.

"Uh-huh." She blew her nose into the tissue I'd given her. "Are people ever allowed to switch?"

"Only in extraordinary circumstances," I said. "Having a roommate is like living with your sister. She might not be your best friend, but you have to make it work."

"But I liked living with my sister," the girl said in a tone verging on a whine. "I wish I still were."

"Why did you come to Barcroft?" I asked. Maybe this wasn't so much about her actual roommate.

"My dad wanted me to. He went here. I . . . I guess I didn't really *not* want to come. But I would've rather stayed with them. I want to be *home*." She crossed her arms and stared out the window. Beyond our reflections in the glass, the new addition to the library glowed in the night, like an enormous, geometric ice sculpture. I could see two people inside gazing back in our direction. For a moment, I thought one was David.

Since spending that morning together installing the shades, he and I had started hanging out a bit—walking to classes, sitting on the steps before the bell, sometimes having a meal at Commons. He'd left a series of notes in my mailbox: The Principles of Spoon Theory. I smiled, thinking of them, forgetting for a moment the girl was waiting for me to say something.

"Well, look at it this way," I said. "You have to change your frame of mind so that from now on, Barcroft is home. When you go visit your parents, you need to think of it that way—as visiting. Otherwise when you're here, you'll always feel like you're *away*, which is kind of an ungrounded way to feel. Right?"

She nodded and sniffled. I offered her the tissue box again.

"So, if you went into Boston next weekend and met someone, and they asked where you lived, you'd say, 'Barcroft,' you know? Instead of . . . ?"

"Greenwich."

"Right. Greenwich. So, to feel like you're in a comfortable, happy home, you need to develop a better relationship with your roommate. Should we write down some ways you might like to talk to her?"

Another nod.

"Don't worry," I said. "We'll get this all worked out."

At nine thirty, I locked the door to the counseling offices behind me and headed to the dorm, enjoying the unmistakable crispness of Massachusetts fall that had blown in this week. I'd looked for Frost House's working fireplace this afternoon, thinking we could start using it soon, and had been surprised to find that it was all bricked up and obviously had been for years. What had I seen that day last fall, when I was deciding whether or not to call the dean? Not smoke from the chimney, sadly.

But fireplace or no, I did still have that lovely, deep, claw-foot tub. As I walked up the porch steps, trying to convince myself that I could concentrate on my homework in a bubble bath, my phone rang. Abby.

"Are you on your way back here?" she said.

"Opening the door now."

"Good," she said, and hung up.

No one was in the common room; somehow, though, the air still snapped with tension, like it was warning me to be on my guard. Voices echoed from down the hall.

Celeste, Abby, and Viv stood in my bedroom, in various postures of hostility—arms crossed or on hips, chins thrust out, feet planted wide. Shards of familiar glossy white-and-green ceramic lay on the floor at their feet, with dried Chinese lantern flowers scattered among the pieces. My stomach plummeted.

"What's going on?" I said.

"Celeste is accusing me of breaking her vase," Abby said.

"Why? What happened?" I asked Celeste.

"She doesn't know," Abby answered before Celeste could speak.

"Jesus." Celeste briefly raised her eyes to the ceiling then looked at me. "I came back from the studio and found Annie standing here with the vase in pieces on the floor. Now she's trying to say David did it? What am I, stupid?"

"I guess so," Abby said. "Because it's Abby. Not Annie."

"Okay, Abby, but you were in here?" I said. For an ugly moment, I remembered the rip in Celeste's skirt and Abby's comments about hoping Celeste would move out. . . . But no, there was no way she'd do something this mean.

Abby held her hands up in front of her. "It was broken when I got here. I swear. I was just borrowing the hoodie." She was wearing a navy-blue sweatshirt of mine that she loved.

"Abby did tell me she was going down to borrow the hoodie," Viv added. "And I didn't hear the sound of something breaking."

"David is here all the time," Abby said. "Bringing her laundry and stuff."

"Why the hell—" Celeste began.

"I know David's around a lot," I said, "but I'm sure he wouldn't have knocked it over and just left it on the floor. And it's not like he's here when Celeste isn't."

"So what are you saying?" Abby asked.

"Nothing." I tried to keep my voice even. "Just that accusing David isn't helping."

"Well, I didn't do it," she huffed.

"Then who did?" Celeste said.

"We've got some strong cross breezes in here," I said, glancing around at the windows, many of which were open. "You're always complaining about them, Celeste. Maybe the vase tipped on its own."

"Right." She used the tip of a crutch to send one of the dried flowers skittering across the room. "You know, I didn't ask to live here. To break up your little party. So I don't see why we can't just live and let live."

Abby sputtered. "We can! You're the one who accused me of doing this."

"Okay!" I said. "Enough!" I dumped my bag on my bed and turned to Celeste. "If Abby says she didn't do it, she didn't do it." I turned to Abby. "David wouldn't have done it." Then to all of them, "Do you guys realize how lucky we are? Instead of being in some big, impersonal dorm, we have this beautiful little house. But if you guys are going to act like this, it's just . . . well, it's going to suck. Am I right?"

I made eye contact with each of them. They nodded unenthusiastically.

"Good," I said. Even though I was annoyed, I didn't want to leave it on this note. "And did you all get my message about what I'm going to cook for the first Sunday dinner? Did it sound okay?"

More nodding. I seemed to be inspiring a lot of that tonight.

"I love your lasagna," Viv said.

"Okay. Well, I don't know about anyone else, but I have a butt load of homework that I haven't even started."

After Viv and Abby disappeared upstairs, I squatted and collected the shards; reaching the floor was tricky for Celeste with her cast. No matter how the vase had broken, I didn't blame her for being upset. But couldn't she have accepted Abby's explanation of what happened? It was as if she was *trying* to make things more difficult here. I handed her the pieces in a plastic bag and, after a mumbled thanks, she headed across the hall to the little room. I swept up the flowers and dumped them in the trash.

When I finally stretched out on the bed, exhausted, my head sank into the pillow so heavily I thought I might never be able to lift it up. For a few moments, I let the room work its magic, tempting me into falling asleep right then, without even taking my clothes off. But I was already stressed out enough by my classes. No way could I afford to skip a night of homework. I had a good three hours or so ahead of me. I dragged myself up and started getting stuff out of my bag. As I rooted around the bottom for a pen, my hand came across something I didn't recognize. I pulled it out, and saw the envelope that David had given me a few weeks ago. Damn.

I knocked on the door to our little study room and then went in.

Celeste sat reading *A Room of One's Own*. (God, if only . . .) The pieces of the vase were spread out in front of her on her desk. She looked up at me.

"I know it was your grandmother's," I said. "Do you want me to try to fix it? I have Gorilla Glue."

"It's in way too many pieces." She put down her book. "It was in the middle of the room, Leena. Not right near the dresser, where it would have fallen."

"Maybe it bounced once, before it broke." I'd seen mugs and glasses do that, instead of smashing at first impact.

She picked up one of the larger shards and ran her finger around the uneven edge.

"I want to keep our rooms locked," she said. "From now on."

I bit the insides of my cheeks. Locking the door in such a small house seemed so aggressively unfriendly. Viv and Abby and I had always gone in and out of one another's rooms, borrowing clothes, books, whatever. . . .

"I know you're upset," I said. "But I wish you'd trust me about Abby."

Celeste was quiet for a moment as she pressed the shard into her fingertip, turning the flesh white. "There's something else," she finally said. "The other day, when I was taking a bath, there was this . . . knocking."

"On the door?" I said.

"No." She shook her head. "I thought so, at first. I thought it was you, so I said I'd be out in a bit. But the knocking didn't stop. Then I realized it was on the wall—not the door. The wall between the bathroom and my closet. Like this." She rapped the desk three times. Waited a second. Rapped four times, then once. An erratic rhythm.

My heart began thumping a little harder, as if responding to her loud beats on the wood. "What was it?" I asked. "A noise in a pipe?"

"No," she said. "Someone was doing it. On purpose."

"What? Who?" Was she saying *Abby* had done this?

"I don't know," she snapped. "It takes me forever to get out of the tub with my cast. I finally hauled my ass out and made it over there, and whoever had been there was gone."

"I don't understand. Why would someone do that?"

"To mess with me. Freak me out."

Okay, *she* was freaking *me* out. "Who would want to mess with you?"

"I just told you, I don't know." Her jaw tightened. "I knew you wouldn't believe me. I didn't even want to tell you. But now, with the vase . . . I'm sure it's the same person. That's why I want to lock the doors."

I tried to think clearly about the best way to approach this before answering. "I'm fine about locking the doors," I said. "If it'll make you feel better, that's not a problem. But I still don't think there's any need to. I think the vase broke by accident. And since nothing happened while you were in the tub, I'm assuming . . . I don't know . . . that it was some other noise you heard. Have you lived in an old house before?"

"Not really."

"Strange noises happen all the time," I explained. "You'll get used to it."

She pursed her lips. "But it sounded so . . . purposeful."

"If someone really did want to mess with you," I said, "that would be a pretty weird way of doing it. Right? I mean, if I were trying to freak someone out, I'd replace their

103

toothpaste with Preparation H, or fill their shoes with pea-nut butter or something."

"Fill their shoes with peanut butter?" Celeste said. "You'd be a crappy freaker-outer."

I laughed, a release of nerves mostly. "You know what I mean. I wouldn't be knocking on a wall. Or breaking a vase, for that matter."

She placed the shard she'd been holding back on her desk. "Yeah. Maybe you're right."

"I'm sure I am."

Feeling like I'd talked her off the ledge, I started out of the room. The minute I was in the hall, though, I remem-bered why I'd gone over to begin with. It took bulldozer force to make myself turn back around. "Celeste?" I held out the small white envelope. "David gave this to me at the beginning of school, and I totally forgot to give it to you. I hope I didn't screw anything up."

She handed it back without opening it. "You should keep it," she said.

"Me? I don't even know what it is."

"The key to his room. Which makes more sense, for his sister to have it, or his girlfriend?"

For a moment, I didn't know what to say. David had a girlfriend?

Then I clued in to her implication. "I'm not his girl-friend," I said.

"I see you guys together all the time," she said. "I don't

mind. I *want* you to get together. I told you that right on the first day. Why else do you think I had him come over to help you hang those shades the other week?"

Oh my God. "You did that on purpose?"

She smirked. "Just moving things along."

I took off my glasses and rubbed the bridge of my nose. "How about this. I'll hang the key on a nail, and then if David's ever locked out, he can know it's here. That's probably why he gave you a copy, right?"

"Okay," she said. "We'll see who's the first one to use it."

I couldn't get out of there soon enough. Back in the bedroom, I lay down and tried to breathe away the tightness in my chest and the ache that was beginning to pulse at my temples.

All of these stories she was constructing in her head! It was just like when we were lab partners—the constant dramas—except now I was one of the people involved. She couldn't just be sad that her vase had broken; she had to make it into a whole mystery with herself as a victim. David and I couldn't just be friends; it had to be a clandestine relationship—orchestrated by her! She thought everyone lived life as out of control as she did, acting on every little emotion. Was she going to do this all semester? Turn everything into more than it was?

Still, as I was having these thoughts, something tickled at the edge of my brain. The knocking on the wall—that was nothing, I was sure. But did I really think a breeze could have blown over a ceramic vase?

I rolled onto my side, facing the window. Cubby stared at me with her big glass eyes. I reached for her, brought her onto the bed.

When I was little, I knew owls were supposed to be wise, so I made up this schoolmarmish voice for Cubby and would ask her questions like she was a wooden oracle.

I think I convinced myself that when I spoke in Cubby's voice, my answers were wiser than they'd otherwise have been.

"Did you see how the vase broke?" I asked her now. "It blew over, right?"

No answer.

"You must have seen it. Was someone in here?"

I looked deep into Cubby's shiny black pupils.

No one, I made her say in her uptight, vaguely English accent. *The room was empty.*

"Thank you," I said, resting her back on the sill.

The room had been empty. Of course it had been. To believe anything else was to be sucked into Celeste's melodrama, and I wasn't going to let that happen.

11

Two DAYS LATER, sitting in my Gender Relations in America seminar, the closer we got to the bell the more distracted I felt.

"So," Ms. Boutillier was saying from the other side of the round table where the seven of us sat, "do you think the author was ahead of his time? Or was he making a remark that was designed to stir controversy and prove that women didn't, in fact, deserve the vote? Did you question his motives when reading?"

I kept my eyes on my text, as if giving her questions deep thought. Really, I was thinking about David.

Over the last couple of weeks, I'd gotten in the habit of leaving by the building's side exit after my seminar. Usually,

David would be coming out of his history class at that same spot. We'd walk over to the mailroom together, check our boxes, stop by senior tea . . . I looked forward to it.

Today, I wondered if I should go out the main exit of Holmes Hall instead. I hadn't run into David anywhere yesterday—the day after the vase incident—and I'd been thinking maybe it would be better if I stopped going out of my way to see him. Just stay away from the freaky Lazar vortex; remove myself from Celeste's rich, imaginative life.

"Leena?" Ms. Boutillier said. "Did you hear those page numbers for tonight?"

"Oh, sorry," I said. "Can you repeat them?" She did, with obvious annoyance, and then the bell finally rang.

I slipped into my canvas army jacket, hoisted my bag over my shoulder, and followed the herd, taking a left toward the main entrance where I'd usually take a right. Then I stopped. David and I weren't doing anything wrong. We weren't doing anything, period. Why play into Celeste's bizarre little game? Also, I wanted to talk to him about what was going on in the dorm. I turned around and headed to where I knew he would be lingering, putting books into his bag.

We swung into step next to each other—my small, blue Chucks next to his bigger, black ones on the shiny checkerboard floor. I imagined Celeste making some comment about the cute couple-ness of it, felt her eyes on us even though she didn't have class in this building.

"How were the genders relating today?" he said.

"You know," I said. "Hostile."

He held the heavy wood door open for me and for a bunch of other people. I passed by him out onto the steps.

"So, I hear there was trouble on the home front," he said, catching up.

"Yeah." I shivered—the sky was gray, the air was damp and cold and bit at my cheeks. "I actually wanted to talk to you about it."

"Senior tea?" he suggested.

"Maybe somewhere more private?"

We were already heading toward the path to the mail-room. I was thinking about a small lounge nearby that was usually empty. I didn't want anyone to overhear me as I talked to him about Celeste.

"Actually," he said, "I have to meet someone later at senior tea. So . . ."

"Oh. Okay." I didn't know why, but this surprised me. Maybe because I hadn't noticed him making any particular friends since he'd been here.

We entered the lower level of the student center and went into the mailroom—a total scene, as it usually was between classes. My box held a coupon packet from local businesses, a flyer for *Buried Child*—the play Abby was in, an Urban Outfitters catalogue, a glossy brochure from my mother's office, and a note to call Dean Shepherd's office. Probably about babysitting.

David came up behind me as I was sorting through

things to keep and recycle. He rested a hand on my shoulder.

"Need a condo in LA?" I asked, waving the real-estate brochure, conscious of the warmth that spread through my body from where he touched me in a way I wouldn't have been if Celeste hadn't made an issue out of it.

"Why are you on a real-estate mailing list?" he asked.

"It's my mother," I said. I glanced at the brochure again. She'd drawn a speech bubble coming out of one of the windows: *Can't wait until you're here!*

I held it out to him and pointed at the building. "That's where she lives."

"Really?" he said. "Wow. Pretty slick."

"Pretty awful," I said, throwing it in the recycling bin.

He gave me a funny look. Sort of . . . pitying.

"That wasn't a statement or anything," I said as we made our way back outside. Ever since I told him about the divorce mess, I'd gotten the impression he thought my relationship with my parents was totally dysfunctional.

"Didn't say it was."

"I know." I fastened a higher button on my jacket to keep the wind out. "I just feel like you might think we're not close anymore. I mean, we're not close the way we used to be, but it's better. I was way too attached to my parents before. The separation had to happen sooner or later."

"I guess," he said, kicking at a couple of acorns on the path. "Seems like they didn't have to make it so traumatic for you, though."

"Maybe." I was kind of annoyed at what he was implying about my parents. "But it all worked out for the best."

We walked up the steps and into Grove Hall, to the same sprawling room where registration had taken place. There was a setup of baked goods, coffee, and tea here for seniors three mornings a week. I waited for an opening in the crowd around the food table—the way we all ate so much, it was as if we hadn't eaten breakfast a couple of hours ago and weren't going to lunch soon—got a pumpkin muffin and a coffee, and met David on a small couch in a corner of the room. He moved his bag off the spot he'd saved for me.

I sat down, shrugged off my jacket, and checked to make sure no one nearby was listening to our conversation. "So, you know about the vase," I said.

"Yup. Am I still a suspect?"

"Don't be silly." I wished Celeste hadn't told him that part of it. "I think it just blew over. Our room has such strong cross breezes, and it was pretty blustery."

"What about Abby?" he asked.

"No," I said, shaking my head. "But that's why I wanted to talk to you. I'm worried that— Well, wait. Did Celeste mention the other thing?"

"What other thing?"

Lowering my voice a notch further, I told him about the knocking noise she'd heard. As I did, the expression on David's face grew more and more concerned.

"Why didn't she tell me this?" he said, pulling his phone

out of his bag. At first, I thought he was calling her, but then I realized he was online, searching for something, following links. "You know that guy she was with over the summer?" he said, still typing.

It took me a second to remember. "The guy in the band?"

"Yeah. I'm just . . . Oh. Here. Hold on." He didn't say anything for a moment, then, "Okay. Good." He turned his phone off and tossed it in his bag. "There's video from a show last night in Amsterdam. He's there."

So David had thought the guy might have followed Celeste here? "Could you really have imagined him doing those things?" I asked, trying to picture a typical rocker guy hiding in Celeste's closet and knocking on the wall.

"It would've been weird," David conceded. "But *he* was weird. Maybe not technically a stalker, but close."

I took a sip of coffee. "I guess dealing with him over the summer explains why she'd be paranoid now." It made me feel a bit better to know that there was something behind her irrationality. "Because I'm sure it was just a noise that the house made, not a person."

"Yeah," David said. "I'm sure you're right."

"Anyway," I said. "I'm worried that from now on, if anything slightly out of the ordinary happens, she's going to blow it out of proportion. Look for someone to blame. Probably Abby. Do you have any suggestions for what I should do to . . . I don't know, make her feel more comfortable in the dorm? And to help convince her that these things really were just random?"

"I can talk to her," he said. "But I bet you don't have to worry. Something else will distract her. Another ill-fated love affair, probably." He smiled a little ruefully.

"And you believe me that Abby didn't break it, right?" I said.

"Sure," he said. "If you say so. I don't even know her."

"You'll get to know her better at the dorm dinner."

"The what?"

It turned out that Celeste hadn't invited him. I'd assumed she had, when she referred to her guest as a "he" a couple days ago. "You should definitely come," I said, trying to cover my surprise and to smooth over the awkwardness. "I'm sorry we didn't invite you sooner."

"That's cool." He was looking at me strangely. "You know," he said, "as long as we're getting stuff out in the open, there's something I need to talk to you about, too."

"There is?" I felt a little surge of nerves at his serious tone of voice.

"Uh-huh. You seem to have a problem, and I'm not sure you realize." He reached forward and softly brushed the side of my head, then grinned as muffin crumbs sprinkled my chest. "Every time you eat, you get food in your hair."

I quickly wiped the crumbs off. "Yeah. That's been pointed out to me before." Shit. My nervous system had had a mini-conniption, wondering what he was going to say and then feeling his hand touching my head and—

"Hey, Leena, David." Simone Dzama, a doe-eyed, environmentally friendly hippie chick, stood by the couch. It was only after she squatted next to David and began talking excitedly about a trip to a green rally in Boston that I realized she was whom he had been meeting. I picked at my muffin as they talked, trying not to listen to them making plans. I studied the shifting sky out the plate-glass windows, then read and responded to a couple of messages that had arrived while I was in class.

Simone finally stood. Before walking away she said, "We should find a time for that other thing, too, David. This weekend or something."

My pulse sped up again, and I knew it wasn't from caffeine.

"Hey." David nudged me.

"I didn't know you were into that stuff," I said. "I mean, enough to go to a rally." *I didn't know you were hanging out with Simone.*

He shrugged. "I'll go if I don't have too much work. Simone's nice. We have English together."

I nodded and took another sip of my now tepid coffee. Obviously, it wasn't just Celeste's involvement that made this friendship with David complicated. I might not want him, but I didn't want anyone else to have him either.

★ ★ ★

With everything that was on my mind, I forgot to call Dean Shepherd until I was on my way to lunch. When I did, Marcia said that the dean wanted to talk to me in person and asked if I could come in at four this afternoon. I told her it wasn't great—I had field hockey at three and wouldn't be done. She said the dean would wait. I briefly wondered why we couldn't just talk on the phone, and why she was willing to stay in the office late for me, but didn't think much of it. I was always happy to see Dean Shepherd.

Some days, I barely got any exercise during field hockey, since I was assistant coaching JVII instead of playing. I wasn't good enough for varsity, and coaching younger kids sounded more fun than a noncompetitive "sport" like "Freedom Movement" or "Boot Camp." Today, though, the team had needed extra players for a scrimmage, and I didn't have time to go home and change before my meeting. I arrived at Irving Hall a mess, in cleats and sweatpants and sweatshirt, bringing along my field hockey stick and the smell of grass, mud, and sweat.

"Sorry I'm so gross," I told Dean Shepherd as I sat across from her. "And you look so nice. I love your blouse."

She glanced down distractedly. "Thanks. Michael gave it to me."

"We're having a dorm dinner soon and if you and Mich—"

"Leena," she interrupted, "I have to pick up Anya in a little bit and didn't call you in here to socialize."

"Oh. Okay, sorry," I said, a bit taken aback.

"A couple of days ago, did you tell Nicole Kellogg that..." She looked down at a piece of notepaper in front of her. The yellow sheet was covered with her loopy handwriting, illegible from where I sat. "... that she doesn't have a home anymore?"

"Nicole Kellogg?" It took a minute for me to remember that she was the crying redheaded freshman I'd counseled. "What? No. Of course not."

"You know how much I trust you," Dean Shepherd said, "but you've got to help me understand what this is about. This girl, Nicole, she's very upset. She's considering leaving school."

"Are you serious? Because of me?" I must not have understood correctly. There was no way.

"What did you say to her?"

I picked up a shiny, leopard-spotted shell from the desk and started running my fingers over it, trying to remember the meeting. "Um, well... She was having trouble with her roommate, not respecting her boundaries, being loud, inconsiderate, you know, normal stuff."

"Mm-hm."

"And I just, I told her that she had to think of her like a sister, who she might not choose to live with, but has to find a way. And that the best way to do that is by trying to communicate right up front about what she needs."

"But did you say something about her home?"

"Just that to be happy at boarding school, it helps to think of school as your home. And your parents' house as just that—your parents' house. Somewhere you visit. Because you don't live there anymore, and probably never will. I mean, right?"

Dean Shepherd's nostrils indented as she drew a deep breath. "Leena, can't you see how upsetting that might be for someone? It's hard enough for her to be away from her family for the first time, but then to tell her that it's not her home anymore? These things have to happen slowly. You don't just break away like that because you've spent a few weeks at boarding school."

I put the shell down, lining it up with a piece of smoky quartz that I'd given to the dean when her husband died. A sick feeling filled my chest. "I guess I see what you mean. But that wasn't my intention. I meant to make her feel better."

"Well, of course. But you said something that came from your personal experience, that didn't help this girl in her situation."

"I . . . I'm sorry. What can I do? Should I talk to her? Tell her she misunderstood me?"

"It doesn't sound like she did misunderstand you. Rather that you used bad judgment in your advice."

I stared down at the grain of the wooden desktop, willing my eyes to stay dry. "So what do you want me to do?"

"I don't think there's anything you can do for Nicole," she said. "I'm dealing with it now. Hopefully, it will blow over, and she'll stay at school. I just want to make sure you understand what you did wrong."

I looked up. "I do. And . . ." I was sure she could see my lips trembling. ". . . I'm sorry."

"All right," Dean Shepherd said with a half smile. "I'm sure it won't happen again."

She began shuffling the papers in front of her. Was there another topic I could bring up? Something to bring us back to the way we usually were?

Before I thought of anything, she said, "Oh—by the way, how's everything in the dorm? One of Celeste's teachers is worried she's seemed kind of tired and distracted this semester. Everything okay?"

"Fine," I said. "She's got a bit of insomnia, but it's better than it was at first." I certainly wasn't going to tell the dean about the problems we were having. That would just give her more proof that I wasn't as good with people as she'd thought. That I wasn't living up to her expectations.

"Okay. Good." She nodded and went back to her papers.

I sat there a moment longer, still feeling like I needed to say something, like I needed to make this better.

"Leena," she said. "You can go now."

I pushed back the chair and stood up. On my way out I noticed I'd tracked clumps of mud all over her rug.

12

I CONCENTRATED ON THE SOUND of my cleats hitting the slate path that crossed the quad—*tock, tock, tock*. I tried not to run, but I wasn't sure how long I could hold in the tears. A girl from Gender class said hi as we passed, and I managed to say it back, my smile straining from fakeness. Okay, I just had to pass Commons and then down the hill and I'd almost be home. *Tock, tock, tock* . . . I reached the driveway, turned in, and there was Celeste. Coming toward me. I wiped under my nose.

"Can't talk," she said, moving as fast as I'd seen her go on crutches. "I am so, so, so late."

Thank God. "When will you be home?" I asked, trying to sound casual.

"Not till after dinner." She almost passed by me, but then stopped. "By the way, thanks for telling David all that." Her voice was heavy with sarcasm.

"Oh. I—"

"You told him I was *paranoid*? What were you thinking? Do you realize the crap I have to deal with now?"

I pulled myself together with my last bit of energy. "Sorry. I was worried about you."

"You don't have to worry about me," she said. "*David* doesn't have to worry about me. I told you that before. I told you to keep your mouth shut."

"Sorry," I said again, but she'd already turned away from me.

I hurried down the side path and up the porch steps, my field hockey stick clattering against them. The minute I burst through the door I knew the house was empty; I could tell by the stillness. And, oh . . . it felt so good to be home. The solid walls wrapped around me like a blanket. I headed straight to my bed, curled up on my side, and hugged my pillow, letting my tears soak into it, trying to muffle the dean's voice echoing in my head. *Bad judgment* . . . How could I have been so stupid, saying those things to that girl? And what if she left school because of me? I'd be responsible for ruining her chance here at Barcroft. All I wanted was to turn back time, to talk to that girl again and say the right thing.

I reached for Cubby and wrapped my hand tightly

around her. *Calm down,* I told myself. I drew in deep breaths as well as I could through my stuffed nose. *You made a mistake. Everyone makes mistakes.* I traced Cubby's feathers with my fingertip—over and over. *It's okay to be upset. You'll feel better soon.*

Through my rough breaths, I heard a noise—the front door opening. I sat up and wiped my face, listened to the sound of someone coming in the entryway. It wasn't Celeste. Her crutches were so distinctive. But whoever it was didn't go upstairs either. Footsteps started across the common room, which meant they were headed in this direction.

I didn't have time to think, just knew I couldn't bear talking to anyone. Quick and quiet, I hurried to the only safe place—Celeste's closet. I pulled the door closed behind me—it made no noise at all—slid through dresses and skirts, all the way to the back, into a corner, Cubby clutched in my hand.

I made it there just in time; footsteps sounded in the room.

I sat very, very still. Who was out there? Viv or Abby, borrowing clothes again? I didn't hear drawers being opened. But it wasn't someone just checking if we were here—they would have left already, if that were the case.

Maybe . . . maybe someone *had* broken Celeste's vase on purpose. Maybe whoever it was was in the room now, looking for something else to do to her. Was that possible? I swallowed, reached forward slowly, carefully, and parted the curtain of clothes, hoping . . . No, there wasn't a keyhole to look through, nothing to—

Click-click.

My body went rigid.

The doorknob right in front of me—it was turning. The door itself rattled.

Someone was trying to get into the closet.

Click-click. I shrank back against the wall, my heart beating like crazy now, beating so hard I was sure the person could hear it through the solid wood barrier between us. What should I do? What *could* I do? I pressed my spine harder against the wall as the doorknob *click-click-click*ed and the door rattled some more. I wondered if I pressed back hard enough whether the wall would open up and swallow me before the door unstuck. *Click, click, rattle, rattle.* My heart was about to stop, it was *thump-thump-thump*ing too hard. I pressed back and closed my eyes, waiting for the inevitable light to stream in. A little kid, thinking, *If I don't see you, you don't see me.*

Rattle, rattle. BAM. Like a fist against the door now. *Click-click, rattle, rattle.*

Maybe the person had ripped Celeste's skirt, too, and had hidden in this very closet and knocked on the wall with the same fist they were now—*BAM*—banging against the door.

I held Cubby up to my face, wrapped both my hands around her, and prayed to whatever nameless entity someone like me who doesn't believe in anything prays to, and then . . .

Nothing.

Wait . . .

Still nothing.

The rattling, the turning—they had stopped before my heart did.

Now, a voice. A male voice, incongruously calm, muffled but still understandable. "Hey, so, I'm here trying to get your laundry bag, but I can't open the damn closet. Is there some trick? Anyway, I'll come by later, I guess. But call if you get this message in the next couple minutes."

David. Leaving a message for Celeste. It was David.

A shudder poured through me. Both relief that no one was doing something bad to Celeste—of course they weren't—but also a moment of panic at the thought of David being the one to find me in here. How would I have explained that I was hiding in his sister's closet?

His footsteps left the room. I sat for a minute, letting my body recover from the scare. Every muscle had been taut, and as they loosened, I even laughed quietly at how ridiculously frightened I had been. I briefly considered taking some sort of calming pill, but then realized that sitting here in the closet was having a similar effect. Surrounded by the smell of my attic and these cool walls, in the now not-quite-pitch dark. Just light enough so I could make out where things were. Being in here made everything seem so far away—what had happened with the dean, my confusion about David. In here, there was a sense of being out of time and place. Safe.

I held Cubby up to my face. "Rough day," I said. "Any advice, O wise one?"

Stay in here, she said.

So I did. I leaned my head back against the wall and let myself just be.

Eventually, though, I realized that Celeste might come home earlier than she'd said. I pushed through her clothes, and as I put my hand on the doorknob, I wondered why it hadn't occurred to me that I might not be able to get *out*, since David hadn't been able to get in. But when I turned the knob, the door opened easily. Like it always did for me. Back in the bedroom, I shut the door again and tried to open it. No problem. Why hadn't it opened for David, after all his shaking and rattling? Was it like when you try to open a jar, and you strain with all your might, and then hand it to someone else and it comes off first twist?

I supposed that's all it was, that I'd been incredibly lucky, and with one more pull, David would have gotten in. It didn't seem quite believable that he hadn't been able to, since he was trying so hard, but I couldn't think of another explanation.

As I stood there with my hand on the door, I said a little thank-you to Frost House, for doing such a good job of protecting me.

13

Ms. Martin's kitchen resembled a construction site, the counters covered with ingredients and cooking equipment for the inaugural dorm dinner. Abby was helping me make vegetarian lasagna, garlic bread, and arugula salad with apples and toasted walnuts, and helping frost the red velvet cupcakes I'd baked yesterday afternoon.

I opened the freezer door of the ancient mustard-yellow refrigerator and took out two packets of spinach I'd stored there. I'd just finished telling Abby how bad I'd screwed up when trying to help that girl Nicole, and how upset Dean Shepherd had been. I'd been worried that talking about it would make me feel like an idiot, that it would bring back all of the horrible feelings. But Abby was so incensed, so convinced I'd done nothing wrong, that I actually felt better.

"I can't believe you didn't tell me this sooner," Abby said. "I would've kicked that girl's ass. And then kicked the dean's ass, too. Maybe I still will."

"Please don't," I said, smiling as I imagined it.

"If she leaves school because of this, she's a total wuss. Good riddance." Abby threw the top of an onion in the trash for emphasis.

"I saw her from across the quad today, so she hasn't left yet," I said. "Can you hand me that?"

She reached for the glass bowl I'd gestured at. "Why'd you lock your room today?" she said as she passed it to me. "I wanted to get back the jeans you borrowed."

I hadn't mentioned to Viv and Abby that we'd started locking it. I'd been hoping that, by some miracle, they wouldn't find out, and that Celeste would change her mind once she calmed down and realized we didn't need to.

"No reason," I said, placing the icy, green bricks in the bowl. Leo the cat rubbed his side against my leg. "I can't pick you up while I'm cooking, cutie. Sorry."

"I'm too heavy to pick up anyway." Abby patted her stomach.

"Ha."

"But seriously," she said. "You never lock your room. There must be some reason."

"Celeste and I agreed that since we're on the first floor, maybe it'd be a good idea." I slid the bowl in the microwave.

Abby was quiet for a moment. "Did she tell you to? Because she thinks I broke that vase?"

"We're just being careful, Abb. I told her you didn't do it."

Abby rinsed a red pepper and set it on the cutting board. Then she said, "I've tried to be nice. What's her problem?"

"She doesn't know you." I turned my attention to the flashing countdown on the microwave. I hated being caught between them like this. "If she did, she wouldn't have accused you to begin with." The microwave beeped. I stirred the spinach into a ricotta-and-egg mixture.

Abby's chopping had slowed to one chop per second. It occurred to me that I had a perfect change of subject. "You know," I said. "She invited Whip to this dinner."

Abby looked over at me. "Whip? Are you kidding?"

I grinned and shook my head. "Nope. I just found out."

"Celeste invited Whip. Why? What possible reason?"

Whip Windham—Spaulding Whipple Windham IV—is an old-school preppie of the madras shorts and bluchers, white-blond hair and thin lips, destined to be a (Republican) member of Congress, variety.

"They're doing some project together," I explained.

"Wow." Abby smiled, bucked up by this amusing piece of news, as I knew she would be. "That's quite a couple. Green Beret and Whippersnapper. Whichever teacher paired them up is my new hero. I'd love to be a fly on the wall while they're working together."

I laughed. "Whip's probably scared to death."

"I assumed she invited David for dinner," Abby said. "Viv told me he's coming."

I stirred more vigorously.

"Leen? I thought we were all only supposed to invite one person?"

"I invited David," I said.

"What? Celeste made you?"

"No. I wanted to." I poured olive oil into a pan on the stove. "He's a really good guy, Abby. You should see how much he worries about his sister. He's not all obsessed with himself, like the other guys here are."

"Yeah," she said, "instead of being obsessed with himself he's obsessed with her. He's in here all the time, carrying her books, her laundry. God knows what else. I don't think it's nor—"

"Abby," I said. "He's my friend. Okay?"

"Oh my God," she said, putting down her knife. "You like him."

"Yeah," I said. "I do. As a friend."

"You want to have his crazy babies!"

"Jesus." I turned from the snapping and cracking pan of hot oil to face her. "You sound just like Celeste."

Abby stared at me, obviously taken aback. "Thanks a lot."

"I mean . . . the way you're blowing this up just to make it into a big drama. We're friends, okay? Sure I have a crush on him, but we're just friends. And if you gave him a chance, you'd like him, too. It doesn't mean anything bad that he's Celeste's brother."

"Okay," she said, picking up the knife again. "Whatever you say."

Whip brought out a silver, monogrammed flask from the inside pocket of his navy blazer.

"My contribution to the evening, ladies." He poured a shot into the can of Coke I'd just given him and offered me the flask.

I sniffed it.

"Grey Goose," he said. "I have a second one. Plenty for all."

Ms. Martin was out until eight at the earliest—that's when we had to be finished in her kitchen—so I added a splash of the vodka to my own can of soda and passed the flask to Cameron. Abby's "date," the guy who was playing Tilden in the play, had canceled; it was the four of us Frost Housers, plus David, Whip, and Cam.

Since we didn't have a proper dining table, the seven of us were seated around the coffee table in the common room. Celeste wore a slinky silver evening dress and a thin black shawl over her shoulders. With Whip's blazer and khaki pants with embroidered whales, they made quite a pair sitting together on the couch.

I went into the kitchen and started bringing out the plates of food I'd prepared. As I brought out the last two,

Whip was saying, "I can't believe they made this place a girls' dorm. I was supposed to live here. My great-grandfather, my grandfather, and my father all did. It's a frigging Spaulding Whipple Windham tradition."

"It's been around that long?" Viv asked.

"My great-grandfather lived here the first year it was a dorm."

"What was it before that?" I said, settling cross-legged on the floor next to David.

Whip took a bite of lasagna, chewed, wiped his mouth, and then said, "A family's house—nothing to do with Barcroft. My grandfather says during his time, all the guys made a big joke of living here because there'd been some hysterical chick—I mean, woman—living in it years before. Like the chick in the attic in *Wuthering Heights*."

"*Jane Eyre*," I said. "You know, Whip, it's not really referred to as hysteria anymore."

"What is it now? PMS?"

"Yeah. Right," I said. My eyes met David's. He gave his a slight roll, then reached over and picked something out of my hair.

Food, already? "Lasagna?" I whispered, appalled.

David grinned. "Kidding."

"He told me this story," Whip went on as I made a face at David, "about how everyone was scared of Frost House because of the rumors about the girl. So they pretended it was haunted or some shit and got all these kids to come over." He took a swig of his drink.

"And?" Celeste said after a minute.

"And what?" Whip said.

"What happened?" Celeste asked.

"What do you mean?" Whip said. "That's what happened. They scared people and got busted for making some freshman piss his pants."

"Sounds like a good time," David said. "Can you pass the salad, Vivian?"

"Yeah," Whip said, apparently not noticing David's sarcasm. "Anyway, it sucks they made it a girls' dorm this year."

"Everyone always thinks Victorian houses are haunted," I said, finishing chewing a bite. "When I was little, my friends were scared to spend the night because we lived in an old Queen Anne and they thought it was creepy. It was so stupid."

"Maybe that was just an excuse," Abby said, "because they didn't want to spend the night with you."

"Very funny." I rolled a bread ball and shot it at her. We were pretty much back to normal after our spat in the kitchen, but I could tell that she was still mad I'd compared her to Celeste.

"What dorm are you in, Whip?" Viv asked.

"He's in Franklin," Celeste said. "It's a nice room. All new furniture. Really swank. I think the mattress is new, too. Good and bouncy. Not like the terrible ones we have here."

Whoa. I glanced at David. He was frozen, his fork halfway between his plate and mouth.

"So, what type of 'project' are you guys doing?" Abby asked Celeste and Whip in a suggestive tone.

"It's for rel-phil," Celeste said. "We're each other's gods."

"You're what?" Abby said.

"We each have to dress the other one as our idea of a god. Then take a photograph, write a paper about physical representations of gods, blah, blah. Whip's going to be naked."

Whip's eyebrows shot up. "Come again?"

"My god does not wear clothes." Celeste reached over and tugged the lapel of his blazer. "Especially not whale pants."

I was thoroughly amused by their interaction; but the look of horror on David's face told me he wasn't.

Whip wiped his mouth with the back of his hand. "I've got nothing to be ashamed of. But there's no way I'm letting photos get out that might ruin my political career."

"Are you serious?" Celeste said. "That would be your objection? Oh, you are so getting naked. I already have this idea for body paint I want to put on you."

A loud clattering came as David reached to put his plate on the coffee table and somehow knocked off a tray of cheese and crackers.

"Damn," he said. "Sorry." He began collecting the things that had scattered on the carpet.

I stood up. "More lasagna, anyone? While I'm in the kitchen?"

"Sure. Great food, Leena," Cameron said, handing me his plate.

"Leena's *my* god," Viv said to the room. "She can cook, build furniture, fix her car, *and* tie a knot in a cherry stem with her tongue."

"You're so modest, Leena," Celeste said. "You make it seem like you're just another pretty, blond prep-school student."

"That's nice," Abby said, turning to Celeste with a laser glare.

"What?" Celeste said. "I just meant that you'd never know she was so talented because she doesn't talk about herself."

"As opposed to you," Abby said.

"That's okay. I know what Celeste meant," I interjected. "Who wants a cupcake?"

"Damn right," Celeste said to Abby, ignoring me. "I know I'm talented and ambitious and if I work hard, I'll be successful. And I don't think there's anything wrong with saying that. Guys get away with bragging all the time."

"You don't know," Abby said. "Anything could happen."

"What's that supposed to mean?" David asked.

"Coffee?" I said.

"What I said." Abby crossed her arms. "Anything could happen that would mean Celeste isn't some raving success."

"Look," David said, "if you're implying what I think you're implying, that's—"

"I think she's just referring to life's unpredictability," I said, my arms now loaded up with dirty plates to bring to the kitchen. "Abby, can you help me here? Please? I'm about to drop something."

In the lovely calm of Ms. Martin's apartment, I took my time rinsing dishes and getting more food for Cameron. While Abby figured out the glass coffee-brewing contraption. I decided not to tell her to lay off Celeste, knowing that she was probably still feeling sensitive. The ironic thing was now that I thought about it, Abby and Celeste *did* have some similarities. Abby completely thought that she had the talent to be a successful professional actress, that stardom was hers for the taking. She'd only jumped on Celeste like that because she thought Celeste had dissed me.

When we got back into the common room, the mood had completely changed. Viv was doing a dance like a football player in the end zone, saying, "Oh, yeah. Oh, yeah," waving her phone in the air.

"What's up, Vee?" Abby said. "Some great-uncle die and leave you his fortune?"

"Better," Viv said. "I got a message from my mother. You know how we have that random Monday off in a few weeks?"

"Curriculum Development Day," I said, handing Cameron his refilled plate.

"Yeah. Do you guys want to spend the long weekend

in New York, *sans* parents? They're going to be in Paris and totally offered us the house."

"Really?" I said. Viv's family has an incredible town house that overlooks a huge park in Brooklyn. "If they won't be there, who'll write our chaperone letters?"

She waved a hand dismissively. "Dad'll write the letters. He doesn't care about rules like that."

"Exdese!" Abby bounced up and down on the armchair as well as the ancient cushions would allow. "Truly exdese!"

"Don't get too excited," Whip said to Celeste. "Viv's house is in an outer borough. Not the city."

"Oh," Celeste said. "I don't think . . ."

A series of darting looks passed among us as we all realized the awkwardness of the moment. Viv and I held eyes for a second.

"Of course you're invited," Viv said to Celeste. "There's plenty of room. And David, you should come, too. Cameron will be there so you won't be totally outnumbered."

"Thanks," David said. "I have to see whether I signed up for a Ride Club trip."

"If you ladies want to get out of the suburbs, I'll be at my parents' on the Upper East Side. You're welcome to come visit," Whip said. "I can send a car."

"You're such a snob," Viv said.

"And what would it take to get *you* out to Brooklyn?" Celeste poked Whip on the shoulder. Her touch lingered.

I sensed movement from my right and when I looked over, David was standing and reaching for his jacket. "I just realized I've got something to do," he said. "Sorry. I totally forgot."

In amazingly quick time, he was out the door.

14

AN HOUR OR SO LATER, dinner was over, Viv and Cameron had banished me from the cleanup stage, and the vodka in my head wasn't helping me decipher what had happened. I couldn't sort out who had been mad or offended and why, and what repercussions there might be, if any, not to mention what the hell was going on with Celeste and Whip. Or Celeste and David. And the trip to New York! God.

I paced around my bedroom, picking things up and putting them down. When I walked by Celeste's closet, I touched the doorknob. The next time, I let my hand rest on it, curving around the beveled glass. My hand turned and I heard the click of the latch and felt the door moving toward me as my arm pulled back. A shudder went through me as the air crept out.

Stepping away for a moment, I peeked into the hall to make sure that Celeste and Whip were in the little room with the door shut. Then I closed the door to the bedroom and locked it from the inside. Following an impulse, I grabbed Cubby off the windowsill.

I left the closet door open a crack so I'd have some light and so I'd be able to hear any movement from the hallway. I sat on the floor and shifted myself into the corner, partially covered by Celeste's clothes, leaving a space for the wedge of light to stream through. I leaned my head against the wall and breathed in the cool, musty air.

I held Cubby up and looked in her eyes, which were catching just a bit of the light. "That was quite a dinner party, didn't you think?" I said to her.

How on earth would I know? I said to myself in Cubby's accent. *I wasn't even there.*

"Oh, right," I whispered. "It got kind of messy. Boys, you know."

Boys, yes. They can be dangerous.

"But cute," I said.

All the same, you need to be careful.

I ran my finger over her feathers, up and down the scalloped ridges.

"It's not like you have to worry," I said. "You're all nice and safe back here."

I'm not the one who isn't safe.

I didn't like the voice she used when she said that. Of course, it was *my* voice. But at the same time, somehow, it wasn't.

The bird tweet ringtone of Celeste's phone disrupted whatever tipsy weirdness I was indulging in. I quickly pushed myself up and out of the closet, brushing the clothes back into place and shutting the door securely behind me.

Her cell lay on her dresser. David's name flashed on the screen. I touched the glittery blue case and thought of him on the other end, pictured him shifting from foot to foot, the way he did, hoping the call would be answered. The tweets stopped.

I put Cubby back on the sill, her eyes facing the window. For once, I didn't feel like having her watching over me. Then I sat on my bed with my head in my hands. After a minute I stood, picked up Celeste's phone, and returned the call.

He answered right away. "Are you done with that jerk, or what?"

"Oh, hi, David . . . it's Leena. Not Celeste. Her phone was right here so . . ."

"Oh. Hey. What's up?"

"Not much. I just wanted to see if everything was okay. You left kind of suddenly."

"Sorry about that. Just something I forgot to do." He paused. "Is Celeste still with that guy?"

"Um, yeah."

"Do you think I should come back over?"

"Come over and . . . ?"

"I don't know. Distract her."

"I think she's okay. You missed dessert. Cupcakes." I checked the time. Still fairly early. "I could bring one over to you there. If you wanted."

There was silence on the other end. "Okay," he finally said. "Sure, if you feel like getting out."

I glanced over at the door to Celeste's closet. What had I been doing in there? "Yeah," I said, "I definitely need to get out."

When I got to Prescott Hall, I phoned from downstairs for David to meet me to get parietals. He didn't answer. I sat on one of the scratchy, yellow ochre couches in the lounge and called a couple more times, feeling progressively more idiotic about the foil-wrapped cupcake in my hands and the nervousness that had wriggled in my stomach on the way over. Obviously, we'd had a misunderstanding. Or had he changed his mind and was now just ignoring me?

I was about to give up when I heard the groan of a door being pushed open. David appeared, carrying a navy-blue laundry bag Santa style, sweaty and apologizing. "I had stuff in the dryer," he said, leading me down the hall to his house counselor's apartment. "And I realized that if I got it now, I could have you bring Celeste her clothes. Took longer than

I thought. Sorry."

"Don't worry," I said, not mad, just relieved.

Prescott has none of the hominess of Frost House, and none of the stateliness of the larger brick dorms. Walking with David to his room after getting parietals, I cringed at the cinder-block walls, the fluorescent lighting, and the nubby brownish-orange carpeting spread everywhere like a fungus.

"Home, sweet home," David said, pushing open the door to a second-floor single.

I guess I'd expected his aesthetic to be more like Celeste's; the lack of decoration in his room surprised me. His comforter was plain black, his sheets and pillowcase light gray with white stripes. He'd hung nothing on the beige walls except a bulletin board, and the fungus carpeting had spread in here, too. Built-in plywood furniture gave the room even more of an institutional feel.

I'd have had no idea David even lived here if it weren't for the photos on the bulletin board: the same snapshot Celeste had of the two of them on the beach with their father, and one of David wrestling on a lawn with three young boys. There was also a large one of a smiling, long-faced woman hugging an enormous black dog. Otherwise the board was covered with notebook paper with ungainly mathematical equations using symbols I'd never even seen before.

I handed David the cupcake and a paper napkin, and didn't say what I was thinking—that I'd kill myself if I had to live in a room like this.

"Thanks a lot," he said. "Make yourself comfortable." He sat on the bed and began unwrapping the tinfoil.

I didn't know where to sit or what to do with myself—David's desk chair had a pile of books on it and I wasn't about to plop right next to him on the bed.

Then I noticed a cardboard box on the floor with a bunch of silvery stuff inside. Spoons.

"Hey!" I gestured at the box. "Can I look?"

"Sure," David said through a bite of cupcake.

I picked it up and rested it on the desk, then began taking the spoons out and laying them next to each other. They were satisfyingly weighty, and all had the same handle design—a loop—but the bowl part was different. There were a few with different-size holes in the middle, one shaped like a small ladle, one with an inverted V-rest on the handle. . . . They looked handcrafted, but not in a bad way—like someone had put care into them.

"These are so cool," I said. "Why are they all packed away?"

"You want me to bring them to Commons?" he asked.

"You should have used one at dinner tonight," I said, smiling.

He finished chewing and wiped his mouth. "Great cake. Your lasagna, too. I'll have to reciprocate sometime. I make killer Pad Thai."

"You cook?"

"Last year, when I was home, my mom was working a lot, so I cooked all our family meals." He tossed the aluminum foil in the trash and picked up his laundry bag. "Until my dad stopped eating anything I'd made, of course."

Oh, right. I hadn't thought about that since he'd first told us, the day we met. Now, knowing how much he cared about his family, it seemed that much more awful—his father thinking he was trying to poison him. Something inside me crumpled, imagining how David must have felt.

"All my paying jobs have been in restaurant kitchens," he continued as he dumped the laundry on his bed and began sorting it into two piles. "Next year, I might just work at this place in New York where I know the owner, make some money."

"Are you applying to schools this year? And then deferring?" I realized that in all our conversations, we'd never talked about his college plans.

"I don't think so. It's . . ." He kept his eyes on the laundry. "It's complicated. There's this professor I want to study with, but I'm not sure I want to go to school full-time, do all the required classes, you know. And the stuff with Pembroke won't help me getting in."

"What happened there?" I asked, since he'd brought it up.

"I plagiarized on a paper," he said. "Stupid. I'd fallen really far behind because I was going home all the time. And I'd been caught before for something else, so I got booted."

"Something else?"

"Illegal parietals," he said, completely matter-of-fact, then looked over at me. "So, what's the deal with this Whip guy? Has he been over to the dorm before?"

"Not that I know of." I turned back to the spoons, trying not to wonder about the girl he'd gotten busted with. "I assume he's just there to work on the project."

"It was pretty obvious he wasn't just there to work on the project."

David was right, of course. And I understood why he'd been upset at dinner—he didn't want his little sister's sex life shoved in his face. But, in the end, wasn't whatever Celeste wanted to do with Whip her own business?

"Whip's not such a bad guy," I said. "Unless it bothers you that he's part of the old-boys' club. I think every male in his family has gone to Barcroft and then Yale." One of the spoons had some sort of dirt on it. I wiped it with my shirt.

"Celeste tends to have really bad judgment when it comes to guys," David said.

"*Most* of my friends have bad judgment when it comes to guys. Except for Viv." I looked over at David and noticed he was tossing a pair of Celeste's lacy underwear into her pile of clean clothes. For a brief second it freaked me out, but what else was he going to do? Of course, he washed her underwear when he did her laundry.

"It's different with Celeste," David said. "Her decisions are . . . self-destructive. Look at that guy she picked this summer." He shoved the pile of her clothes into a bag and set it on the floor. "She never listens to me about guys. But maybe . . . maybe you could say something."

"About Whip? What would I say?"

"You're the peer counselor," he said. "I'm sure you can think of something."

"Yeah, but in peer counseling, people come to me," I said, feeling a little uncomfortable. "Honestly, I'd feel weird saying something without having noticed anything bad going on."

He nodded. "Yeah. I get that." And then, without explanation, he grabbed his jacket and keys off the desk and said, "Okay, let's go."

"Go?" Back to Frost House?

He held the door open and herded me with a nod of his head. I followed him to the far end of the hallway and up two flights of a dim, concrete staircase until we reached a big metal door with a sign that said EMERGENCY ONLY. ALARM WILL SOUND on it. Between WILL and SOUND someone had drawn a line leading to the scrawled word *Not*. And, sure enough, as David pushed the door open, no siren blared. He led me out onto the flat, expansive roof, the sky opening up above us. Dark and starry.

"Wow," I said, stating the obvious. "It's beautiful up here."

He crossed over to a rectangular raised area, about the size of a small bench, then sat and patted the spot next to him. We barely fit on it together, so I had to sit with my body pressed against his. For a few minutes we were both quiet, staring up at the stars. I felt the crisp night air sneaking around my neck, and the heat off of David's body seeping into mine, smelled the mulch of fall and his spicy scent.

Eventually, he was the one to break the silence. "I thought going to school with her was going to be great," he said. "But . . . in some ways, it was easier to be apart. Because I can't always make everything okay for her. And even though I know that, I can't help trying."

"You're such a good brother," I said, melting a little at how vulnerable he sounded. "She's lucky."

He gave a brief laugh. "Don't think she'd agree."

"She would."

"You know . . ." He shifted forward, leaning his elbows on his knees, and turned his face toward me. "I've been feeling kind of bad about something."

"What?"

"The other week, I didn't mean to say your parents aren't good parents, or anything like that. I think I was, well, being kind of protective of *you*."

"Oh," I said, remembering that he had sounded judgmental about them. "That's okay."

"No it's not. I'm not your brother."

"I wish you were," I said.

"You do?" He didn't attempt to hide the surprise in his voice.

"Growing up I was always happy it was just me and my

146

parents," I explained. "But maybe the divorce wouldn't have felt so much like a total . . . destruction of the family if I had siblings."

"Oh," he said and, then after a pause, added, "but you don't really want *me* as a brother, right? Because, no offense, I don't really want you as a sister."

His words sent a rush of warmth through my veins. I stared down at my feet and smiled. "No, I guess not."

"You *guess* not?" He nudged me.

"Well, it'd be kind of like having a bodyguard," I said. "Someone to save me from men in whale pants."

"Oh, God," David said in an amused voice. "If it makes you feel any better, she's just as harsh about my choices."

I reached down and scratched one of my calves, and made myself ask the question I wasn't sure I wanted answered. "Did you, um, did you have a girlfriend at Pembroke? The one you got busted with?"

"Not really."

"Not *really*?"

"I never had a girlfriend so much as, well . . . friends who were girls." He gave an exaggerated cough.

"Oh. Why? Were you making self-destructive decisions?" I said, ignoring the queasy sensation in my stomach. Of course a guy as good-looking as him was a player.

David laughed. "Maybe. I didn't give it too much thought at the time. Just did what I wanted to do."

I could imagine Jake or Theo saying the same thing

about how they'd treated me, and was considering asking David whether the girls had appreciated his selfishness when he said, "I wouldn't be that way now, though," in a new, more serious tone of voice.

"Oh?" I said.

"Definitely not." He sounded so sure.

"That's . . . that's cool."

"What about you?" he said.

"What about me?"

"Where do you stand with the whole boyfriend thing?" Was I imagining it, or had he somehow found a way to press even closer to me? Having a conversation when I was near enough to share his breath was kind of difficult. The distraction of the pulsing and fluttering in my body . . .

I adjusted my glasses, swallowed. "I went out with a couple different guys, freshman and sophomore year. Now, this semester at least, I kind of don't want to deal. I have so much else to think about. I know that sounds lame, but . . ."

"So, that's it? You're just . . . not interested?"

Wait, did he mean in general, or in him?

"I . . ." Breathe normally. Speak normally. "This fall, I've put a moratorium on dating. I'm so stressed-out about colleges, and keeping my grades up, and everything. I'm going to reassess after break."

"A moratorium?" he said.

"Yeah." I nodded, feeling like an idiot.

"That's too bad," he said. Or, at least, that's what I thought he said, but my blood was rushing so loudly in my ears I wasn't quite sure. If it is what he said, why was it too bad? Because of him? Because it meant we couldn't be together?

"So do you really think Celeste and I should go to New York with you guys?" he said, interrupting my spontaneous combustion. "What if she and Abby end up killing each other?"

Given my own fear about the dynamics on the trip, I was surprised by my immediate response. "You should definitely come," I said. "You can ride down with me. It'd be much more comfortable for Celeste than the bus."

"I've seen your car," he said. "Can it make it to New York?"

"Didn't you hear Viv?" I said. "I can tie a cherry stem in a knot with my tongue *and* fix my car."

"Simultaneously?" he asked.

I laughed, then checked the time on my phone and immediately jumped to my feet. "I didn't realize how late it was. I have to go."

After stopping back by his room to pick up Celeste's laundry, David walked me downstairs to the front entrance of the dorm. A group of senior guys were playing Nerf basketball in the common room.

"Hey, Leena," Matt Halpern said. "Pretty late for parietals, isn't it?"

"She *came* earlier, dude, so now she's going," one of the

other guys said. They snorted and jostled one another. I couldn't look at David's face.

"Thanks again for the cake," he said as he opened the door. He was positioned so I had to pass just inches from him to get out. I didn't want to go outside, but those stupid guys could see us standing there.

"Leena?" he said.

The planes of his face were sharp and strong in the harsh fluorescent light, but his voice was soft. "Yeah?"

"I understand it's an awkward situation, but if you can think of anything to say to Celeste, about that guy, I'd really appreciate it. Only if you feel comfortable."

Gazing at me with those eyes, he could have asked me to do just about anything and I would have agreed.

"I'll try," I said.

"And . . . the moratorium. It's only one semester, right?"

"Yeah," I said. "One semester."

Suddenly, that sounded very, very long.

15

I MADE IT BACK TO FROST HOUSE with forty seconds to spare before sign-in, sweaty and breathing hard after running the whole way from Prescott carrying the bag of laundry. As I scribbled my name on the sheet, I noticed that Whip had signed out only fifteen minutes ago. Not a development I'd be reporting back to David.

I wasn't quite ready to be inside, and definitely didn't feel like dealing with Celeste, so I dropped her laundry bag in the common room and sat out on the porch in one of the Adirondack chairs. I stared up at the sky over the trees and tried to bring myself back to the roof. I didn't want to worry, right now, about anything that had been said. I just wanted to remember the feeling of my side pressed against his. The warmth and solidity of his arm, his torso, his thigh . . . The unmistakable reaction inside me and on my skin. How could something so passive—just sitting there next to another body—feel so good in so many different ways? A sense of complete safety combined with that giddy flitter-flutter that thrummed all the way to my toe tips.

"Someone there?" Ms. Martin called from her front doorway.

"It's me, Leena," I called back. "Sorry. I'm here on the porch."

She padded around the corner, wrapped in a bathrobe. "I wanted to make sure it was one of you girls."

"Just me," I said, standing. "But I'm going in now."

I went inside, and when I tried to open the bedroom door was surprised to find it was still locked. I got out my key and slid it in the lock, pushed the door—

"Leena?" Celeste's voice called out from somewhere. Not the bedroom.

"Yeah?" I said, turning around.

"Can you . . . can you come in here?" She was in the bathroom. Probably taking one of her frequent nighttime baths.

Figuring she had forgotten something—she had a hard time getting out of the tub, and was always needing me to bring her a razor or towel or something else—I tossed her laundry bag in our room and went in. She was sitting in the bath, a thin layer of bubbles covering the surface of the water. Her cast was propped up on her special bath stool, in its plastic bag. Her other leg was bent, her arms wrapped around it. There was something not quite right about her face. Her jaw muscles were tense, her skin paler than usual. She looked like she might be trembling.

"Are you okay?" I said.

She shifted positions slightly to show me: a bright red mark seared the back of her left upper arm. I knelt quickly by the tub. It was a burn. The size of a baby's fist. Not blistered, but still obviously painful.

"What happened?" I asked.

"I . . . I was sitting here while the water was running," she said. "And I guess . . . I guess I bumped against the faucet. I don't remember. It happened so quickly, and then it hurt so much."

"That's from the faucet?" I said. "The water must have been so hot."

She shook her head. "I was trying to cool the bath down. Only the cold water was turned on."

"You must have turned the wrong handle."

"I didn't." Then she said it again, louder. "I didn't. I know which handle I turned. This wasn't my fault."

The faucet couldn't have burned her if it was running cold water, obviously, but there was no point in me fighting with her. What mattered was her burn.

"Let's drain the bath," I said. "And then you need to hold your arm under a stream of cool water. I'll cover the faucet with a facecloth." As I did, I found that the metal wasn't hot

153

at all. The bathwater wasn't especially hot either. How long had she been sitting here? I didn't ask, just handed her towels to wrap over her legs and her shoulders, so she'd warm up. Her whole body was shaking. "You should take Tylenol for the pain," I said. For once, she didn't say no to my suggestion of medication. I left her for a moment and went back into the bedroom.

After getting a couple of pills from my stash, I happened to notice that Celeste's beetle photo wasn't hanging in its usual spot. This wasn't so strange; for some reason, ever since that first day, the frame had been prone to falling off the nail. But this time, I didn't see it on the bed where it usually landed either.

I wasn't sure why this made the hairs on the back of my neck prickle, but it did.

"Leena?" Celeste called.

"One second," I called back. "Just finding the Tylenol."

I quickly scanned the room and spotted the photo lying awkwardly on the floor across from Celeste's bed. With growing apprehension, I walked over and picked it up. The photo itself was fine. But one corner of the black frame had chipped badly, revealing the lighter wood underneath the paint. Following an instinct, I checked the wall. About two feet up from where the photo had been lying, there was a black mark on the white surface, where the corner must have hit.

The frame hadn't been placed on the floor.

It had been thrown.

My body stiffened. What had gone on here while I was with David?

"Leena?" Celeste called again.

I set the frame on her bed, then returned to the bathroom and handed Celeste the Tylenol and a glass of water from the sink, an anxious thumping in my chest. "What happened to your photo?" I asked carefully.

"Huh?" She took the pills and handed me back the glass.

"The beetle photo."

"Did it fall again?" she said. "Can you grab my robe?"

"You weren't in there when it . . . fell?" I said, letting her use my arm for stability as she climbed out of the tub.

"No." She slipped her right arm into her silk robe and held the fabric closed in front, then twisted to look at her burn. "Do I need to bandage this or something?"

"I'll do it."

I got supplies from my first-aid kit in the medicine cabinet, my thoughts spinning. If Celeste really didn't know what I was talking about, did that mean someone had snuck in our bedroom and thrown her photo while she was in the bath, or with Whip, and she just hadn't found it yet?

After applying antibiotic ointment to her burn, I tore off a piece of tape and affixed gauze across it. She'd seemed so vulnerable: sitting in the tub, all skinny and trembling. How would she react if she knew that while she'd been in there, someone had done that to her artwork? Would she accuse

Abby because of the way they'd been sniping at dinner? I bit my cheeks and wondered if maybe . . . maybe it would be better if I didn't tell her at all. At least, not now, while she was already shaky.

"There," I said, smoothing down the final piece of tape. "It's not actually that bad, I don't think. Just hurts."

"Thanks," she said.

I was on my way out when she added, "Leena? Don't tell David about this."

For a minute I thought she meant about the photo. But, no. Her burn. "Okay," I said, not seeing any reason he needed to know.

I shut the bedroom door behind me and sat on the bed with the photo in my hands, studying the damage. Then— pulse racing, knowing Celeste was right across the hall—I rummaged through my bag for a black Sharpie and began coloring in the chipped area on the frame. At first, the color was too brownish, but after a few layers it built up to black. If I looked closely, I could tell there was a variation in the surface; once it was hanging I thought it would be okay, especially if she didn't know to be looking for it.

After I was finished, I couldn't even entertain the idea of doing the homework I had left from the weekend. I went straight to bed. As I lay there in the dark, all I could think about was who would have done that to Celeste. The door had been locked; they would have had to climb through a window to get in. They would have had to *break in* to our bedroom—*my* bedroom. Picturing it, I couldn't ignore the anger beginning to burn at the center of my chest.

This wasn't how Frost House was supposed to be. None of it—the tension at the dinner, worrying about what was happening here in the room. It was supposed to be a sanctuary.

I brought Cubby onto my chest, wishing again, like I had with the vase, that she could tell me what she'd seen. If I didn't know what had happened, how could I know what to do to make it safe again? I concentrated very hard on her eyes, trying to see the answer.

It will never be safe while she's here. Cubby's voice was inside my head, quiet.

"It's not her fault," I told myself.

Everything is her fault. She has to go.

I looked through the dark at Celeste's side of the room: her hat collection, her flamboyant wardrobe, the beetle photo . . . and I wondered. One thing I knew was that she needed to be the center of attention. Was it possible that she was doing this all herself, so she would be the center of attention in the dorm? Was that what I was trying to tell myself, by saying it was all her fault? Maybe she'd ripped her own skirt, broken the vase, thrown her own photograph. And just pretended to be the scared victim.

Well, if she had, then hanging the photo back up and ignoring it was the best thing I could have done.

16

THE NEXT MORNING, I pretended to be asleep when Viv came to get me for breakfast. I absolutely shouldn't have missed bio—especially not an unexcused absence—but the only, only place I wanted to be was in my room. It was going to be one of those shockingly bright fall days, and the early sun shone in through the trees, filling the whole space with warmth. I liked knowing that if I was here, the room was safe. No one could come in except those rays of sunlight.

I lay curled up on my side with my comforter piled on top of me and tried to think about yesterday's events without getting worked up. I needed to talk to someone about what was going on. But who? Not David, or Abby, or Dean Shepherd. Viv was a possibility, but she hated keeping secrets, and I'd have to ask her not to tell anyone. I was even considering my mother, when I had another idea. Trying not to get my hopes up, I looked at the clock and calculated. . . . Yes, it should be the perfect time. Without another thought, I opened my laptop and checked to see if she was online, then called.

I almost cried when Kate appeared on my screen, all the way from Moscow, wearing her favorite Violent Femmes T-shirt and playing with her ever-present wire mandala. Viv and Abby and I had talked to her occasionally as a group, but it was hard because of the time difference, and because she wasn't online often.

"Leena Thomas," she said with a smile. "You look like hell."

The minute I started talking, it all rushed out in a waterfall of words, everything that had happened with Celeste and Abby and David from the beginning of the semester, so many things—I realized now—that I'd been keeping to myself.

Kate listened and nodded and kept up a steady rhythm with her hands, flipping the three-dimensional wire form into different geometric shapes. I could tell she was thinking hard because of how quickly her hands moved.

"It seems to me," she said, "from thousands of miles away, that you're tangling a lot of things all together. I don't actually think there's anything you need to be worrying about."

"Really?" I said.

"The one thing you need to make a decision about is whether to tell anyone about the photograph, right?"

The weight of all the worries I had made it seem much more complicated than that, but I supposed that was the only actual decision to be made. "Right," I said.

"Okay, I'm trusting that you can really tell it hit the wall hard enough to have been thrown. So, in that case, either . . . one." She stopped playing with the mandala and held up a finger. "Someone snuck in the room and threw it to be mean to Celeste. Or two—" Another finger. "Celeste threw it herself, for God knows what reason. Right?"

"I guess."

"You don't sound sure," she said. "Those are the only options I see. Unless you think a ghost did it or something." She smiled.

"Don't go all Viv on me," I said, rolling my eyes.

"Okay," Kate said. "So let's say we know it's option one. Someone was mean to Celeste. The question is, should you tell her? How would she react if you did?"

No mystery there. "Freak out. Accuse Abby. Get even more paranoid."

"So she'd get scared? Would anything *constructive* come from it?"

I imagined Celeste reacting and didn't see it leading anywhere good. "No. I don't think so."

"Okay, so that solves that. You don't tell Celeste." Her

hands went back to their rhythmic motions.

"But maybe we should be reporting it, to the dean or something?"

"It's not like they're going to fingerprint the frame and windowsills to figure it out." Kate paused for a moment, her thick, black brows lowered. "You're *sure* someone would have had to come in through a window? It seems so . . . unlikely."

"The door was definitely locked," I said. "And only me, Celeste, and David have keys."

"David has a key?" she said, leaning forward. "You don't think he—"

"No!" I said immediately. "Not to mention, he was with me." A thought—David's lateness to meet me at his dorm—flickered through my mind. But I forced it out. There was absolutely no way.

"Okay." Kate sat back again. "So, about telling the dean or whoever. I don't think you should. They wouldn't investigate; all they'd do is ask Celeste who doesn't like her. And we know the answer to that."

"Abby."

"Right. Now—"

"Kate, you don't think there's any chance she'd have done this stuff, do you?" I asked in a quieter voice. I knew the answer, just needed to hear her say it.

"Abby?" She screwed up her face, annoyed. "*Please*. I can't believe you'd even ask me that. Now, let's take option two, which, from all you told me, is much more likely."

Option two: Celeste threw the photo herself.

Kate continued, "If that's the case, you've actually done all you can do. You already asked her what happened to the photo. If she did it herself and pretended not to know about it, maybe she was just embarrassed. In any case, there's some reason she didn't want to tell you, so . . ." She shrugged. "What else can you do?"

I sat for a moment and processed what Kate had said. Basically, she was saying that no matter what happened to the photo, I should let it go.

"But . . . I feel like I should be doing *something*," I said. "Take some sort of action. I don't want to feel like there's all this bad stuff going on in my room and I'm just sitting here all la-di-da."

Kate stared down at her mandala for a minute. "Well, you can't keep Celeste out. But you could lock the windows, too, I guess. With the doors and the windows locked, if it's someone else, they won't be able to get in."

I nodded. Lock the windows. I could do that.

"You knew she'd be like this," Kate added. "You told me right from the beginning, it's always something. So maybe you need to just let her have her little dramas. You're not your sister's keeper. Or David's sister's keeper. Sit tight and ignore it as much as possible until I come flying home to you."

"You have no idea how much I wish for that day," I said.

We talked for a little while about other stuff, and then

Kate had to go. Before she logged off, she said, "Oh, and Leena? Would you just jump David's bones already?"

She was gone before I could respond.

On Mondays, I had a free period after Calculus and would help carry Celeste's books to Rel-Phil. That afternoon, as we walked across the quad, the sky was blue and the air was knife-pleat crisp. Barcroft looked like a picture in a prep-school catalogue, students everywhere, lounging on the expansive lawn, playing Frisbee, taking their time getting to their next classes.

I felt so much better after talking to Kate. She was so logical and unflappable. I was going to take precautions— locking the windows and doors—but otherwise, it was out of my hands. I still felt angry that it was happening in my home, but at least I didn't feel the weight of solving everything.

"Good day for KSM," Celeste said. Kill, Screw, or Marry. Whenever we saw a group of three people—sitting together, walking together, whatever—we each had to pick one to kill, one to sleep with, and one to marry.

"Okay," I said.

Students sat in clusters all over the wide marble steps of the chapel as we walked past. We'd just KSM'ed a group of freshmen when a new threesome sat down: Simone Dzama, Mr. Bartholomew, an English teacher, and David. My heart did a nervous jump at the sight of him; my body had a flashback to how it had felt on the roof.

"Exempt," I said immediately.

"No one's exempt," she said. "You know the rules."

"Come on, Celeste."

"Don't be so uptight." She stopped walking. "I'll even go first. It's an easy one. Kill Simone, marry Mr. Bart, screw David."

I looked at her with a grimace.

"What?" she said. "I'm not going to kill or marry my own brother."

She was trying to shock me. I should have been used to it by now. "Okay," I said, "Kill Mr. Bart, sleep with Simone, marry David."

"If that's your plan, you better hurry up." Celeste gestured with her chin toward the steps. "You'll be out of luck on both counts."

Simone had a hand on David's shoulder and was laughing, her long legs—with striped knee socks and bare thighs—stretched out in front of her. David stared, apparently mesmerized. A lump settled in my stomach.

"So, what's up with you and Whip?" I asked, turning away. Because of the distraction of her burn and the photo, I'd never asked her last night.

"He looks surprisingly good in body paint," she said, "if that's what you mean."

"So, you had fun?"

"Jesus, Leena." Celeste glared at me. "David's obviously

already using you to do his dirty work."

My face flushed. "He worries about you."

"I know," she said. "That's the goddamn problem." She turned toward the steps and called, "Hey! David!" He looked in our direction and she beckoned him over. Crap. What was she planning?

David said something to Simone then grabbed his bag and walked over.

"What's up?" he said.

"You guys are annoying me," Celeste said, gesturing at the two of us. "That's what's up. All this delay. Dilly-dally, twiddle-twoddle. It's annoying."

The flush in my cheeks flared hotter. "Celeste—"

"No. Wait a minute." She reached into her bag I was holding, brought out a bunch of papers, and began shuffling through them. "I don't know what the holdup is, but . . . here. A catalyst." She separated out a sheet of white paper. David reached for it but she hid it behind her back and turned to me. "The other day, David brought me papers he'd picked up for me at the office," she said. "But a couple of his own things were mixed in the pile." Now she held out the sheet for us to see.

The syllabus for David's English class.

"So?" I said.

Celeste turned the paper over.

On the back, David had done a bunch of doodles: a remarkably realistic eye, a glass of water, a cartoon cat . . . My immediate thought was, *Wow. David can draw.* A split second later, though, my brain made sense of the largest doodle on the page. An elaborate graphic version of a name—in black ballpoint pen, a name turned into an almost Celtic twisty-turny hedge of intertwined, swooping strokes.

Leena.

My breath stopped.

David grabbed the paper from Celeste. "What the hell?" he said, shoving it in his bag. "Who cares?"

"Yeah," I said, recovering enough to jump to his defense. "So he doodles. Big deal."

Celeste snorted. "Anyone who has ever been in love knows the primal urge to doodle the loved one's name."

"You're unbelievable," David said, shaking his head. "I'm outta here."

"It's just a name on a piece of paper," I added, to assure him I wasn't making a big deal out of it.

David walked away without looking again at either one of us.

"I'm doing this for your own good," she called after him. "Don't you want to actually live life, instead of just thinking about it? Instead of focusing on everyone else?"

David didn't turn around, just held up a hand giving Celeste the finger. People on the path had stopped and were staring.

"Thanks for ruining a nice friendship," I said as his figure receded.

"He'll get over it."

We started walking again. I couldn't believe I wasn't making her carry her own bag after that little episode. And I couldn't believe that instead of just being angry, some of what I felt coursing through my body was actually excitement. I didn't want to let her know that, though.

"Has it occurred to you that if something *were* going to happen between me and your brother, it should happen at its own pace?" I said.

"No," she said plainly.

I shifted her bag on my shoulder. "Well, has it occurred to you that if something *were* going to happen, the fact that you are so suspiciously, *overly* gung-ho about it would give someone like me second thoughts?"

"Huh." She seemed to consider this. "No."

"It is a little weird," I said. "Your insistence. Just tell me—why do you want us to get together so bad? Do you have some ulterior motive?"

She stopped walking and looked at me. "Okay. Yes, actually, I do."

Of course. I raised my eyebrows.

"I want you to get him off my back," she said.

"What?"

"I want him to have someone he can take care of so he'll stop spending every free minute wondering who I'm hooking up with or whether I'm losing my mind or whether I took a crap yesterday. Is that so weird? I have enough to worry about without worrying about him worrying about me."

Her voice and face made it clear she was telling the truth. I didn't quite know how to respond.

"I just know," she added, "that if he had the right girlfriend, not just some fling, he'd be the best boyfriend ever. It's not like I randomly picked you. I really, honestly think you'd be great for him. Don't you think he'd be great for you?"

I stared at her some more, at the almost pleading look in her eyes. "You sound like you're trying to sell your used car," I said finally, laughing a little.

"Leena," she said, smiling now, too. "I promise, he runs really, really well."

As I walked away, after leaving Celeste at the religion building, I found myself unable to contain a huge smile. Celeste's reason for wanting us to get together *wasn't* that weird. And despite feeling bad about David's embarrassment, I couldn't help feeling a giddy jolt of excitement when I thought about what had happened on the quad. I actually broke out into a skip.

For once, I wasn't the one doing the elaborate name doodles. They were being done about me.

David called me that evening. "So, that was awkward," he said.

"Yeah," I said, hugging a pillow to me, "you could say that."

"Sorry she's such an ass," he said. "I wasn't mad at you when I walked off like that. I just couldn't believe her. Of course, I should have acted like I didn't care. That would have been much better. She's like a three-year-old throwing a tantrum. She really is."

"I know."

"And, you know, that wasn't—"

"Don't even worry," I said. "I doodle all the time. Totally random stuff."

"Because I respect the moratorium," he said. "So I wouldn't ever, you know, ask you to compromise that. Even in my fantasies."

"Uh-huh," I said, smiling, because the way he said it was insinuating just the opposite.

"The seriousness of the moratorium must be respected," he went on. "Celeste wasn't aware of it, I guess."

"I guess not," I said. And I closed my eyes and hugged the pillow tighter, and dared to think that something good—something very good—might have come from rooming with Celeste Lazar.

My favorite part of books and movies is almost always the "before." The beginning, before whatever upends the characters' lives has happened—*before she knows he's a vampire, before the spaceship arrives* . . . And for me, the next week or so had that same sort of feeling. I knew, almost for sure, that something was going to happen with me and David. I wasn't sure when—maybe not immediately; I hadn't shed my stress about how much work lay ahead of me this semester. But still, the air was filled with the thrill of possibility.

Every time we talked—not about anything serious, just the usual conversations about classes and homework and stuff—there seemed to be a little more physical contact. But nothing to push us over that line. Nothing that meant I actually had to deal with the complications of the situation. Just . . . the beautiful before.

And as for what had happened with Celeste's photo, well, Kate had reassured me as much as anyone could have. Not that I forgot about it, of course. I was vigilant about locking the windows and doors whenever I left. But I'd pretty much decided that her theory was correct: Celeste had thrown the photo herself, and had been too embarrassed to let me know. And all I could do was sit tight and wait for the semester to be over.

17

"BUT HOW DO YOU MANAGE EVERYTHING?" I said to Marika, my co-counselor. "I mean, how do you have time for all your work, plus this, plus soccer, college stuff, and a girlfriend? It seems . . . impossible."

I'd decided to take advantage of a lull in activity at the peer-counseling office and had been asking Marika's opinion about my "friend's" dilemma—to get involved in a relationship or not— while she practiced yoga poses on the carpet.

"I don't know," Marika said as she balanced in tree, arms stretched over her head. "I don't really think about it. It all just happens." She looked at me as if I might have a brain deficiency. "You do realize a lot of people have relationships while living full and productive lives?"

"But what would you do if Susanna dumped you, right before midterms or something?"

The door to the office flew open. Abby breezed in and dropped her bag on the floor. "I need help." She placed the back of her hand on her forehead in a swoon.

"I'll take this one," I said.

Abby followed me into one of the two small, private rooms adjoining the main one.

"I have to warn you," I said as we settled into the plush purple armchairs, "I may not be qualified to treat mental disturbances as deep as yours."

"That's understandable," she said. "I just wanted to tell you the plan for New York." She kicked off her shoes and drew her legs up. "You still have an honor-roll day left, right?"

I nodded. "Two." Barcroft has the ironic policy of awarding honor-roll students with two days the next semester that they can officially take off of classes.

"Cool. So, we're going to beat the traffic by driving down on Thursday night," Abby said. "We'll have an extra day in the city. And the best thing is that Viv's mom got us tickets to the new play where Nate Warren does this whole scene naked, on Friday night, so this way we could be there in time for that. Nate Warren naked, in the same room as us! Can you believe it? I am so psyched. *Beyond* psyched. It'll be the best trip ever. Can I have a Life Saver?"

I fished a pack out of my pocket and handed it to her.

"The thing is," I said, "I'm supposed to drive David and Celeste, and David obviously doesn't have honor-roll days—he wasn't even here last semester. I don't know about Celeste."

"So?" Abby said. "They can find another way down. We're giving them a free place to stay, isn't that enough? I mean, why are they even coming? Don't they know Viv was just being polite?"

"I'll think about it," I said.

"What's there to think about?" Abby said. "I'm not going to let your perverse sense of obligation get in the way of you having a good time. *Nate Warren*, Leen!" She had stood up and was mock-shaking me by the shoulders. "Nay-kid!"

Her face was so serious that I had to laugh. "Okay, okay. I'll let them find another way."

Days went by, though, and I couldn't bring myself to tell David or Celeste. I didn't know why not driving them felt like such a big deal. It wasn't. But at the same time, I worried that they'd take it as a definite statement about not wanting them there. Abby wanted me to make that statement, obviously. She didn't know what was going on with me and David. My own fault, for being too chicken to tell her.

The dilemma wrapped itself up into a constant knot in my gut. I needed to get it over with. Finally, one day I ran into Celeste on my way home from dinner and steeled myself to do it. But the whole way back to the dorm she was talking

173

excitedly about a guest artist who had come to her portfolio class and had loved her work, and I couldn't get a word in at all.

When we entered Frost House the loud clangs of the radiator filled the common room.

"Thank God the heat is finally on," Celeste said.

"Yeah," I said, "I spoke to maintenance about it. The way to do it is talk to them in person, instead of just submitting a work order."

We reached the bedroom. I fumbled in my pocket for my room key. *Just tell her.*

"Celeste . . ." I turned the key and pushed open the door. "I don't want—"

I froze. Scattered debris covered an area of the bedroom floor stretching from Celeste's closet more than halfway across the room. "What the hell?" I flipped on the overhead light. Twigs, twine, dried grass, dirty ribbons. Nests. Or what used to be nests. I took a few careful steps. The closet door was wide open. Inside, a cardboard box on the high shelf lay with its top facing front, flaps agape. More remnants from the nests were below the box, caught among Celeste's dresses and skirts.

Celeste hadn't moved from the doorway. Her face was pale, mouth small.

"The box must have tipped over," I said. My heart hammered.

"And this happened how?"

"Maybe by accident," I said. "The box tipped when you were getting something? But didn't spill until—"

"By accident?" She looked at me. "How can you say that? Don't you see?"

"What?"

She pointed at the floor. "Can't you see what it says?"

I surveyed the scraggly mess. Then it came together, into two big letters.

GO.

18

A SHUDDER BEGAN AT MY NECK and spread throughout my limbs. I shook my head a little, forced myself to see it as just a jumble, a jumble that somewhat resembled the letters. It was a random mess. It had to be.

"That's not on purpose," I said. "You're seeing what you want to see."

"What I want to see?" Celeste said in a tone of disbelief.

"Well, what you're scared to see. Why would someone do that?" I asked. "Who would want you to go?"

She stared at the floor. "I don't know."

"Like finding shapes in clouds," I said. "You can see what you look for." I squatted down and began filling my cupped palm with thin twigs and bits of twine. "Don't worry," I said, "I'll be careful."

"What does it matter now?" Celeste's voice was tight. "Do you know how long this all took me?"

"Collecting the nests?"

She nodded. Her chin trembled. "And then I wove other materials into them. It's a whole project."

I picked up a narrow purple ribbon, a length of unspooled cassette tape . . .

"Who would *do* this?" she said.

"The door was locked."

"It wasn't an accident, Leena. I know what I saw."

I swallowed. "David and I are the only other people who have keys."

"It wasn't David."

"I know. I didn't mean that. I meant that I think there's another explanation." I sat back on my heels. "Maybe the house has mice or rats. In the closet." I didn't know why I was even saying this. Mice or rats hadn't thrown the photo the other day. Should I have told her about that? Should I tell her about it now? It would upset her even more, but maybe she needed to know.

Celeste collapsed on her bed and held her head in her hands, then began rocking back and forth.

I looked down again, picked up a fragile clump of materials that had stayed together and set it aside. "Some of this might be salvageable," I said hopefully.

The squeaking of bedsprings stopped, and Celeste let out

a cry. "I can't take this anymore! I can't! What do you think I should do?"

"What do you mean?"

"I hate it here!" She flung her arms out. "I hate this room. I have to talk to Dean Shepherd, tell her I need to move."

Defensiveness flared inside me. "This doesn't have anything to do with the room," I said. "If someone is doing this to you, they'd do it wherever you lived."

She was quiet. I knew I'd sounded mean. "Another dorm wouldn't have all these windows," she said.

"What does that have to do with it?" I asked.

She didn't answer.

"These things that are happening have nothing to do with the room," I said again. "If you really think this is someone, then the best thing to do is ignore it. Don't give them the satisfaction of caring. Right?"

She wiped her cheek and leaned forward to pick up a clump of nest. "How can I not care? I worked so hard on this, Leena. This is *me*. Why would someone punish me like this? It doesn't even matter if the mess said some stupid thing or not. They ruined my work."

She was crying for real. I stood up from the floor, sat next to her, and put an arm around her shoulders. "Hey," I said. "It's okay."

"I can trust you, right?" she asked, her voice shaky and thin. "You'd tell me if you knew who was doing this, right? I just, I'm so sick of it. And I'm . . . scared. You know. It's all so mean. Like someone *really* hates me. More than Ann—Abby, I think."

It's all so mean. "We're just talking about the vase and this, right?" I said.

"That rip in the skirt, too," she said. "You said you didn't do it." She looked out the window. "I can feel them watching, you know? Waiting till we're gone so they can do this stuff. David and you are the only people I trust. And I can't even tell David how upset I am, because he'll worry."

"You still feel like someone's watching you?" I said, a heavy dread descending on me.

"Sometimes," Celeste continued as if she hadn't even heard me, "when I open the closet . . ." She motioned toward it with her head and spoke quietly. "Sometimes I feel like whoever it is is in there. I have to look through all the clothes, you know, to make sure no one is hiding. But it's like I *feel* them."

My stomach constricted. I had sat in the closet a couple more times recently, just for a little while when I needed to clear my head. And although I'd never done it while she was in the room, it was as if she'd sensed I'd been in there.

"Celeste," I said, "you realize that you sound a little . . . irrational? No one's watching you."

"So, what?" she said. "You think I'm . . . what, imagining it? Don't tell me I'm making it up. This stuff is real, this stuff that's happened to me."

"Honestly?" I said. "I think that you had a hard summer, dealing with your boyfriend. And a hard year, with your dad. I think that some weird, bad stuff has happened to you in this room. And it's freaked you out."

Celeste's eyes rolled up and she stared at the ceiling, as if trying not to cry again.

"Maybe you should talk to someone," I said.

"A therapist? They'd just stick me on some medication. Don't . . . don't tell anyone I have these feelings, okay? Not the dorm, or David. Okay? Please. It's really important."

She gripped one of my hands in both of hers. They felt cold, bony.

"I just think it would be good if you talked to someone," I said.

"You don't understand," she said. "With a father like mine, people—everyone—they're just waiting for me to crack up. And I can't do anything without everyone thinking I tried to kill myself or whatever. And I've done stupid stuff in the past, and now it's like, if they . . . you know . . . I don't get the benefit of the doubt. Please, Leena. *Please*. It's not like I'm making up these feelings from nowhere. This stuff happened."

I remembered the horrible feeling after I'd tried to hurt myself in eighth grade, when my parents would stare at me with these expressions like they were worried I was going to crack into a thousand pieces at any moment.

"Please, Leena," she said. "I'm not crazy. I'm not." Her

voice was stronger. "Promise you won't tell."

"Okay," I said. "I promise. But you have to promise to let me know if it doesn't get better. Okay?"

We agreed.

Later, as I was about to turn off my bedside lamp, Celeste came into the room wearing the Moroccan caftan she slept in. I couldn't remember the last time she'd gone to bed while I was still awake. As if reading my mind, she said, "Maybe I'll be able to sleep. Now that the heat is on." I didn't point out that she hadn't been able to sleep when the weather was warm either.

She lingered at her mirror, smoothing cream on her face, brushing her hair. Finally, she turned off her light and headed toward her bed. On the way, she paused in front of the slightly open closet door. After a second, she kept walking. She sat down on the comforter, laid her crutches on the floor, glanced at the closet again, stood up, closed the door.

This didn't bode well.

"Do you want something mild to help? Just tonight?" I said.

"No, thanks."

When the lights had been off for a minute, she said, "You . . . you know I was speaking . . . *metaphorically*, before. Right, Leena? I don't really think someone's in the closet. I was just trying to describe what it's like, to feel like someone wants to hurt you. You know that, right? I don't really think someone's in here or whatever."

I hesitated. "Sure," I said. "I know what you meant."

Sleep came easily for me, as it always did in that room, even though I was picturing those scattered nests, telling myself they'd been in a random pattern. It was deep, as well, so I had no idea how long Celeste had been shouting when I woke up.

"Get off! Get off of me!"

Without my glasses and in the darkish room, I panicked—someone was on Celeste's bed! "Hey," I cried. "Stop!" But as I leapt up and hurried across the floor, I realized it was her arms thrashing underneath the covers, not another body. I turned on the light.

"Celeste." I placed a hand on her shoulder. "Wake up."

She sat straight up. "I'm awake," she said. Her face shone white and glistened with sweat.

"It's okay," I said. "You were having a nightmare."

"No, I wasn't," she said. "I wasn't. Someone was here." She turned her head back and forth, searching. "I was awake."

"You're okay, Celeste." I sat down and moved my hand to her back. "No one was here except me. It was a bad dream."

She shook her head. Her pupils were huge, swallowing up her irises. "It wasn't. It wasn't. Someone was here. Someone's always here."

"Shh," I said. "No one was here. It's okay. You're just upset, from before."

"Before?"

"The conversation we had, earlier."

We sat in silence for a moment, my hand absorbing the tremors from her body.

"Are you okay to go back to sleep?" I finally said. "I swear, no one was in here except me."

She gathered her quilt around her shoulders. "Can you hand me my crutches?" she said.

I did. She stood up and made her way out of the room. With her stooped posture, the blanket around her shoulders, and the sunken, haunted look in her face . . . well, I wondered if, when I'd promised not to tell anyone about her fears, I'd made a promise I shouldn't keep.

The next day, I couldn't get that image of her out of my mind. As my teachers talked on, I kept hearing her voice—so much fear in it. I didn't know what to do. Before last night, I'd settled into thinking that Celeste was doing the things herself because I couldn't imagine who else would have. But yesterday her surprise—her horror—had seemed so genuine. Nothing made sense.

The first time I saw her was in the afternoon. She was sitting on the main quad underneath the statue of Samuel Barcroft, listening to music and writing or drawing in her sketchpad. Part of me wanted to head in the opposite direction, pretend I didn't see her. But I had to deal with this sometime.

I walked up and waited for her to take out her earbuds.

"So," I said, sitting next to her on the base of the statue. The granite pressed cold and hard underneath me. "How do you feel?"

She shrugged. Rhinestone-studded sunglasses hid her eyes. "Okay," she said. "Sorry for all the commotion last night. God, David couldn't believe it when I told him the cat did that to my nests."

Wait, what? "The cat?" I said.

"Oh, right. I didn't tell you yet." Her voice was breezy and crisp as the autumn air, as if this was all perfectly normal. "I realized this morning it must have been Leo. I'm sure he smelled the materials and jumped up there. Batted them around the room."

"But . . . he doesn't ever leave Ms. Martin's apartment, does he?" I said, totally confused. "And the bedroom door is always locked."

"He must get out sometimes," she said. "I think I've seen him. And the door's open when we're in the bathroom, or the common room."

"Oh," I said. "Okay. So, you don't think it said—"

"Leena." She moved the sunglasses onto the top of her head and stared at me, her eyes slightly bloodshot and somehow bluer than ever. "It was the cat."

In that moment as we sat there looking at each other, I knew she was asking me not to fight her on this. To agree to say it was the cat. I didn't know, though, whether she had done it herself, and this was her way of saying that she'd screwed up and let's just move on. Or whether she really did want to believe what she was telling me. Either way, I knew she was saying that she didn't want me to worry about her.

Looking back, maybe I should have fought her on it. But I know why I didn't: She was giving me exactly what I wanted. I wanted to put all of the anxiety behind us. To know that there was nothing wrong with Celeste except her usual melodramatic tendencies. To know that I didn't have to worry about what was going to happen the next time I opened the door to our room. I wanted it to be a sanctuary again.

"You're probably right," I said. "The cat."

19

A WEEKEND AWAY FROM FROST HOUSE would be good. For all of us. Right?

At least, that's what I told myself as I packed and unpacked every item of clothing I owned, trying to figure out what would be appropriate for New York, and as I tried not to admit that what I really meant by *appropriate* was something that would appeal to David, and as I struggled not to keep dwelling on all of the fights that might or might not happen and all of the possible ways this could turn into an enormous disaster, and as I debated whether I should fill the gas tank tonight so we wouldn't have to waste time in the morning, and as I remembered Abby's reaction when I told her and Viv I couldn't come early. . . .

186

We'd been at Lorenzo's Pizza, just the three of us.

"It's David, isn't it?" Abby'd said. "You're trying to hook up with him."

"I just don't feel like it's fair to strand them without a ride," I said, avoiding her question. "It would be an incredible hassle for Celeste to take the bus with her leg."

"Have you always been such a Goody Two-shoes?" Abby tossed down her pizza slice. "Fine. Do whatever you want. Drive down on Saturday. Maybe we'll run into you somewhere in the city."

She stood up, pushed her way out of the booth, and stomped to the restroom.

I bit my bottom lip. "I'm not trying to piss her off," I said to Viv. "Can you help her chill out about this?"

"I don't know," Viv said. "She's pretty jealous."

"Jealous?"

"Of Celeste. You know, because it seems like you've sort of chosen her over us."

I rested my head in my hands. "God save me. I have enough to worry about without this." I looked up at Viv's reassuringly placid eyes. "I'm not choosing Celeste. It's not a contest."

"I know," Viv had said. "I'm just explaining where she's coming from."

Aargh! I zipped my duffel shut—whatever was in there would have to do. I locked the bedroom door and went into the closet with Cubby, then took a small oval pill to calm my out-of-control nerves.

I held Cubby up. "Sorry," I whispered. "You're not coming with me. You have to guard the fort."

You shouldn't go either. It's dangerous. I didn't speak out loud for Cubby's voice now. Just imagined her in my head. Sometimes surprising myself with what I made her say.

Like just then. Of course I was going to New York, but Cubby's words gave me a brief fantasy—spending the weekend here, in Frost House, alone. I hated to admit it, but if I'd had a choice, that's what I would have picked. There were so many ways in which the trip might go wrong. Although . . . I was excited about spending the time with David. Scared, yes, but excited, too.

"Should I just forget about my moratorium?" I said. It had been feeling stupider and stupider lately.

He doesn't care about you.

"That's not true," I said.

It is true. He's just like the others.

"No, he's not." He wasn't, was he? He was all those things that made him a good brother—loyal, protective, honest. And much older than Jake and Theo when I'd hooked up with them. He was almost nineteen.

He'll hurt you.

At these words, the excited tingling in my limbs turned to a cold numbness. Coziness became claustrophobia. Why was I telling myself this? It's not what I expected. Not what I wanted.

He'll hurt you, Leena.

I pushed aside Celeste's clothes and stumbled back into the room, slamming the closet door shut behind me, my chest wound tight. I sat down on the bed, pushed Cubby to the end of the windowsill. I put my hands next to me on the mattress and tried to steady myself. Reality crashed into my head. What had I been doing? Sitting in a closet, talking to a piece of wood?

I took slow, steady breaths. Okay, nothing was wrong here. It was just a way I was accessing my subconscious. Something about the way the closet's smell reminded me of my fort in Cambridge. Something about how comfortable I was in there was bringing out the way I really felt about stuff. That wasn't so strange, was it? I'd felt a connection to that little space from the first day of school. Obviously, it was tapping into my brain in a way a neurologist could probably explain.

Deep down, I was scared. Scared of being hurt by David. This shouldn't have surprised me. I'd been telling myself for so long to stay away from boys. But life was about overcoming fears, wasn't it?

I went to bed early and expected my nerves to wake me up before my alarm. Instead, I hit SNOOZE. Repeatedly. When I came to a fuzzy consciousness, there was a hand on my shoulder, nudging me.

"Mmmph." I turned my head into the pillow. "Neurons not firing."

"C'mon, Leena. It's late." It was David's voice. "Where's Celeste?"

I remembered—New York. I sat up, wiped drool off my mouth. "What time is it?"

"Seven thirty. You were supposed to pick me up half an hour ago. Where's Celeste?"

"Seven thirty? Shoot. I don't know. Across the hall?"

David walked into the hallway. I grabbed some clothes and hurried to the bathroom. I couldn't believe I'd overslept, today of all days. I'd promised Viv and Abby that we'd get an early start so they wouldn't be stuck at the house all day, waiting for us. I'd have to call and tell them we'd be late. I took a quick shower, threw on jeans and a hoodie, cursing myself the whole time. When I went back in the bedroom, Celeste was piling clothes on her bed. I watched her with my arms crossed. Couldn't she have done this yesterday?

"Is your bag still where I put it when I moved your stuff in?" David asked, looking over at her from by the closet.

"I guess," Celeste said.

"What are those?" David pointed at a couple of bruises on her lower thighs. Celeste pulled her skirt down to cover them.

"Nothing," she said.

"What are they?" he pressed.

She rolled her eyes. "I don't know. Maybe from when

things got a little frisky with Whip. Okay? Like that answer?"

"He hurt you?" David said.

"Jesus! No. I bruise easy. Don't you remember? From all our games of tickle monster?"

"I never hurt you like that," David said.

"I bruise easily, too," I said, sensing that their conversation was rapidly deteriorating. I rolled up my sleeve and pointed at a blue-yellow blotch on my forearm. "This one, I don't even know what it's from. Field hockey, maybe, but I don't remember it happening."

Neither of them said anything else. Just stared at each other as if I wasn't even in the room.

The next time Celeste spoke was as I backed the car out of the driveway.

"I am so fucking happy to be getting out of this place," she said.

The silence between Celeste and David lasted through getting coffee at The Mean Bean, and past multiple exits on the Mass Pike. Celeste may have been happy to leave Frost House, but all I could think about was how much I'd rather be back there alone than here in the car, trying to ignore the obvious tension.

Somewhere near Sturbridge, I heard a small snore from the backseat. I felt as if I was being released from thumbscrews.

"Is she asleep?" I asked quietly.

David twisted around and watched her for a moment. "Yeah, she is."

"So," I said once he was facing front again, "what's with all the weirdness?

Before answering, he turned up the volume of the music a bit. "She used to cut. Before Barcroft, but I get nervous when I see bruises. It's stupid, I know."

"Oh," I said, understanding better now. I thought of her burn, and how she'd asked me not to tell him. That must have been why. She was worried he'd assume she'd done it on purpose.

"How has she seemed to you?" he asked. "Aside from letting that asshole abuse her."

"I don't think he's *abusing* her," I said gently. "I think she was just trying to get to you. She's seemed . . . okay. Really upset about what happened to her nests, of course. Honestly, I don't see her that often. You should ask *her* how she's doing." That was true. Ever since that event with the nests, she'd spent more and more time in the little room, and out of the dorm entirely. I wasn't sure where or when she was sleeping.

David turned around again to look at Celeste, then rested a hand lightly on the back of my neck, sending a jolt of electricity all down my spine.

"I've been really looking forward to this weekend," he said in a low voice.

"Yeah. Me too. It'll be fun." I knew that my tone didn't match his. But since that disturbing episode in the closet,

I'd gotten more and more worried that maybe I was headed toward a big mistake. How did I know whether to trust my gut, or my rational mind?

"Is there anything *special* you want to do while we're there?" he said. Up and down, his fingers traveled the length of my neck.

He's just like the others. I gripped the steering wheel tighter as I passed a massive Jordan's Furniture truck. "Left on Spit Brook, right on Daniel Web-stah."

"What?"

"Jaw-dens Funicha Weah-house. The radio ads? The guys have those crazy accents?"

"Leena."

"What?" My mouth felt dry.

"I just wanted to see if we're, you know, both looking forward to the same sort of weekend."

I decided to switch lanes and flipped on the windshield wipers instead of the turn signal. I fumbled with the controls while saying, "I, um, I don't really know. . . ."

He took his hand off my neck. "Sorry. I thought . . . I guess I've been misunderstanding. I knew you didn't want to get involved this semester, but I thought . . . the way we've been acting. Sorry. I guess I'm just stupid."

A moment of silence went by. I heard Celeste breathing in the backseat. Suddenly, something clicked. The reason I was so convinced he wouldn't be able to have a relationship, the reason I was so scared. It was more than just worrying he'd be like the other guys.

"Maybe you don't have room to care about anyone else," I blurted out. "Maybe that's why you haven't wanted a real girlfriend. You spend so much energy on Celeste and your parents, which I love, I love that you're so good to your family. But maybe . . . maybe you don't want anyone else. Maybe you'll realize that once you're with me."

I held my breath, waiting for his answer.

To my surprise, David started laughing.

"What?" I said. "What's so funny?"

"That's exactly what my shrink used to say. About expending all my emotional energy taking care of my family. Not saving any for friends or girlfriends."

I smiled. "Really?" I said. "Wow. I'm good." I glanced away from the road for a minute and our eyes met.

He put a hand on my knee. "I don't think you have to worry about it, though," he said. "I'm feeling pretty energized. Plenty of energy. No problem there."

My palms felt sticky on the wheel. "Really?" I said.

"Really. Also . . ."

"What?"

"Not that I wouldn't, if you needed me, but you don't seem like you need anyone to take care of you. You're pretty good at doing it yourself."

I didn't say anything, but I loved that he thought that. Sometimes I felt like it was the furthest thing from the truth.

"So . . ." I said.

"So?"

He was now stroking my leg with his thumb. A smile took over my body. Oh, God—every single one of my cells was smiling. I put a vision of Cubby's disapproving eyes out of my mind.

"So maybe I could, I don't know, suspend my moratorium," I said. "On a trial basis, of course."

20

"WASN'T *THE EXORCIST* FILMED HERE?" Celeste said when I pulled up in front of Viv's family's house in Brooklyn. It's a four-story limestone town house, right across the street from Prospect Park, with a bowed front, Gothic carvings, and an imposing archway over the double door.

I would have laughed, but I was too stressed about the fact we were more than an hour and a half later than I'd originally said we'd be. I'd called Viv a few times and had tried to get them to go do something without us. But she'd insisted they were happy to wait.

A blond girl about our age answered the doorbell. "Come in, come in. They're upstairs," she said, hustling us into the marble foyer and pointing at the staircase ahead. From her

196

accent, I figured she was the Swedish student who helped with housework and cooking in exchange for a room. She looked at Celeste's cast. "Maybe you want the elevator?" she said. "Yah? Cool. You come this way."

David and I carried our bags up the three flights, "accidentally" bumping into each other a number of times. We found Viv, Abby, and Cameron sitting in the Parker-Whites' less-formal living room, watching one of the Spider-Man movies.

"Hey." Viv unwound her limbs from Cameron's and came over to give me a hug. "Long drive, huh?"

"Sorry," David said. "My fault. I suggested an alternate route that turned out to suck."

That wasn't really why we were late, of course—it had been my fault for oversleeping. He was taking the bullet for me, probably because it had been so obvious in the car that I was worried they were going to be mad. I had a sudden urge to hug him. As if sensing this, he placed a hand on the small of my back.

"I wish you guys hadn't waited for us," I said.

"Viv's idea," Abby said, not looking away from the TV, even though a commercial was on.

Celeste appeared in the doorway. David took his hand off me to move a bag that was in her way.

"I hope you guys are hungry," Viv said. "We stocked up at the farmers' market this morning. I got those dilly beans you love, Leen, and good bread and cheese. A ton of stuff."

"Actually," I said, feeling a spike of guilt, "we kind of ate in the car."

"Oh, okay," she said. I could hear her disappointment. "Well, it's a gorgeous day. What does everyone want to do? Abby, Cam, turn off the TV, losers."

It turned out that none of us had really thought about what we wanted to do in New York, except Abby, and everything she suggested involved tons of walking. I kept having to point out that Celeste was on crutches.

"Okay," she finally said to me, "how about we sit on our asses and do nothing? Does that work for you?"

"No, I—"

"How about we split up?" David said. "You guys go do what you want. Celeste and I will be more mellow."

People exchanged looks. "Sounds good," Abby said.

So now I had to pick whether to spend the day with David or with my friends? This wasn't part of the plan.

"You're coming with us, Leena, right?" Abby said.

"Umm . . . I . . ."

Viv cut in. "Wait a minute. I've got an idea."

Viv conferred with Miss Sweden for a minute, then the two of them wrangled some sort of metal contraption out of the hall closet. It turned out to be a collapsible wheelchair that belonged to Viv's grandfather.

Celeste stared at it. "You want me to ride around in that? In Manhattan?"

"It might be kind of annoying," Abby said. "The sidewalks are so crowded."

"Try it," Viv said.

Celeste sat down and wheeled herself slowly forward. "It's hard to maneuver."

"We'll push you," I said. "We'll take turns."

"Promise you won't push me down any stairs?" she said.

"Promise," I said.

"At least not on purpose," Abby added. Then she looked around at all of our horrified expressions. "Just kidding! Jeez."

Who knew a wheelchair in New York could be so much fun?

We didn't only take turns pushing, we took turns riding. Much to their mothers' annoyance, we used small children and strollers in the Central Park Zoo as a moving-obstacle course. We had time trials down the park's corridor of massive elm trees.

At one point, David pushed Abby in a tight little circle until she was laughing and screaming and begging him to stop. When he did stop, she caught her breath and gathered her hair back in its clip. Our eyes met and she smiled. The first real smile I'd gotten from her in a long time.

Even Celeste seemed like she was relaxed and having fun. A whole group of Japanese tourists must have mistaken her for a movie star because they asked if they could have their picture taken with her. Of course, she obliged, taking off her coat so her fabulous outfit would be visible.

We ended up at a matchbox-size Indian restaurant in the East Village for dinner. The ceiling and walls were decorated with so many flickering, multicolored Christmas lights it was like being inside a kaleidoscope. Along with the frenetic Bollywood music, the table full of curries, and everyone talking, it was sensory overload of the best kind. At the end of the meal when the bill came, David took out a credit card and handed it to the waiter.

"How much do we owe you?" Viv called over the blaring strains of the sitar.

"I'm taking care of it," he said.

"What?" I said. "No way. That bill must be huge."

"Yeah, man," Cameron said. "I wouldn't feel right."

"Look," David said. "It's not a big deal—this place isn't expensive. Just saying thanks for the weekend."

When the waiter brought the receipt back for David to sign, I said, "Are you sure? Let me give you some cash, at least."

"Leena," he said quietly, folding up the yellow copy and placing it in his wallet. "I'm trying to impress you here. You're not making it very easy."

"Oh." I stared down at the tablecloth, a stupid grin on my face.

The temperature outside had dropped. None of us were dressed for it, and I shivered in my thin coat as we stood on the sidewalk, debating what next. Without a word, David draped his hoodie over my shoulders. I moved closer so I was leaning slightly against him, and rested like that until a minivan cab big enough for all of us came down the street, and we decided to head back to Viv's house for the time being. During the ride, Celeste suggested we go to a bar in a remote, waterfront neighborhood in Brooklyn that she'd been to over the summer with Band Boy. She promised they wouldn't card us, and if they did, I was the only one without a fake ID.

"Will there be guys?" Abby asked. "Cute guys?"

"Actually," Celeste said, "there's a sign on the door that says Ugly Guys Only. Is that a problem?"

"At least Cameron and David will be able to come in," Viv said.

Everyone laughed. I settled back against the comfy seat and closed my eyes. We'd made it through the day and no one was fighting.

David was sitting next to me. I felt his hand, warm on my knee. He squeezed it and I squeezed his hand and I thought, *Maybe we should just die right now, in a car accident.* Because it didn't get better than this.

21

DESPITE CELESTE'S ASSURANCE we wouldn't be carded, I wasn't taking any chances. Back at the Parker-Whites', I put on my nicest jeans and a black turtleneck sweater that made me look older and more sophisticated, and pulled my hair into a twist at the nape of my neck.

"You look like a librarian," Celeste said from the bed she'd claimed.

We were sharing a room here, too, with twin beds, framed photos of Japanese temples on the walls, and a massive golden Buddha statue watching from the corner.

Insisting I could do better, she had me try on one of the many dresses she'd brought—a red-and-black-pattern vintage Diane von Furstenburg. The silk stretched over me, cool and slinky, and seemed to fit. Then I looked in the mirror.

"No way," I said immediately, taken aback by how exposed I felt. This sort of dress—tight, low-cut, curve-enhancing—was obviously designed for someone with a different sort of build. Or, rather, a different sort of personality. And definitely someone with different footwear, I thought, looking across the room at my selection: scuffy, brown, lace-up boots or Chucks.

A knock came at the door. Celeste said, "Come in," at the same time I said, "One minute." Her voice must have been louder because the door opened. David stood there.

"Wow," he said.

I crossed my arms in front of my boobs. "I was just trying it on," I explained. "I'm not wearing it."

"Really? Why not?" He turned to Celeste. "It's yours, right? You should give it to Leena for good. To wear on a daily basis." I blushed as he grinned at me.

"It was Mom's," Celeste said. "I'm not *giving* it to anyone. What did you want, anyway?"

David's smile faded. "I actually need to talk to you."

"I have to use the bathroom," I said, picking up on his serious tone of voice. "You guys can talk in here."

I decided to wear my hair down, and just a little mascara and lip gloss, so I didn't actually have that much to do in the bathroom to waste time. I ended up posing in front of the mirror, trying to appreciate David's opinion of my new look.

I liked that he'd been so enthusiastic, but wearing something so sexy and sophisticated still felt strange: as much of a lie as my friends' fake IDs. Not to mention, it seemed more than a little weird to be trying to look good for a guy in his mother's dress.

Before going back to the bedroom, I glanced in the medicine cabinet to see if anything had been abandoned there. While my doctor prescribed me antianxiety pills for emergencies, I occasionally snagged a few other types from my and my friends' parents—only when it was obvious they weren't actively taking it. Nothing here, though.

Eventually, I figured I'd given Celeste and David long enough. Celeste stood in her black lace underwear, surveying the remaining clothes in the closet.

"What do you think?" She held up a fifties aqua-blue diner waitress dress and a black top that looked like it was made of ribbons.

I pointed to the aqua blue.

"Eh. I think the black," she said.

Celeste rehung the blue dress and hopped toward the bed. Her eyes were bloodshot.

"Everything okay?" I asked.

She sat down and began wriggling the top over her head. I noticed that there were a couple of bruises on her torso, too. Like the ones on her thighs. Were they really from Whip? I'd thought she was just saying that to annoy David, but maybe they were. I couldn't imagine how else they might have happened. What did people do to each other in bed that would make bruises? Did it feel good at the time?

"Celeste, you okay?" I said again.

She pulled the top down. "Yup," she said. "That David. He always likes to make sure I'm in a cheery mood when we're going out." She shook out her hair. "You know, you don't have to wear that just because he said you should. I can tell you're uncomfortable in it."

"I think I will," I said, running a hand over the smooth fabric. "It's fun to wear something different for a change."

"Hmm." She stood up to admire herself in the mirror and I realized that the black ribbon top was actually a dress. Sort of. It barely reached below her underwear. "You might be right, you know," she said.

"About?"

"David. Your hesitation."

"What do you mean?"

"Well, I guess if you guys wanted to be together it would have happened by now. Right?" She turned so she could see herself in side view. "Maybe I tried too hard to push you together, for selfish reasons. Maybe you're not his type. I made it all up in the beginning, saying that he liked you. He's that way with anyone who has boobs."

"Oh. Maybe," I said, just to end the conversation.

This new attitude of hers was completely bizarre. And the only possibility for what caused it, that I could see, was that she was jealous. She was used to being the center of David's universe. As much as she *said* she didn't want so much attention from him, maybe now that David was acting blatantly interested in me she was having second thoughts.

"Do you think my bruises are too obvious in this dress?" she asked.

"It's a bit short," I said. "You could wear leggings under it. Although, not over your cast, I guess."

"Too short? You mean, too sexy?" she said. "I'm just following your lead."

She *was* jealous. For a minute I considered not wearing the wrap dress, so I wouldn't be the target of these digs all night. Then I remembered the expression on David's face. *Forget it. Let her deal.* I sat on my bed, shoved my foot in my boot, and pulled at the laces.

When I finished tying up both boots, Celeste was still looking at herself in the mirror, holding the dress up a little bit so her thighs were bare. After a second she let it drop, then turned to face me. I was dreading her next comment about David, but instead she said, in a strange, tight voice, "What do you think's happening in Frost House right now?"

After the six of us convened downstairs all dressed and ready, we called a car service—the Brooklyn version of a cab—to take us to the bar. We split into two groups; I went with the Lazars. Somewhere during the ride, I wondered if Celeste and David were members of a Mafia family and their little private talk had actually been about setting me up for a hit. Because after driving through a couple of normal neighborhoods, our car crossed under an expressway, into an area with warehouses and dilapidated liquor stores. Eventually, we turned onto a cobblestone street.

"I didn't know cobblestone streets still existed," I said as the car jostled forward. "This area's pretty desolate, huh?"

A pair of skinny dogs trotted alongside us for a minute before sliding through a gap in a barbed-wire fence into an abandoned lot.

"I bet I could find some great stuff for projects here," Celeste said. I prayed she wasn't going to tell the driver to stop so she could pick up a desiccated rat carcass or something.

Earlier, when she'd asked me what I thought was happening in Frost House, I'd been spooked by her tone. And by the question.

"Nothing," I'd said. "Seeing as it's empty. Right?"

She'd seemed surprised I'd even answered, like she hadn't meant to ask it at all. "Of course," she'd said. "I was kidding."

The driver took a left on a street that was lined with parked cars. On one side was the water. On the other side was a small, dark storefront with a neon sign of a dolphin curved around an anchor. Above it was a sign that said BAR. We tumbled out of the car and walked up to the door. As David held it open, warm light spilled out along with the sounds of low voices and live music. Bodies filled the long, narrow space; a band was squeezed in the middle of the crowd. We worked our way inside and found Abby, Viv, and Cameron just taking off their coats.

David and Viv said they'd get our drinks. The rest of us pushed through the room, past where the four-man band was playing Johnny Cash–type music. No one seemed to give us a second look, but we were definitely the youngest people there. We ended up in a back room that was a little less crowded and noisy. A group was just leaving a round, red leather booth, so as soon as they got up we claimed it. The space and everything in it seemed to have been here for a hundred years—walls and shelves were filled with artifacts: from delicate models of old clipper ships, to figurines of the Marx Brothers, to real shark jaws. I loved that everything about it felt genuine. Not at all what I expected from a bar in New York.

David and Viv appeared minutes later with an assortment of beers. I waited until Celeste and Abby had picked, knowing they'd be the two to make a fuss if they didn't get what they wanted.

"So, is everything okay?" I asked David quietly, during the first lull in our group conversation. He was sitting on my left, solid against me. "Whatever you needed to talk to Celeste about?" I glanced over; she was talking to Viv. "She seemed upset earlier."

"Sort of okay," he said, tugging on the corner of his beer label. "I got a call from our mother. Our father's not doing too well."

"I'm sorry. What's wrong?"

"Bad reaction to a new drug," he said. "Something for a trial."

I studied my dress. How long ago had Mrs. Lazar worn it? When her husband looked at the red-and-black pattern, had his brain seen it the way mine did? Maybe he was already seeing things differently, finding meanings and messages in the geometric forms, instead of just thinking how good the dress looked on his wife.

"I don't want to talk about it tonight," David said, startling my mind off the track it had been going down.

He reached over and smoothed my hair behind my ear. Our eyes met and a whole conversation seemed to pass between us in an instant. I was only snapped out of it by a clunking noise on the other side of the booth.

"Back in a minute," Celeste said as she hopped off.

My hands rested on the table. David reached over and began fiddling with my bracelet. His thumb brushed against my wrist.

"Have I told you how great you look?" he said, his mouth by my ear.

"Yes," I said. More a breath than a word.

"What are you guys talking about?" Abby called from across the table.

"Nothing," I said. "David was just saying he misses Barcroft."

"Yeah, right," Cameron said. "How do people live

through senior year? The freedom is so damn close. I swear, I'm not going to make it."

"We make it through by having weekends like this one," Viv said, giving him a big kiss on the cheek.

Cameron lifted his beer. "To weekends like this."

"To weekends like this," we all echoed, clanking our bottles together.

We went around making several other toasts until our bottles were drained. Viv and Cameron got up and took our orders. With nothing to drink, the natives were restless.

By the time they returned with beers, so was David. Twenty minutes had passed; there was no sign of Celeste.

22

"I HAVE TO GO TO THE BATHROOM ANYWAY," I said to David. "I'll find her."

I made my way up and down the narrow front space, pushing myself between people and dodging the band members' guitar necks. I checked all of the seats. I figured out where the women's bathroom was and knocked on the door. From inside, I could hear the sounds of someone being sick. Damn.

"Celeste?" I knocked again.

After a bit, a voice that was definitely not Celeste's called out, "Can you wait a minute?"

Finally, I asked the bartender if he'd seen the girl on crutches recently.

He nodded as he squeezed a lime into a cocktail shaker. "She was talking to a guy. He bought her a drink. Everything okay?" He gave me a funny look, and I got the sense he was about to ask for my ID.

"Yup," I said, turning around. I wasn't sure it was okay, though. What the hell was Celeste doing? Who was this guy who bought her a drink? She'd been in such a strange mood earlier. And all she had on was that borderline-pornographic dress.

I made one last round of the front room, then pushed open the heavy wood door to the street. A thick mist and the briny smell of the harbor hung in the air. I heard the clank of a bottle.

A girl and a guy sat on the pavement to the right of me, leaning against the wall.

"You waiting for a car service, too?" the guy asked me.

"I'm looking for my friend. She's on crutches."

The woman pointed toward the water, bracelets jangling on her arm. "They went that way. To the pier."

I started walking down the cobblestone street, trying to ignore my nervousness. In the middle of nowhere, in a neighborhood that didn't seem particularly safe, and Celeste off with some guy. I kept thinking about what David said about her self-destructive decisions. I kept thinking about those bruises.

Then I thought about her strange fit of jealousy. Maybe my flirting with David had pushed her to get together with some random guy, just to feel wanted, or to get David's attention back.

I came to the end of the street and heard rustling noises from down by the water. A damp, fish-scented breeze blew my hair across my face. I hoped to God the noises were from Celeste and not some waterfront rats. Or rats climbing all over Celeste's body.

"Celeste?" I said loudly enough to scare them off.

More rustling. "Mmm?"

I could now make out her shape, sitting next to someone else on a big slab at the edge of the shore. I picked my way over rocks and chunks of concrete and waterlogged scraps of wood.

Surprise and relief hit me at the same time when I saw whom she was sitting with. "Whip! Hey! How did you get here?" I asked.

"This amazing innovation," he said, lifting a cigarette to his lips. "It's called a cab."

"I think I've heard of that." I turned to Celeste. "I was just checking to make sure you were okay."

"Let me guess," she said. "David sent you."

"No. We were all wondering."

"My brother," Celeste said to Whip, "has an irrational fear that if I'm ever out of his sight, I'll do something stupid like sit on a darkened waterfront with a totally untrustworthy male. While drinking alcohol. And smoking. So he has to send out his little minion to check up on me."

"You said you'd only be a few minutes," I pointed out, annoyed.

Celeste ignored me and kept talking to Whip. "Maybe she'll get to give him a blow job for the information she brings back."

My mouth fell open. "I—"

"The word's always been Leena doesn't do stuff like that," Whip interrupted. "I know plenty of guys who'd be happy to hear otherwise."

"David did not send me out here," I snapped. I wasn't even going to address Whip's comment. "I came on my own because I couldn't find you inside and I was worried. I don't know where I ever got the idea that Celeste Lazar couldn't take care of herself. Maybe it's because every time I leave you alone in the dorm I come back and some horrible thing has happened to you."

"God, Leena," Celeste said. "I must have really hit a nerve. Did you already service David tonight? In the bar bathroom, maybe?"

"I'm sorry," I said. "Is that your job?"

Oh my God.

The words rang in the air. I could not believe I'd said them. I didn't know where they'd come from.

"Snap!" Whip said.

Celeste didn't say anything. I was about to apologize when she starting making a strange noise. It took a second, but then I realized what it was. It was laughter. She was practically convulsing.

"Oh, sweet Jesus," she said once she'd calmed down. "I had no idea you could be so funny."

Was she being serious?

"I shouldn't have said that," I said. "I'm sorry."

"No," she said. "It was funny. Really. I'll tell David. He'll think so, too."

I knew perfectly well David wouldn't think it was funny. And I had a feeling Celeste knew he wouldn't think it was funny, too.

"Look, just forget it. It wasn't funny. Anyway, do whatever you want. I'm going back inside. It's freezing out here."

I tugged open the door just as David was coming out.

"What's going on?" he said. "Did you find her?"

"Yeah. She's okay." Seeing David made me feel bad for what I'd said to Celeste, the tasteless joke. I prayed that she'd forget and wouldn't repeat it to him. "She's down by the water, with, uh, Whip."

"Whip? What the hell is he doing here?"

"I guess she called him," I said.

"You just left her out there with him?" David started to brush by me. The door closed behind him.

"David." I gripped him by the forearm. "She's fine. They're just sitting there."

"Are the bruises not enough proof for you that this is a really bad idea?" he said.

"Isn't telling her *not* to do something the worst approach?" I said. "The more you tell her not to be with Whip, the more she'll push it with him. Right?"

"That's your assessment?" David said. "Reverse psychology. Very tricky."

I took my hand off his arm. "Don't be such a jerk. I'm just trying to help. If you want to know the truth, I don't really feel like being in the middle of this sibling drama. But I don't want to see you getting all upset at each other, either, especially when you might just be being overly protective."

David looked out toward a bell clanging in the fog on the water.

"She likes to do the unexpected," I said. "It's too obvious for her to date some artistic, emo guy."

"I don't need you to tell me about my sister," David said.

"Then why do you ask me about her all the time?" I pushed by him and opened the bar door, my eyes burning. Before going inside, I said one last thing in his direction. "Do what you want. Go down there and beat him up. That should help things."

"So you think I should just do nothing?" he said. He sounded not mad, but genuinely upset.

"David," I said. "You know that Celeste survived three years at Barcroft without you. I think the best thing you can do is to leave her alone and concentrate on your own life."

He stared out at the low *clang-clang-clang* of the bell. The neon sign cast a soft, red glow on his face.

216

"What happened to all of that energy?" I said. "The energy that was going to go toward something other than worrying about her?"

"The energy?" he said, looking back at me.

"Yeah. In the car, remember? Where'd it go?" I tilted my head. "If you find it, I'll be inside."

23

WE ALL STUMBLED INTO the Parker-Whites' town house some-time after two a.m. Celeste disappeared up the elevator immediately, alone. Whip had gone back to Manhattan.

"Hungry, hungry, hungry," Abby said. "How can I be so hungry?"

We moved en masse to the kitchen. Usually, I'd have been psyched to raid the pantry, but my stomach was too tied up to eat much. After our little . . . *conversation* outside the bar, David hadn't gone to find Celeste and Whip; he'd come inside right after me, and had sat close and apologized and touched me in the ways that are socially acceptable in public—hand on knee, arm across shoulders, foot on foot. It had all been suggestive of more to come, and now here I was, confronted with a whole night in front of us, and nothing stopping us from spending it together.

Eventually, Viv and Cameron went upstairs.

"Want to watch a movie?" Abby said.

"Nah," I said. "I think I'll go to bed."

David stood up and stretched his arms over his head, showing his stomach. "Me too."

"Your loss," Abby said.

Should I follow David to his room? I wanted to just as badly as I didn't want to. We padded up the stairs next to each other. When he turned off to go to his room on the third floor, I hesitated a minute.

"So," I said. "It's late."

"Yeah," he said. "But it is New York. Right? City that never sleeps?" He raised his eyebrows in an expectant look. An adorable, expectant look.

"I'll be right down," I said, sounding more sure than I felt.

I was sure about one thing, though. I wasn't going to his bedroom wearing his mother's dress.

I stopped in the bathroom first, and Celeste was asleep—or pretending to be asleep—by the time I went in the bedroom to change. As I slipped into my tank and boxers (Would he expect lingerie?) the words I'd tried to banish from my mind nagged at me: *he'll hurt you; he'll hurt you.* By the time I tiptoed down the carpeted stairs, the Indian food and beer and those stupid words churned in my stomach.

David had left the door to his room ajar. He lay on the bed—a full size—propped up against pillows, reading. He only had a small table lamp on, so the room was mercifully dark. I was embarrassed not to be wearing a bra, and I knew I looked tired and not especially pretty. And I should have showered. He was probably expecting a clean girl in a nightie.

Walking toward the bed was like walking into a final exam I hadn't studied for. Not a final, I told myself. A mini-quiz. Because it's not like we were going to go all the way or anything. He wouldn't assume that. Right? I wasn't planning on waiting until marriage, but I wasn't planning on doing it tonight either.

"Hey." I perched on the opposite side from where he lay.

"Hey." David put the book on the bedside table. He was wearing striped boxers and a white T-shirt.

I placed my hands on the bedspread to wipe off some of the clamminess.

"Why don't you sit up here?" He patted the pillows next to him.

I slid over. I could feel a deep seismic rumbling in my body. Shaking on the molecular level. I'd never been in a bed with a guy before. Not like this, at least.

I swallowed to try and get some wetness in my mouth. "I'm kind of . . . kind of nervous," I said, figuring he'd notice anyway.

"That's okay," he said. "So am I."

"You are?"

"Sure."

But I knew he wasn't, at least, not nervous like I was. So nervous that all I could think about was being at home, safe in my room, or better yet, safe in a deep, dark closet. I started thinking of what excuse I could possibly make—cramps, my period, demonic possession—to get out of there. I swallowed again.

He reached over and gently took off my glasses, placed them on the table. He brushed the hair away from my face. I moistened my dry lips. I could feel my pulse throbbing even in my palms.

Then David's lips were on mine. Soft, sweet, fuller than they looked. Gentle but insistent as they moved. Oh, kissing! It had been so long, I'd forgotten the intensity. Warmth poured through every cell of my body. His hand held the back of my head. I touched his shoulder, firm and alive under the soft T-shirt. I slipped my fingers up inside the sleeve, touching his smooth, smooth skin. He must have showered; he smelled like citrus and grass and . . . boy.

Kissing harder, now. I recognized the flavor of natural cinnamon toothpaste. And then his tongue. Darting. Tasting. The bright green toothpaste I used probably caused cancer. *What? Don't think about that now!* I tried to stop thinking and let myself enjoy the kissing, as I had been a minute ago. But then I felt David's hand inching its way closer to my breast. And then it was on my breast, the side of my breast, pressing against it, moving slowly. And I lost track of the kissing and wondered how hard he would have to be touching me to leave bruises like the ones on Celeste.

Stop it! Think about the kissing. Or the touching. Not about his sister. But then I didn't want to think about the touching either, because he'd moved the hand underneath my tank top and was playing with my breast, swirling his fingers around it, cupping it, kneading, *needing*. I was glad we were on our sides so that his second arm was trapped underneath him. It was so intense, his hand, like it couldn't get enough of what it was doing. Images of Celeste with someone's hands kneading into her darted into my brain. Hands pressing too, too hard. Hurting. David was going to hurt me.

"Relax," he said. "Is this too much?"

I realized that I was shaking, quite noticeably. Like a stray kitten out in the cold.

"Um, yeah. Maybe. Sorry."

"Don't be sorry." He reached down and pulled the covers up over me. "Turn on your side."

"I am on my side." Even my voice was shaking. I didn't know what was wrong with me. I'd never had a reaction like this before, had always loved fooling around. If anything, I'd had to force myself to stop before I'd gone further than I wanted, because it felt so good.

"Other way," he said.

I turned the other way and felt him spoon his body behind mine. His arm held me close. I tried to just breathe easily and calm down. I tried to ignore his hard-on, firm against me. I was so embarrassed. He'd never want to do this with me again. Who would?

"I'm sorry," I repeated.

"Shhh . . ." he said as he ran his hand up and down my arm. "We can just lie here."

"Really? You're . . . you're okay with that?"

I felt him kiss the back of my head and snuggle even closer, his arm wrapped around, protectively. Was there something wrong with me, I wondered, that I liked this so much better than the actual fooling around? *He'll hurt you.*

"You don't know," I whispered.

"Huh?" David sleepy-grunted into the back of my neck.

"Nothing," I said. "Just . . . good night."

His arm squeezed me more tightly. I pressed against him and wished that, like Dorothy, I had a pair of ruby slippers to click, click, click. . . .

24

IN THE MORNING, I didn't have time to be anxious. My body and David's body had found each other before I'd even really woken up. When I swam to total consciousness, we were kissing with a heat that my nerves had made impossible the night before. I was on top, straddling his hips, pressing against him, only the thin layers of our clothes between us, now kissing his neck and inhaling his gorgeous morning skin, which smelled like sun even though the blinds were drawn. The way I felt—it was as if while I'd been asleep, someone else had entered my body.

The minute I had that thought, though—the minute I was aware enough to analyze—a switch was flipped. Just like that, my muscles tightened. My nerves rebelled. And the shaking started again. Jesus. What was wrong with me?

"You okay?" he said when we broke away for a moment. "You seemed okay with it. I didn't mean . . ."

What was I supposed to say? That I'd been okay until I actually woke up? "I . . . I'm fine," I said. "I just have to get up for a minute." When I said it, I realized it was true—I needed to pee. Bad.

I sat on the toilet seat and wrapped my arms around myself. I was conscious of the sound of pee hitting water and hoped David couldn't hear it. After flushing, I looked at myself in the mirror. I stared into my pupils and tried to hypnotize myself into a state of calm. *You chose this. You want this.*

"You're incredibly sexy," David said as I walked back across the room. He'd opened the blinds; the morning was gray and blustery.

"No I'm not," I said reflexively. I sat on the edge of the mattress.

"Hey. Tattoo." His fingers lifted up the hem of my tank top. "Nice."

"Thanks." I smiled down at the top of his head as he inched forward and then placed his lips against my tatt. I shivered. He pulled back, rested his head on my thigh, stared up at me.

"The way you looked last night, in that dress?" he said.

The way I looked in that dress. His mother's dress. The dress his sister loaned me. His sister, who was in a bedroom in this very house. His sister, who was jealous of the way I looked in their mother's dress. *Stop it, Leena!*

"What time do you think it is?" I asked. "We should probably get up."

David propped himself up on one arm and grabbed his phone off the night table. "Ten fifteen," he said. "I guess we should."

"Can you hand me my glasses?" He did. I slipped them on and stood up. "See you downstairs?"

Back on the fourth floor, Celeste's bed was already made and there was no sign of her. Thankfully. I took a steaming-hot shower. My body still felt jarred from the physical intensity of being with David. With a clearer mind, I considered the strangeness of having woken up in the midst of it. It really was like my body had made a decision, bypassing my conscious brain. I rubbed lather over my skin and tried to imagine my hands were David's. Tried to imagine enjoying it. I had to get over my nervousness. That shaking thing couldn't happen again.

Before getting dressed, I put on my glasses and stared at my naked body in the full-length mirror. It wasn't a dislike of my figure that made me nervous about being with David. Sure, I had my issues, but whatever. So what was it?

I turned around and looked at my butt, my back—my eyes stopped scanning and focused. My tattoo. I turned my gaze from the mirror to my actual body. Normally, I didn't see myself naked with my glasses on—in the tub or shower I was half blind. So I couldn't remember the last time I'd given the tatt a clear-eyed appraisal. It had changed. The colors didn't glow with that depth of pigment that had made it really look like stained glass. Now they were washed out. And the black lines had thickened and bled. As if David's kiss had reacted with the ink.

Damn. It wasn't the most expensive tattoo, but it wasn't cheap either. And I'd taken such good care of it. I kept staring, as if it was going to change back before my eyes.

When I was sufficiently sure it wasn't going to, I dressed and followed the smell of bacon downstairs, into the kitchen.

Viv stood at the marble countertop island, cracking an egg into a bowl. At the table, Abby sat hunched over a mug of coffee and Cameron leaned back in his chair, reading the paper.

"Morning, sunshine," Viv said. "Eggs? Veggie bacon? Home fries?"

"Mmm." I got myself some grapefruit juice from the fridge then sat down next to Abby. "Hungover?" I said to her.

She nodded. "A little. Need food."

"Hey," I said, "have either of your guys' tatts faded or bled?"

"Nope," Abby said.

Viv turned from the stove. "Cam? You see my butt more than I do."

"Looks good to me, baby," he said.

I swirled the juice around in my glass. "Mine looks like hell."

"Go back to the place," Abby said. "They can fix some stuff."

"I will. Where's Celeste? Did she eat already?"

"Haven't seen her or David," Viv said.

"David's getting up." I tried to keep any suspicious notes out of my voice.

I wasn't successful. All eyes turned toward me.

"And you know this how?" Viv asked.

I would have lied, but my smile and blush told the story. "We just, you know, hung out."

Abby rested her head on the table. "Why do I always have to be right? Why, why, why?"

"So where's Celeste?" I said. "She's not in the bedroom."

Viv ate a bite of eggs off her spatula then recommenced using it to stir. "Yesterday she asked me if she could take some pictures around the house. Maybe she's doing that."

Honestly, at that point, her absence just seemed like a gift, one I wasn't going to question too strenuously. Especially not after David came into the room, fresh from a shower and looking ten times hotter than I'd thought before, if that was possible. I was sure I could get used to that fooling-around stuff. I was just nervous I'd do something wrong, probably. Push the wrong button, pull the wrong lever. It had been a long time since I'd been with a guy, after all. And I'd never

228

felt as excited about anyone as I was about David. That was probably it: overexcitement.

Viv served us breakfast and we passed around the best sections of the Sunday *New York Times*. David's foot found mine under the table. I skimmed through the real-estate section, fantasizing.

I was happy to ignore Celeste's absence for as long as possible. After a bit, though, David got antsy. He called her cell and it went straight to voice mail. For once, I wished he wasn't such a caring and thoughtful brother.

"Maybe she went to the park?" Cameron said.

"In this weather?" I said, then turned to Viv. "Is Annika around? Maybe she's seen her."

"Nope. Saturday night and Sunday she has off."

David and I decided to look through the house. It didn't take us long to figure out she wasn't here—unless she was hiding, which, I hoped, was beyond even Celeste. The whole thing was giving me a flashback to the bar last night. Maybe we were going to find her sitting in an alley behind the house, smoking with Whip.

"What should we do?" I asked David, annoyed that this was how we were spending our morning. "Walk around the neighborhood and look in cafés and stuff?"

"I think we should wait for her here," he said. "If we go out and she comes back, she won't be able to get in the house."

I went to my bedroom to grab a sweater. As I did, I

checked around to see if I could tell what type of clothes Celeste had worn, in case that told us anything. I quickly realized I should have thought to check earlier.

Everything was gone.

All she'd left was a piece of paper folded over one of the hangers in the closet with a scrawled note: *Back to Barcroft. Sorry, took the dress with me.*

"She's what?" David said, placing his glass of orange juice down without taking a sip.

"Gone," I said in disbelief. "Back to school."

"What? Why?" Viv said, collecting dishes to be washed. "She seemed okay last night. Was she upset or something?"

"I have no idea." I thudded down in a chair.

David picked up his cell, sent a message. Called, left a voice mail telling her to call back immediately.

"Do you think she took the train?" I said. "Or bus? I mean, what a hassle with her bag, and her cast. What do you think we should do?"

"She's a big girl," Abby said, looking at us over the top of the Style section. "Can't we assume she knows what she's doing?"

No one said anything. The last thing I *wanted* was to spend another minute worrying about her, but it was just so strange.

"Since it's bad weather," Abby continued, "I think we should go to that movie. It starts in twenty-five minutes.

But the theater's a quick walk, right, Viv?" She folded up the newspaper with loud snapping noises.

"Yeah. Ten minutes," Viv said.

"And we can go to that museum you read about after," Abby said.

I looked at David, could read in his face right away that he didn't feel right going out without hearing from his sister. I didn't think I'd be able to concentrate on a movie either.

"You guys go," I said. "David and I will stay here. We can meet you later at the museum, okay?"

Abby pushed her chair back and stood up. "Whatever. Hope you have fun."

Despite the fact that it was the afternoon after our first kiss and first night together, our time alone was not at all cozy or romantic. We spent most of it staring at David's phone. I attempted the *Times* crossword puzzle but had trouble concentrating well enough to make a dent in the clues.

I was trying to remember who wrote the short story "The Lottery," seven letters, when the phone finally rang. But it wasn't David's; it was mine. And it wasn't Celeste.

"Leena?" Dean Shepherd said. "Sorry to bother you."

"That's okay," I said, surprised. "What's up?"

"Sorry if there's noise around me," she said. "I'm in the parking lot at Whole Foods—dinner party tonight. But I just got a strange message. Apparently, a maintenance worker was called over to Frost House to help a student with something. And since no students are supposed to be there . . ."

A maintenance worker? "Uh, I guess that's something to do with Celeste," I said.

"Celeste?"

"You know how we all came to New York, to Viv's house?" I said. "Well, Celeste has sort of, well, she left early."

"What?" A car honked near her as she spoke. "Why?"

I ran my finger along the side of the place mat, feeling David's eyes on me. The only possibility we'd come up with was that Celeste was having some overblown reaction to us getting together. I couldn't exactly tell that to the dean. "It's kind of a misunderstanding," I said. "I'm not quite sure why. She left early this morning."

"And came all the way back to Barcroft? Alone? On crutches?"

"I guess." It sounded so ridiculous. I didn't blame the dean for being confused.

"Did Viv's parents take her to the train station, or something?"

"No. I mean, we don't really know."

"Well, I don't quite understand, Leena, and don't have time to talk about it right now. But I'll go to Frost House on my way home from running errands and see what's going on. In the meantime, please have one of Viv's parents call me."

I could have lied. I could have told her they were out, or whatever. But I didn't. At the moment, it didn't strike me as that big a deal. Dean Shepherd loved me. She trusted me.

And Celeste was the issue at hand.

"They're actually not around," I said. "They got this last-minute trip deal to Paris so they went. But Viv's housekeeper is here, or was here, I mean, yesterday, and took great care of us."

"They aren't there?" she said.

"No."

I could hear a sigh of annoyance. "I'll call you back after I've been to Frost House. In the meantime, you and whoever is with you—Vivian and Abigail and whoever else—are going to pack up and drive right back here."

Drive back to Barcroft? Today? That's when I realized the mistake I'd made. My stomach turned inside out.

I slumped against the back of my chair. "Abby is going to kill me. K-I-L-L, kill me. Now that Dean Shepherd knows that our chaperones aren't here, she's making us come back to school. She sounded really pissed. We're seniors. I didn't think she'd care. And everyone knows chaperone letters are bullshit."

"What's going on with Celeste?" David asked.

I explained about the maintenance worker being called to the dorm. "I shouldn't have told her," I said, then rested my cheek on the cool table. "I am so dead."

I was in my room folding clothes into my duffel when my phone rang again.

"I found Celeste," Dean Shepherd said. "She was the

one who called maintenance. I can't discuss anything now, Leena, but please come find me at home the minute you arrive back on campus. I need to talk to you."

"I know," I said. "I'm sorry about the thing with Viv's par—"

"It's not about that," she said.

"It's not?" I rested my full bag on the floor.

"No," she said. "I want you to tell me what has been going on in this house."

25

DAVID AND I HIT A TRAFFIC JAM on I-91. The kind of jam that even in the best of circumstances would make me want to get out of the car, slam the door, and walk.

With the mood I was in, I thought I might literally explode. Having to spend one more minute than necessary trapped in the car, helpless. No chance to make anything better. Just a relentless cycling in my head of all the ways this was beyond bad. And I kept picturing Viv and Abby and Cameron stuck in the traffic, too. I couldn't stand it. I wished I hadn't left Cubby—with all of my pills—at Frost House.

"What?" Viv had said in a whisper when I called to tell her what had happened with Dean Shepherd. "You're saying

235

we have to leave? Today?"

"I know it sucks," I said. "Why are you whispering?"

"We're at that museum—the Museum of Sex," Viv said. "Can you believe there's a Museum of Sex? Anyway, I don't want Abby to hear. She's going to have a fit."

"Tell her and Cameron how sorry I am. At least we got a couple days in the city."

"I guess," Viv said, not sounding convinced. "I was keeping it a secret, but I got us tickets to Letterman tomorrow."

"Really? God, I'm so sorry."

"Yeah, well, I am, too."

Sitting in the car, I couldn't get Viv's voice out of my mind. And we'd only moved about five feet in the last ten minutes.

"What is wrong?" I yelled, hitting the steering wheel. "It's a Sunday. Who are all these stupid people?"

"Hey." David laid a hand on my knee. "We'll get there."

He had been much calmer than me after we'd found out Celeste was definitely back in the dorm. Even though we were still confused about why she'd left, and why she wasn't answering our calls, he kept saying, "I know it's a pain in the ass, but at least she's safe."

I refrained from telling him that with everyone so mad at me, I didn't care if she was safe at school or the victim of an alien abduction. Actually, I did care. I'd have preferred the alien option.

I fiddled with the radio, trying to find a traffic report. "By the time we get there, I'll have to interrupt Dean Shepherd during her party."

"She's the one who told you to come talk to her. She can't be pissed if you do."

Bad song, worse song, commercial . . . "Do you think I should call Viv again?"

"I think you should try to relax."

"You keep saying that!" I snapped off the radio and glared at him. "Do you have any idea how much this sucks?"

"I know it sucks," he said. "I just don't think getting upset does any good."

"How can I not be upset?" I said. "This is a really, really shitty situation your sister's put me in. Put us in. I mean, I know it was stupid of me to tell Dean Shepherd about Viv's parents, but I shouldn't have even been talking to her. If Celeste hadn't run away—"

"Leena—"

"And I don't even know why the dean wants to see me tonight! Maybe Celeste made it sound like we did those things to her. Like we broke her vase and ruined her art project." I couldn't say it to David, but maybe she'd even told the dean about the nests spelling out *GO*, about how someone wanted her to leave. Maybe she'd blamed everything on Abby.

"Why would she do that?" David said.

"I don't know." I gripped the steering wheel and focused my eyes on the Greyhound bus ahead of us. "Because Celeste always wants to be the center of attention, right? And that's exactly what happened in the dorm. And what happened this weekend! Maybe she even did it all herself—the vase, the nests. So she can be the victim, just like she wants." Blood pounded in my ears.

"Yeah," David said. "That occurred to me."

"What?" I turned. He met my eyes with complete calm.

"I was worried, at first," he said, "that she might have broken the vase herself."

Any words in my mouth evaporated. He'd been thinking the same thing I had? "Oh," I said eventually. "Well, did you . . . did you ask her about it?"

"I didn't have to."

"What do you mean?" I glanced forward, drove a few yards to close the gap that had opened up. Looked back at David.

"I didn't have to ask," he said. "Celeste told me. Not that she *did* it. That she *didn't*. She's not stupid. She knew I'd suspect her."

"Oh." This was all such a surprise. "And you believe her?"

"Yeah, I do." He pointed at the windshield. "Bad accident."

Up ahead, the left of four lanes was closed to bypass a mess of police cars and ambulances. David and I fell silent as we inched up to the scene. Three totaled cars sat at varying angles on the median.

"They're using the jaws of life," I said. "Someone must still be in that car."

"Uh-huh," David said. Then his hand covered my eyes,

knocking into my glasses. "Oh, man. Don't look."

"David! I'm driving." I batted his arm.

"Well, keep your eyes straight ahead. Trust me."

I did, but couldn't help asking, "What is it? A body?"

"You don't want something horrible to be the thing you remember from this weekend, do you?" he said.

"As opposed to remembering my own personal disasters?" I said. "God, we're at a total standstill again."

"Hey. Look at me for a sec." He rested a hand on my shoulder. "I'm sorry about this mess," he said. "I'm really, really sorry for my sister's part in it. I am. But about what you said before—Celeste is *not* always the center of attention. At least not the center of *my* attention. Understand?"

I nodded.

"And this might turn out to have been a pretty important weekend," he said. "So you should work on remembering the good parts."

"Important?"

"No?" he said. "Nothing that happened strikes you as important? Nothing's changed?" His gaze lingered on my lips.

I glanced at the road, looked back at David. "Maybe you should refresh my memory."

He moved his hand to the back of my head and eased me forward into a long, soft kiss. This time, instead of adding to my worries, the heat and intensity obliterated them. In that moment I knew, despite any self-sabotaging nervousness, this was what I wanted.

26

THROUGH THE WINDOWS of Dean Shepherd's cozy, shingle-style house, I could see people gathered in her living room—standing in clusters, eating, drinking, laughing. . . . I ran my fingers through my hair, tucked it behind my ears, and rang the bell.

The dean answered the door holding a glass of red wine. "Leena," she said. "I was beginning to worry about you."

I wanted to tell her how nice she looked in her silk, kimono-style dress. I wanted to tell her David and I had finally gotten together. I wanted to be one of the people invited to the party, not the student interrupting it.

We had to pass through the living room to get to her home office. The smell of onions and garlic cooking poured from the kitchen. The Cinnabon I'd eaten for dinner sat like a brick in my stomach. I said hello to Mrs. Fleissner, an English teacher, and Mr. Prince, a theater teacher, self-conscious about my too-long-in-a-car appearance. I didn't know the other guests by name, but I could feel everyone looking at me with curiosity. Had the happenings in Frost House been fodder for their party conversation? Hard to say, since I didn't even know what the happenings were.

Dean Shepherd shut the office door behind us. Stacks of paper filled every surface. She took a messy pile off a chair and asked me to sit, then placed her glass of wine on a bookshelf, as if she'd be too tempted to down it during our conversation.

"So," she said, sitting. "Have you been back to the dorm yet?"

Was that a trick question? "No." I said. "Well, I dropped David off there to see his sister. But I didn't go in. You told me to come straight here."

She folded her hands together on the desk. "I know I was vague on the phone. I didn't want to get into it until I saw you in person."

"It sounded serious."

"When I went to look for Celeste, the dorm was a wreck."

"A wreck?"

"Your section of the house. It looked like a tornado had hit it. Clothes everywhere. Boxes in the middle of the hallway."

"Did someone break in?" I asked, suddenly a bit panicked. I'd left my laptop there, my only valuable jewelry—

"No," the dean said. "Celeste did it. She was moving all of her stuff into the tiny room with your desks, and your stuff into the room with the windows."

"She was what?"

"Moving your things, so you'll have separate rooms."

"Oh." I didn't know what to say. "That's weird. We've never talked about doing that. She did all of this on crutches?"

"That's what she'd called the maintenance worker about—to help her. But there were other things. I noticed some dried blood drops on the floor. Honestly, the whole place looked like a crime scene." Her pointed stare made me feel like I was the suspected criminal.

"What did Celeste say?"

"She was very cagey. She said she was moving rooms because she didn't like being in a bedroom with so many windows. Apparently, the blood was from a cut she got while moving the stuff."

"I guess I'm not surprised she wanted to change the room setup," I said. "She hates that bedroom."

The dean's eyebrows drew together. "There must be something else going on here, Leena. Why would she have left your trip like that, without telling you?"

"I haven't spoken to her, so I don't know," I said. "The only thing I can imagine is that . . ." Peals of laugher filtered in from the next room. I waited until they stopped. "David and I are kind of, well . . . you know. Involved."

"You are? Since when?"

"It's pretty recent. Anyway, maybe it has something to do with that. Maybe she felt out of place or uncomfortable."

Dean Shepherd rested her forearms on the desk and leaned in. "I don't want to miss a warning sign that something more serious is going on. Given Celeste's family situation, and her accident over the summer, I can't just ignore what seems like troubling behavior. You're sure there's nothing else I need to know?"

I hated not to tell the whole truth, but I wanted to talk to Celeste, to find out what this was really about. And talk to David, too. If something were wrong, he'd expect me to tell him first.

Like a kid, I crossed my fingers under the desk. "Well like I said, she's never been comfortable in our bedroom. She can't sleep in it. She has nightmares. I don't know her well enough to know if it's really the room, or if she'd have this trouble anywhere. I'm pretty sure the main problem is me and David, though. They're really close, you know."

"I know," Dean Shepherd said, sitting back in her chair again. "Okay, well, I'll trust you to let me know if you notice anything else, Leena. Although, I'm sure I don't need to tell you that you've seriously compromised my trust by lying about your chaperones this weekend."

"I'm really sorry," I said, relieved that I seemed to have weathered the storm. The meeting hadn't been nearly as bad as the scenarios I'd imagined—Celeste telling the dean she'd been persecuted all semester. "Being seniors, you know, it just didn't seem like that big a deal. Over the summer our parents leave us alone all the time."

"The rules at Barcroft apply just as much to seniors as they do to underclassmen. You know that."

"I know." Blah, blah, blah . . . I supposed she had to say all of this.

"I haven't checked, but I believe this is the first strike against everyone involved. Luckily. So, you'll meet with the disciplinary committee, but it won't lead to anything as serious as expulsion."

Her words hit me like a slap. "The disciplinary committee?" I said. "Really?"

"Of course. What did you think?"

What did I think? I thought she'd write it off as a stupid, but harmless, mistake.

I thought I was special.

I stood at the bottom of the narrow stairs, looking up at the closed door to Viv's room waiting for me at the top. I hadn't yet seen Celeste or the supposed disaster area. In the common room, the only sign of something amiss was a black garbage bag with Celeste's violet comforter inside. It smelled like rotting fruit. I couldn't imagine why, and didn't really care. The only thing I cared about was being alone in my room. But I knew I had to face Viv and Abby first. If I delayed telling them, it would just be hanging over my head for longer.

I forced myself to lift my legs. Step. Step. Step. My hand felt heavy as a cement block when I raised it to knock on Viv's door.

"Yeah?" Viv answered.

"Can I come in?" A question I never would have bothered asking before tonight.

There was a pause. "Whatever."

Viv and Abby sat together on the bed, each holding a mug of tea. Normally, I'd have joined them, but I knew better, especially from the looks on their faces.

"You guys made it back okay?" I said, standing awkwardly just inside the doorway.

"Obviously." Abby said. "Seeing as we're here."

"I'm so, so, sorry, you guys," I said. "But I didn't have any control over this. I didn't know Celeste was leaving."

"No control?" Abby said. "Seems to me you're the one who told the dean about Viv's parents. In other words, the one who ruined our weekend."

"I'm sorry," I said again. "I feel terrible. I'll do whatever I can to make it up to you guys."

"What do you want, Leen?" Viv asked in a tired voice.

I drew a deep breath. "I talked to Dean Shepherd. And she said that we have to meet with the DC. But because it's our first offense, we don't have to worry about being kicked out."

"Kicked out!" Abby sat up straighter. "Are you kidding?"

"I said we're *not* going to be kicked out."

"But it's a first strike?" Abby said. "You know what that means? No drinking, no smoking, no illegal parietals or sneaking out at night. No anything! During senior year! If we're caught doing anything, we're kicked out. We might as well be handcuffed to our desks!"

"I know. I'm sorry. It sucks."

Viv's hand flew up to her mouth. "Oh my God."

"What?" Abby said.

"Oh my God," she repeated.

"Viv. *What?*"

"Cameron," Viv said, her voice quiet. "Freshman year. Before we were together. He was busted for drinking."

"He's on probation?" I said. How could I not have known that?

Viv nodded.

A weight dropped in my gut like a cannonball.

"Viv," I said. "You know I didn't mean—"

She pressed one hand against her eyes and waved the other in my direction. "Just go. Okay? Go."

"Please, Viv, I—"

Abby glared at me. "What part of 'go' don't you understand?"

Thankfully, the door to what was now Celeste's bedroom was closed. I'd have locked it from the outside if I could.

246

Trembling, I took Cubby off the windowsill and opened the door to my closet, momentarily jarred by how uncomfortably large and bright it seemed, empty of clothes. But then the smell and the soft air reached for me, and I knew it was still the same. Celeste had dumped my clothes from the other room in a pile; it only took me a few moments to hang them up—everything except my ankle-length puffer coat, which I spread on the floor in one corner. The space wasn't nearly as full as with Celeste's wardrobe, but it would do. I scooted into the corner with the puffer as a cushion. No more worrying about Celeste walking in on me. And I didn't foresee Abby or Viv coming to visit anytime soon. The thought made my throat swell. I breathed deeply, inhaling the familiar, comforting scent.

"What am I going to do?" I said to Cubby.

The ring of my phone from my pocket startled me. I only answered because it was David.

"How'd it go?" he said.

It took me a second to realize he meant the meeting with Dean Shepherd. "Okay," I said.

"Really?"

I bit the inside of my lip, remembering. My voice trembled. "Well, sort of." Then I started to cry. "Can we . . . I'm sorry, can I just talk to you tomorrow? I can't really deal right now."

"Of course. Are you okay, Leena? Have you seen Celeste?"

"No. Not yet." And whenever I did would be too soon.

"I'm sorry. I really have to go."

I hung up, took off my glasses, and pressed the heels of my hands against my eyelids to try and make it stop. But the tears were too strong for that. I lifted off Cubby's head. My fingers fumbled with the baggies of pills. I set aside ones I didn't want. Found the one I did.

"Everything is ruined," I whispered even though there was no need to be quiet anymore.

You're here now, she said. *It's okay.*

"But Cameron . . . . I've ruined his *life*. And Viv'll never forgive me."

Shhh . . . You don't need her.

I wanted to believe what I was telling myself. Wanted to believe I'd be all right. But I knew it wasn't true. Of course I needed my friends. They were . . . everything.

Bit by bit, a calm settled over my body. My tears stopped, and I slept. A deep sleep, not the sleep of someone who's worried she might have lost three of the most important people in her life.

The sleep of someone who knows she's come home.

part two

27

I SLEPT IN THE CLOSET UNTIL surprisingly late the next morning. When I stood up, my limbs and spine hurt as if I'd spent the night digging a deep hole; my head ached so much I was ready to jump in the hole and be buried. I immediately took a couple of Tylenol. As the pills scraped their way down my dry throat, the events of the night before came back with more clarity, making my stomach hurt, too—the kind of ache that no medicine could help. I grabbed a clean towel and shuffled into the hallway. Celeste was just locking the door to the little room, dressed to go outside in a short, plaid wool cape, miniskirt, and the green beret. As if everything was perfectly normal.

"Hey," I said.

She turned to face me. Dark hollows shadowed her eyes, her skin was dull, lips chapped—aside from her pulled-together outfit, she looked as bad as I felt. I'd thought I was going to have trouble controlling my anger, but much of it drained away.

"What happened?" I said. "We were really worried."

"I took the Fung Wah Bus to Boston," she said. "Bummer with my leg, but only fifteen dollars."

"You know that's not what I meant." I leaned my back against the wall. "Why didn't you talk to us before leaving? You do realize we're all going to disciplinary committee because of this?" Silence. "Cameron might get kicked out." Saying those words made me want to vomit.

"You weren't in the room. How was I going to talk to you?" she said, scratching inside the top of her cast.

"Was it because of me and David?"

"Because it turned out you're a slut like the rest of them?"

"Excuse me?" I said, standing up straight again. "Not that it's any of your business, but nothing much happened."

"Of course it's my business. He's my brother."

"Exactly," I snapped. "He's your *brother*, not your boyfriend or husband. You get pissed when he asks about *your* romantic life."

She didn't respond, just resumed scratching. How could she be so cavalier about this?

"Look," I said, trying to retain some sort of composure.

I couldn't stand any more fighting. "David and I are going to be hanging out, like you've wanted all semester. So I need to know why you're so upset. I mean, you out-and-out told me you wanted us to get together. Is it . . ." I didn't quite know how to ask if she was jealous without implying she was in love with her own brother. "Are you concerned he won't have as much time for you?"

Scratch, scratch, scratch. She didn't look up as she spoke. "Of course not. I already told you I wanted David to have a girlfriend so he'd get off my back."

"Okay, well . . ." I couldn't force her to admit to it. And what good would it do, anyway? At this point, I wasn't going to break up with David to make her feel better. "Dean Shepherd is really worried about you. She wants to know what's going on. Why you came back early and everything. And why you moved out of the big room."

That got Celeste's attention. "I told her why," she said.

"Because you don't like all the windows? She didn't buy it. Well, she didn't buy that you'd have come back early from New York to do it."

"What did you tell her?"

"Just that maybe you'd been uncomfortable that David and I were together."

Celeste's mouth dropped open. "What, like I wanted him for myself?"

"No! Not like that," I said. "It was the only reason I could think of."

"You didn't tell her about . . . you know, the stuff I told you before, did you?"

"No." I hugged the folded towel closer to my body. "But Celeste, if that's why you switched rooms, if you're really still having those strange thoughts—that someone's . . . watching you, or trying to mess with you—maybe we should tell someone."

She shook her head. "You promised you wouldn't. You *can't*. I told you how bad it would be for me. And I told you I felt better the next day. That was just a bad night, before I realized the cat had done it. I blew it all out of proportion. You promised, Leena."

"I know. But things change."

"You know what's changed?" she said. "I *slept* last night. Comfortably. I told you I didn't like those windows the very first day. And then with all the other weird stuff that happened . . . Can't you see why I freaked out in there? Now I don't have to worry."

Her exhausted appearance didn't match this version of events. "Are you sure?" I said. "Why is your comforter in the trash?"

A flicker of something—fear? panic?—passed across her face. "David didn't take it yet?" she said. "It got wet and mildewy while we were gone. Rain through the windows. He has to wash it."

"The windows were shut," I said. I'd locked them all before we left.

"They leaked," she said. "A welcome-back present from the house."

Enough to get her bed that wet? "Was someone in our room while we were gone?" I asked.

"No," she said, rubbing her eyes. "No one. Look, I switched rooms to give you some privacy and because I can't sleep over there. What's the big deal? You don't mind, do you? Why would you mind? It's better for both of us."

"I guess," I said. And, truthfully, having my own room was the one good thing that had come from this mess. "But the way you did it . . ."

"I shouldn't have come back early," she said. "I'm impulsive. You know that. And, okay, maybe I wasn't expecting things with you and David to move that fast. I thought you— Whatever. It's not important. I shouldn't have left. And I'm sorry. But I'm fine. This new room arrangement is going to fix everything."

"Okay," I said. "Okay."

I shut myself in the bathroom and stood under the shower and made a decision. Celeste had been very clear, again—if something was wrong, she didn't want me interfering. She wanted her own room, her separate life. And that's what I'd wanted right from the beginning, wasn't it? The less I knew, the less I had to keep from David. She hadn't shown any concern for the rest of us when she'd come back from New York like that, no matter what her reason. So, fine. Our own rooms. Our own lives.

I spent most of the day with David, a large part of it lying on his bed as he tried to distract me from worrying about Abby and Viv and the disciplinary committee. We listened to almost everything on his iPod—from James Brown to Eminem; he described in detail the gourmet meal he wanted to cook for me one day soon; he tried to explain the math he was doing (all I really understood was that it was called topology and had something to do with a donut and a coffee cup being the same thing); he told me stories about better times with their father. All of this interspersed with sweetly intense bouts of kissing. He was obviously trying to distract himself, too, from worrying about Celeste, because by midafternoon he'd asked me "how I'd thought she seemed" one too many times.

I propped myself up on my elbow. "New rule," I said.

"Rule?" David said. "Are your rules as strict as your moratorium was?"

I punched his shoulder. "Listen. Seriously. Now that you and I are, you know, *together*, I really think it's best if you . . . if we don't talk about your sister as much. I don't want to always feel like I'm your source of information. Okay? I want to keep things a little more separate." For an instant, I had the horrible thought that maybe the only reason he even wanted to be close to me was to find out stuff about his sister, but then he said, "Yeah, you're probably right." He ran a hand through my loose hair, fingers getting caught in a tangle. "Could get messy."

"So, good rule?" I said, relieved.

"Good rule."

The six of us met with the disciplinary committee on Tuesday. Later that night, in some sort of masochistic haze, I decided to listen to Viv and Cam's show on WBAR, but there was a guest host. I supposed they wanted to spend their last night together alone.

Cam had to leave school on Wednesday.

The rest of us, as promised, had gotten probation.

Walking across campus Wednesday afternoon, I saw Cameron's car—filled with belongings—in the parking area next to his dorm. He and Viv stood outside of it. Even from the other side of the Great Lawn, I could tell by the stoop of her shoulders and Cameron's hand stroking her back that Viv was crying.

I dropped my gaze to the ground and hurried along, the path becoming a muddy, gray blur.

Once I got home I headed straight for the closet. I wanted to know that it would be okay, that I'd be okay, even without Viv, like I'd told myself in here the other night. I stroked Cubby's feathers. I just needed to know that I could get past how much it hurt.

In here you can, her voice said.

On Thursday, Dean Shepherd told me she wanted me to step down from peer counseling.

"You understand," she said. "We can't have the mixed message of someone in a leadership position like that getting into trouble." There was a hint of sympathy in her voice, but it didn't do anything to make me feel better.

I couldn't hide my desperation as I spoke. "What if I just step down as cohead? But keep counseling? Could I do that?"

"Maybe next semester. I doubt it, though," she said.

Had I thought she'd sounded sympathetic a moment ago? Because now, I didn't see how there was any chance she felt anything but derision and disappointment. The horrible feeling it gave me was even worse than knowing I wasn't a part of my program anymore. I hated myself more than she ever could.

Later that day, David and I took a walk through the arboretum at the edge of campus. A few trees were still lit up with flame-colored foliage; mostly, I saw the brown leaves under our feet. I told David how I'd messed up not only my friendships with Viv, Abby, and Dean Shepherd, but also my one meaningful extracurricular. I told him I had nothing left.

"What about me?" he said, sounding hurt.

I wrapped my arm around his waist and squeezed.

Thank God. I had David. And I had my house.

I was incredibly relieved that my room was tucked in the back, and on a separate floor from Viv's and Abby's, so I didn't have constant reminders that Frost House was now a divided territory. I couldn't have handled listening to their muffled voices and laughter, or the sounds of their sock feet on the wooden floor going back and forth between each other's rooms. As for Celeste, in the days since we came back from New York, I'd barely seen her. My space was truly my own and I wasn't going to let the opportunity go to waste.

The Saturday after we got back, I made a rare call to my dad to ask if I could buy some supplies at Home Depot on his credit card. He said yes—probably partly out of shock at hearing from me, and partly because he always likes to support home improvement.

As I walked across the store's parking lot, I found myself scanning the cars for his orange Subaru, even though this Home Depot was about an hour from his condo. Going to any sort of hardware store without him never felt quite right.

I began in the paint department. After a long period of deliberation, I chose a very light sky color, called "Blue Heaven." I got brushes, rollers, trays, Spackle, and drop cloths. I considered buying a ladder, but they were too expensive, so I decided I'd just borrow one from maintenance.

Next, I found all the supplies I'd need for wall-mounted shelves.

In the garden department, I chose tulip and daffodil bulbs to plant in the backyard that would bloom next spring, and a couple of houseplants to hang in my room, along with the necessary wall brackets.

Then I got an egg-crate–foam-mattress pad and a brass, sliding bolt lock.

The closet needed an upgrade, too.

28

"ALL I'M SAYING IS THAT I don't want you in my room anytime soon."

"Nice," David said from the other end of the phone. "This is how you treat me?"

I scooped some more Spackle onto my knife. "I just want it to be a surprise. Give me a couple of weeks. Then you can be over here whenever you want. I promise."

"All right," he said in a tone of resignation. "What are you doing tonight?"

"Studying, I guess."

"Want to come over and do it here?"

"If you let me get some work done," I said, scraping the whitish paste over another small hole in the wall. "I've got to seriously start working if I want to have any chance at Columbia. I've never been this behind before."

"Speaking of Columbia," he said, "Paul, the guy who owns the restaurant I might work in, wants to meet with me over Thanksgiving. So I was thinking you could come down and we could spend a couple of days in the city together."

When I'd mentioned to David that Columbia was on my list of long shots, he'd started talking as if it was a given that we'd want to be in the same city. Every time he talked that way, I wanted to die of happiness. We'd only been a couple for a week, but I already felt like he was a central fixture in my life. I couldn't believe I'd even hesitated. Our togetherness seemed so obvious, and inevitable. Sort of like the way I'd felt when I'd moved into Frost House.

I spotted some holes midway up the wall that needed to be filled. "That'd be great," I said, stepping up on the chair. "But I always go to Abby's parents' place for Thanksgiving."

"Do you think you'll do that this year?" he asked carefully.

I hadn't even considered the possibility that I wouldn't. "Probably," I said. I'd gone the last three years. Her parents owned a bed-and-breakfast farm in Maine. I loved visiting them. Abby had to have forgiven me by then. Right? I wasn't sure how many more weeks I could take with her and Viv not talking to me. Or even how many more days. . . .

"Well, if you come to New York," he said, "you can check out where I might end up living. This guy Paul knows is going to be subletting his place and it would actually be affordable if I get a roommate."

"A roommate?" I scooped a bit more Spackle from the bucket.

"Yeah. With New York prices, I'll be lucky to have only *one* roommate."

"Huh. I wonder if . . ." My heart thudded harder and faster as I strained to reach the next hole.

"If what?"

"If I'd have to live in a dorm at Columbia. I mean, maybe I'm being crazy, but what if we shared a place?"

"Lived together?"

Crap. Why had I said that? Same city is one thing, but this would probably completely freak him out. "Yeah, forget it. I was just thinking that financially, it might . . . but I'm being—"

"No, Leena. It's a great idea. I'd love to have you as a roommate. Obviously."

"Really? You would?" I said. "Because living with you is probably the one thing that would make me psyched to leave Frost House."

All of a sudden, the earth tipped. I saw myself falling before it happened, then it did happen. The chair toppled backward. My cell and Spackle knife flew out of my hands. I pitched toward the floor, hit with a thud, landing partially on top of the overturned chair. Pain flared through me.

"Shit," I said. "Oww!"

I rolled onto my side. After a second, I inched over and grabbed my phone.

"Are you there? Leena? Leena?" David was saying.

"Oww. I fell. It hurts."

"Are you okay? Jesus, you scared me."

"I think so," I said, though I was shaking pretty hard from the shock. I pulled myself up and walked wobbily over to the bed.

"What happened? Are you okay? Should I come over?"

"No. I'm okay. I don't know what happened." I rubbed my hip. "The chair tipped. I guess I shifted my weight funny."

I didn't tell him that, actually, it felt like I'd been pushed.

I stared at the chair, searching for some evidence of what had happened. It looked perfectly normal. Still, I didn't trust it enough to climb back up on it. After I'd physically calmed down, I decided to work on the closet instead, cutting down the foam and installing the lock. Once I had the foam down to the right size, I covered it in an extra tapestry and nestled it into the space. It fit perfectly. I'd even cut out one corner to accommodate a metal scrollwork grate in the floor. I wasn't quite sure but assumed the grate had some purpose. Maybe it let air up from the basement, which would explain the way it had stayed cool on hot days. I took a couple of throw pillows off my bed and tossed them in.

Installing the lock required a bit more patience—measuring, drilling holes. When I'd finished, I stood inside the dark closet and slid the small bolt back and forth, back and forth, happy with how smoothly it worked. I left it in the locked position, turned on the small camping lantern I'd bought, and curled up on the mattress, enormously pleased with my new setup. Still a bit achy, though, from my fall, I reached for Cubby, opened her up, and found a pain reliever.

"David wants us to live together," I said.

That's not going to happen.

Cubby's words came to me easily now whenever I was in the closet. Like I'd realized before, the closet—its smell, its familiarity—was what let me into my subconscious. I didn't even need Cubby here, although I usually still brought her in; she made me feel less alone.

"I have to leave here," I said. "And living with David would be the best thing I could imagine."

I'd never mean to hurt you.

"Hurt me?"

All I want is to protect you. If you can't do it yourself.

You are *myself,* I thought. I shivered and reached up to unlock the door.

Don't go, she said.

I was pretty sleepy. I let my arm fall back down.

There's nothing wrong with admitting you're weak, she said.

I *had* given into David, when I said I wouldn't.

In here, she said, *it doesn't matter. Nothing matters.*

My head felt strange, heavy. If nothing mattered, then it wouldn't be a problem for me to just lie down, take a little nap. . . .

29

FOR THE NEXT COUPLE OF WEEKS, I divided my nonstudying free time between being with David and working on my room. Because painting edge-work around windows is so much more difficult than covering big areas of open wall, it took longer than I expected. But the meditative quality helped keep my mind off how much I missed Viv and Abby. And, in the end, the effort was worth it. With the paint, plants, shelves, and a new furniture arrangement, it was the nicest room I'd ever seen at Barcroft. I could tell how impressed David was when I showed him. "You did this?" he kept saying, eyes all lit up. He was still talking about it the next day as we sipped coffee at senior tea.

A change of expression on his face made me glance over

my shoulder. Abby was headed in our direction.

"I think I'll give you some space," he said.

I brushed muffin crumbs off my lap and tossed my napkin in the trash.

"Hi," I said as Abby stood in front of me. I scooched over on the small love seat. "Want to sit?"

She shook her head. Her nails were newly painted deep purple. I was suddenly conscious of my chipped and uneven ones. All the work I'd been doing wasn't conducive to pretty fingernails.

"I want to make sure you know that you're not coming home with me for Thanksgiving," she said, crossing her arms.

"Oh? I hadn't really been thinking about it." I was surprised the lie made it past the grapefruit-size lump in my throat.

"Well, you need to make other plans."

"Don't you think, maybe, we'll . . . we'll be okay by then?" I folded my hands so my nails, which looked more disgusting by the minute, weren't visible. "And, I mean, I always go with you. It's our tradition, right? Remember last year, how funny your mom was with the turkey? Remember, you did that imitation of her during dinner?"

I dared to look up, and thought I glimpsed a bit of a softening in Abby's face. She shrugged. "Yeah, but . . . just make other plans, okay?" She turned to walk away, the black-and-white wool skirt we'd bought together at Urban Outfitters swishing against the top of her boots.

"Abby," I said. I didn't know what I was going to follow it with. I just couldn't stand for our interaction to be so brief. For it to end like that.

"What?" She turned back to me.

"You should come downstairs and see all the stuff I've done in my room," I blurted.

"What stuff? Something to do with all the noise you've been making?"

I nodded. "Celeste moved across the hall, you know, so the room's just mine until Kate gets back next semester. I painted, built some stuff. If you and Viv want to come down and hang out, we don't have to worry about Celeste being there or anything."

Abby shook her head. "I can't be—"

She stumbled sideways with a jolt. Ponytail Guy, her crush from the beginning of the semester, had snuck up and hip checked her.

"Hey," she said, regaining her footing. "Watch out." I could tell by her smile she didn't mean it. Something was going on with them, obviously, and I didn't know anything about it.

"Did you get what Brighton was saying about that whole thing with peripeteia or whatever," Ponytail Guy said. "The Aristotle stuff?"

"Yeah," she said. "Why? You want me to explain it to you, dum-dum?"

"If you've got a minute in your busy schedule."

"I might." Abby cast a distracted glance in my direction.

"So, see you later?" I said.

"Yeah, later." She nudged Ponytail Guy as they walked away. "You really don't understand Aristotle?"

After dinner that night I spent a couple of hours cleaning and re-reorganizing so everything was just how I wanted it. (How could I have thought those Ball jars filled with pebbles and shells looked good on that shelf? Way too Martha Stewart.) Then I went upstairs for the first time since I'd told them about my meeting with the dean.

I knocked on Abby's door.

"Go away, Viv!" she called.

Were the two of them in a fight now? "It's me," I said. No response. "I wanted to know if—"

The door cracked open and Abby slipped out, shutting it behind her. Her hair was all mussed up, her cheeks flushed pink.

"What do you want?" she said in a rough, low voice.

"Is someone in there?" I said. "Ponytail Guy?"

"Shhh!" she whispered. "Yes. Now what do you want?"

"Just for you to come see my room. But you can come down after he leaves, obviously. Or tomorrow. Sorry to interrupt!" I gave her a smile and started to head down the stairs. I'd taken a few steps when she spoke again.

"Don't you get it?" she said. I stopped and looked back

up at her. "You made your choice, Leena. All semester. You chose Celeste over us. And you screwed everything up. You can't just come back now . . . like . . . I don't know . . . like nothing happened."

"You're blowing this all out of proportion," I said. "And it had nothing, *nothing* to do with choosing Celeste over you. Never."

"That's not what the facts say." She rested her hands on her hips. "Why don't you think about it from our perspective for once?"

"Abby, I know I screwed up. I feel terrible. But can't we just have it out and be done with it? Get in a fight and make up?"

"Not as far as I'm concerned. And Viv is the one whose boyfriend is gone, so I wouldn't count on her either."

I didn't know what more I could say. "Okay, well . . . let me know when you're ready to talk." My back was to her when I heard her voice again.

"You should know that we're thinking about moving out next semester."

"What?" I swung around to face her.

"You heard me. We'd both rather be somewhere else. I don't know if they'll let us. But we're looking into it."

"But . . . but Celeste won't even be living here next semester! Kate will. The four of us. Like we planned!"

Abby reached to open her door. "It's too late, Leena," she said. "Maybe Kate will stay here with you. Viv and I don't want to." And with that, she disappeared.

I pressed my hands against the walls of the narrow staircase. It felt like they were closing in, shutting out air. I tried to breathe into my tight lungs and stepped down. The floor at the bottom looked so far away, then veered up toward me, then fell back down. *Just one step at a time,* I told myself, keeping my gaze on my feet now. *Step down and breathe. Step down and breathe.* When I made it to the bottom, I took my hands off the walls and forbade myself from turning around. I knew what I'd see: the walls of the staircase collapsing toward each other, closing me out for good.

The pain was physical. My whole body hurt as I crawled into the closet. I lifted off Cubby's head, took one, then two of the strong oval pills that would help me relax, and waited for some of the pain to go away because I wasn't sure I could stand it. I hadn't felt this desperate since not knowing what to do about my parents, since feeling like my life was crashing apart. It was the type of hurt that felt like it wouldn't ever let me go, that I'd carry it with me for the rest of my life.

I breathed in the soothing air and pressed my cheek against the cool wall, wishing I could just become a part of it. I let the pills seep into my cells, telling myself I'd feel better soon, that help was coming. And it did. I'm not sure how long it took, but the pills and the quiet and the walls of the closet worked together to build me back up. And eventually, what had happened drifted away into a haze of unimportance.

"Everything's easy in here," I said, lying down now, staring up into the dark. "If I don't feel it, is the pain still there? Like the tree falling in a forest? Because I should care about Abby and Viv. But in here, I don't."

In here, none of that matters. What you don't feel doesn't exist.

"I like that," I said. "That's how it should be."

30

DURING THE NEXT WEEKS, my ability to concentrate almost vanished with the last of the tree leaves. Responsibilities faded into a sort of background noise that only rarely got loud enough so I'd pay attention. Not that I stopped attending class or doing homework, or that I wasn't aware that college apps and interviews were looming, just that I felt sort of numb when I tried to care about any of it. Occasionally, I'd realize that I needed to pull myself together—when I got a B minus on an English paper, for example—but most of the time I couldn't work up enough energy to make a difference.

Some colleges sent interviewers to campus. Columbia was one. The morning of my interview I woke up with the sudden realization that I'd done nothing to prepare. Hadn't I received a Columbia catalogue? And hadn't my college counselor given me a handout with interview tips? Well, if I'd ever had either of these things, I couldn't find them. So instead of going to my Gender Relations seminar, I read everything I could on the Columbia website and printed out a few online lists of the most popular college interview questions.

After lunch I went home to change clothes and gather myself. I chose a black miniskirt, black tights, and a charcoal-gray turtleneck sweater. Then I went into the closet.

I turned on the camping lantern and settled into the corner with my list of possible questions. For a moment I closed my eyes and felt the calming effect of the space seeping into my mind and muscles. Everything was going to be okay. I had plenty of time to prepare. I just needed to concentrate.

I assigned Cubby the task of interviewer. I didn't need her in here to hear her voice, but I'd have felt stupid being interviewed by the walls.

Why do you want to go to this college? she began, her schoolmarm tone perfect for the role.

"I don't," I said, then laughed. "No, wait. I don't think that's a good answer. Ask me again."

Why do you want to go to this college?

Even in here, without the pressure, my mind was blank. I couldn't say, *Because I need to live in New York so I can shack up with my boyfriend.* Not to mention that I'd read on the website that first-year students were supposed to live on campus. (There had to be a way around that, right?) Such a basic question and I couldn't even think of an answer, couldn't remember why Columbia had been one of my top choices this past summer. My eye twitched. Okay, I'd come back to that one.

I moved on to the next question.

What do you think you can bring to this college?

"Uh, I guess I bring a concern and caring for the . . . the health of the community. I'll talk about starting peer counseling here." I didn't think I had to mention that I was on hiatus from the program.

What is your biggest weakness?

"Hmm . . . I'm supposed to say something that's really a strength."

You don't know?

I pulled my turtleneck up over my chin. "My biggest weakness?" I had plenty of weaknesses, but none of them seemed like the type I could spin into strengths.

This one isn't a strength.

What did that mean? What was I trying to say? "If you're trying to make me less nervous for my interview, it's not working."

I pushed Cubby aside. This wasn't the time to be worrying about all of the things that were wrong with me. Maybe trying to anticipate questions was stupid. Not to mention, my body was beginning to crave a nap, the way it often did after lunch. Resting was probably a better plan than making myself more nervous about the interview. I slid down and curled up with my head on a pillow, and let my mind go blank, a slight ache pulsing at my temples. The minutes ticked by. My limbs felt heavier and heavier. At 1:45 I made a motion to stand up, but I couldn't bring myself to do it. It was like a multiple snooze-button morning. I kept trying to get up, but my mind kept dragging me down.

"I don't want to go," I said. And I knew what I meant. There were many ways it was true. I didn't want to go to the interview. I didn't want to go to Columbia. I didn't want to go anywhere.

No one is making you, Cubby said.

"But I have to." I pushed into my palms, hoping I'd be able to raise myself up, hoping I wouldn't be able to.

You don't have to. You can stay right here.

David found me in the backyard where I was finally planting the bulbs I'd bought at Home Depot.

"Leena." He crossed the yard with quick, long strides. "What's going on? Why didn't you answer my calls?"

"Sorry. I've been out here for a while." My cheeks, cold from the damp fall air, heated up.

"Didn't you have your interview at two?"

"Mm-hm." I turned my attention back to the hole I'd been digging for the next bulb. An angular stone blocked my trowel from going deeper. I reached down and worked it out of the hard earth.

"So . . ." he said. "How'd it go?"

"Okay."

276

"Just okay? C'mon, you've got to give me more than that."

David leaned his knees against my back. His hands raked through my hair, tingled my scalp. The affection intensified the guilt in my stomach.

"Good. It was good." I nestled a lumpy tulip bulb in the hole. "Harder than I thought, maybe." I couldn't possibly tell him the truth: that I'd been twenty minutes late. And that my interview clothes had been rumpled and wrinkled from my time in the closet. A raw breeze slid across my scarfless neck. I shivered.

"Hard? What kind of hard?" David said.

Why couldn't he leave it alone? I filled the hole with soil and smacked it down with the back of the trowel, then brushed my hands together. I stood up and turned to face him.

"Look," I said, "you're not going through all this college stuff, so maybe you don't get that it's really not a fun topic." My voice had an edge to it.

His lips parted for a moment. "I'm just asking because I'm psyched for next year. That's all. Did it . . . did it not go well?"

"I'm going inside. It's cold." I walked around the side of the house. David's steps crinkled dry leaves behind me.

"Leena," he said. "Wait . . ."

My throat tightened. David had no way of knowing it was myself I was angry at. He followed me inside, down the hall.

Hot water from the bathroom faucet cut through the blackish soil on my hands and swirled it down the drain. Warmth flooded up from my hands and through my body as if the boiling liquid was running directly through my veins.

"I'm sorry," David said from outside the bathroom door. "I just—"

"I can't hear you," I called over the whoosh of water. "I'll be out in a minute."

I turned off the tap and dried my pink hands on a towel. Afternoon sun filtered through the bathroom's small stained-glass window, a window not so different in style from the one drawn on my skin, the one that continued to fade, as if my body was trying to forget the memory of my old room. The late sun cast a red-and-blue glow on the wall above the tub. The chalky white paint absorbed the color like a bloodstain.

I *did* want to live with David next year, didn't I? Why had I jeopardized that by screwing up my interview? Twenty minutes late is unheard of. Unthinkable. A big, red X on my application folder.

What had Cubby told me when I'd been in the closet after my interview? *You'll end up where you're supposed to be.* A good philosophy to live by.

I found David waiting for me on my bed.

"Did you get parietals?" I asked.

"I checked before. She's not home."

"David." I stood next to him instead of sitting down.

"You know we can't risk getting busted."

"When has she ever, *ever* come back here?" he said. "Not once." He reclined on an elbow and patted the bed with his other hand. Reluctantly, I shrugged off my jacket and sat next to him. He reached his hand under the back of my sweater. The cold touch sent tentacles creeping up my spine. I lay down so he'd have to move it. But he took my shift as an invitation to lean over me, to remove my glasses, to place hands alongside my shoulders and start kissing.

I want this. I want this. I had to repeat this over and over in my head whenever we fooled around in Frost House. For some reason, at David's dorm, I was completely relaxed. I loved every moment of touching him, and being touched. And loved that we were having fun without going further than I wanted, which, for now, meant we hadn't had sex. But here, in my own room, my skin never felt quite right with someone else's hands on them. My heart would pound, but not in a good way. My mind wandered . . . began to picture things like Celeste's cockroaches lying right where we were. And, I hated to think it, because it made me feel like Celeste, but I had a bit of a sensation that someone was watching us. Probably because I knew she could be right outside the door at any time.

I rolled out from under David and reached for my glasses. "I'm sorry," I said. "I'm just too paranoid. It's not worth getting kicked out."

He sat up, his face flushed, readjusted his pants. "So you

want me to leave?"

"I don't *want* you to." I leaned over and nuzzled his cheek, rubbed my nose in the warm crook of his neck. Did I want him to leave? He smelled so good. And when he left, it would just be me. "I don't know," I said. "I'm just freaked about the probation thing."

"That's all it is?" he said.

"Yeah."

I gave him what I meant to be a quick kiss but it turned into a long, hard one. For a moment, my body hummed and squirmed and wanted to be against his. This time, he pulled away.

"If I'm leaving, it has to be now." His lips glistened, deep pinkish red.

I considered changing my mind. It had felt so good, for a moment there. But then, behind him, I caught a glimpse of something. The closet door was open just enough so you could see my mattress. Usually I was so careful. I couldn't believe I'd left it open like that.

"Yeah," I said. "You'd better go."

THE FOLLOWING FRIDAY was the start of Barcroft-Edgerton weekend, our weekend of sports events with our rival school. Old bedsheets, spray painted with war cries and crudely drawn pictures, hung between windows on the big, brick dorms along the center quad. *What Do We Eat? RED MEAT!!!! Red = DEAD. Go BIG BLUE!!*

At the beginning of the semester I'd imagined Frost House working together on a banner. Ha. I readjusted the strap of my book bag and kicked at a lacrosse ball hiding under a cover of sunset-colored leaves. I leaned over to pick up a quarter, and when I stood back up, the quad spun before me. I closed my eyes to regain balance.

When I opened my eyes, the world stood still again. In

the days since my Columbia interview, I'd been taking a regular dose of pills to counteract my constant "What now?" anxiety. Dizziness was a possible side effect, but I'd never had it happen before.

"Leena?" A girl's voice came from behind me. I turned and saw red hair sprouting from under a navy Barcroft baseball cap. Nicole Kellogg. She stood with a short, curvy girl—another freshman.

"Nicole, hi," I said. We hadn't said more than a word in passing to each other since the counseling session. I'd considered talking to her about it, but eventually—when it was obvious she wasn't leaving school—I didn't care enough to bother.

"Hi," she said. "This is my friend, Sera."

Sera and I exchanged heys.

"I was wondering if you have hours anytime soon?" Nicole asked. "You know, office hours."

"I'm actually not counseling for the rest of the semester," I said.

"Oh my God." Nicole brought a hand to her lips. "It's not because of me, is it? That whole thing was totally blown out of proportion by my hysterical parents. I felt so bad you got in trouble."

"Her parents are total whack jobs," Sera added.

"No." I shook my head. "I was busted for illegal off-campus. Stupid. Anyway, Dean Shepherd thought I should take a break from the leadership position, blah, blah, blah."

"Oh. Good," Nicole said. "I mean, not good, but—"

"I know what you mean," I said, giving her a smile.

"Well," she said, "would you maybe have a few minutes to talk to me sometime anyway?"

"There are other counselors, Nicole." I was sure Dean Shepherd wouldn't want me to have anything to do with Nicole Kellogg.

"But I know you. And it's actually not about my own problem." She fiddled with a button on her peacoat. "It's, like, I just need advice about how much to butt into someone else's life."

"Oh." I checked the time on my phone. Could the dean get mad (madder than she already was) if I talked to Nicole as a friend? I was almost too tired—too drained—to care. "Well, I have about an hour. I'm walking to town, and if you want to walk with me . . ." I glanced at Sera. "Unless you want to meet alone, Nicole. I have time after the assembly this afternoon."

"That's okay," Nicole said. "Sera knows about it, too."

The three of us shuffled through blankets of dried leaves. Winter would be here soon, and then spring, and then . . . God. Which other New York schools should I apply to? I needed to do some serious research. David kept asking about it.

"So, it's like this," Nicole said. "I'm in that freshman PE class, you know? Where they try to drown you?"

"Sure," I said. "We hated it. Abby told them submersion

in water was against her religion."

"Abby?" Nicole said.

I waved my hand. "No one. Sorry. Go on."

"Well, when I was using the locker room a couple of days ago," she continued, "I saw this girl in the showers, and she didn't look too good."

"You think she might have an eating disorder?" I said.

"No. It's not that." We reached a crosswalk. Nicole readjusted her baseball hat, fussed with her hair. When the sign changed to WALK she spoke. "I don't know. Maybe I shouldn't be gossiping about this."

"Nicole," Sera said, stretching out the last syllable. "It's not gossiping."

Nicole drew in a breath. "Okay," she said. "Well, this girl had, like, bruises all over her body. I don't know. Like someone's hurting her."

"Maybe she's on the girls' rugby team?" I said. "Have you ever watched one of their matches? They're totally brutal."

"I really doubt it," Nicole said. "Her leg's been in a cast all semester."

Nicole never mentioned Celeste's name. I don't know whether she even realized I knew Celeste. But once it was clear that's who she meant, I told her not to worry. That I'd figure out what was going on. I also told her not to spread this to anyone else. I was upset that she'd already told Sera, and who knew how many other people.

I continued on to town alone, my book bag not the only weight on my shoulders. Since Celeste and I rarely saw each other now, I had been trying to think about her as little as possible. Especially since when I did see her, she looked harried and tired. I'd heard her call out in the night, too, through her door. So I knew she was still having nightmares.

One thing Nicole said that struck me was the fact that Celeste had been showering at the gym. She wasn't playing a sport, of course. So why would she be at the gym? Was she hoping to keep me from seeing the bruises? I tried to remember the last time I'd had to wait for her to get out of the bathroom so I could use it, the last time I'd seen her coming out in a towel. But I couldn't. Whenever I was in my room I had my door closed, and if I heard her in the hall, I usually made a point of waiting to go out.

Sure enough, when I got back to the dorm and checked, I saw she'd taken away her wire basket of shampoo and soap. Her toothbrush still rested in the holder. That was the only sign of her in the bathroom. For some reason she was using the shower at the gym. And for some reason, she was covered in bruises.

Of course, they could be from Whip, like she'd said before. But I had my doubts. This had gotten to the point where I'd have to tell someone else—David or the dean. First, though, I wanted to know what I was dealing with.

* * *

I knocked on her door. "Celeste? Are you in there?"

I tried the knob. It wiggled only the slightest bit. Locked. I'm not Nancy Drew at heart and didn't entertain thoughts of lock picking or anything like that. I decided to just wait until Celeste was back and go in while she was there. It's not as if I knew what I'd be looking for, anyway. Just, something . . .

I'd given up and had moved on to writing a paper about the unreliable narrator in Nabokov's *Pale Fire* when it occurred to me how stupid I was being. I had the key from before she'd changed our living arrangement. Duh.

Celeste's windowless room was nighttime dark. I ran my hand over the rough plaster wall until I felt the switch. I held my breath and flipped it.

I don't know what I expected. Nothing as obvious as whips and chains, of course. Something more subtle—a clue . . . One wall was covered with sketches and notes. Her hat collection sat piled in a corner. Shoe boxes sat in stacks, labeled on the side with notes like *Bugs—done; Bugs—to do; Nests.* All perfectly normal—for Celeste, at least.

Under her desk, there were six large, white candles, with deep enough depressions at the top that I could tell they'd been burned quite a bit. Candles were definitely not allowed in dorm rooms, so she was risking something by having them, which was odd. But nothing to do with bruises, clearly.

I turned off the light and closed and locked the door

behind me, simultaneously relieved and disappointed.

David was standing in the hallway.

"What were you doing in there?" he asked.

"Oh, hi!" I shoved the key in my pocket. "I was just look-ing for my Barcroft sweatshirt. I thought I might have left it in the closet when we switched rooms. I wanted to wear it to the assembly later."

"No luck?" His words, and his eyes, were steel hard. Because I'd been in there without Celeste?

"Nope," I said, ignoring his strange reaction. "What's up? Should I get parietals?"

"That's okay." He ran his fingers through his hair. "Is there something you want to tell me, Leena?"

So it wasn't me being in her room that had made him mad. A pressure started in my chest. "What do you mean?"

"Don't pretend you don't know what I'm talking about. You're just making it worse."

Celeste's bruises? Was that what he meant? "David," I said, "I really don't know what you mean. Honestly."

"I *know*, Leena," he said. "I know you were an hour late for your Columbia interview. An *hour* late."

"No, I wasn't," I said, stiffening. "Who told you that?"

"Doesn't matter. Is it true?"

"No!"

David raised his eyebrows.

"Twenty minutes," I said. "I was twenty minutes late."

"Still. You're never late. Why would you be twenty

minutes late for something so important?"

"It was an accident. Why are you so mad? Please, don't be." I reached out and touched his arm, but he brushed my hand off.

"Why am I mad? Leena, if you cared about being in New York with me, you wouldn't have screwed up the interview. And you lied to me about it, too."

"I didn't screw it up," I said. "The interview itself was fine. Look, don't you want to go in the bedroom to talk?" Honestly, I didn't know how the interview had gone. Once I arrived I was in such a state—blurry from sleeping, panicked at being late, nervous about being unprepared—that I barely heard myself answering the woman's questions. It was probably a moot point, anyway. Columbia had been a long shot. And I had blown it.

"Not particularly." He leaned against the wall and rested one foot on top of the other, his arms tightly crossed. I was in sock feet, and he seemed to loom over me in a way he didn't usually. "That's a whole other thing, the bedroom," he said. "You're different in there. Here. In the dorm. You're always so preoccupied and nervous. The other day you couldn't get me out of here fast enough. When's that going to change, Leena? Maybe you just don't want to be with me, is that it?"

I grasped his arm, but he shook me off again. Roughly. My elbow jolted back into the edge of the door. Pain fired through my nerves. "Of course I want to be with you," I said, trying to ignore the sharp pulsings. "Maybe I've been weird,

288

but don't you know what a hard semester this has been for me? With Viv and Abby and Dean Shephard all disowning me? Thank God I have you! But maybe that's why I've been acting weird, if I have been." My heart pounded. I couldn't lose David, too.

But you will, Cubby said. The words, her voice, came to me out of nowhere.

"What about when we fool around?" David said. Had he heard Cubby? Had I said that out loud? "We're talking about moving in together. I can't imagine you've been like this with other guys."

"No," I said. Why had I imagined Cubby's voice? "No, I haven't."

"Doesn't that tell you something? That this has all been a big waste of time?"

"No, that's not it. I promise. I haven't been like this with other guys because I haven't been with any other guys."

David shook his head as if he was clearing water from his ears. "What do you mean? I thought you dated a couple other people?"

"Yeah, but we . . . I . . . I only got together with them a few times," I said. "They wouldn't . . . they wouldn't really count in the scheme of things. They weren't relationships."

David hesitated. "Well, that explains a lot."

"What? Why I'm so incompetent?" I said.

"No, no. Come here." He held his arms open. I hesitated a moment, then let him wrap them around me. "It helps me understand why it makes you nervous. I thought it was me."

"David." I tipped back my head to look up at him. "I'm scared to death to leave school at the end of the year. And the only thing that makes it seem bearable is that I'll be with you."

"Really? Because it seemed so strange about the interview . . ."

"I know. I don't know what that was about, honestly. It was weird and not like me, and I didn't even want you to find out. I think maybe I was so nervous about it that I freaked."

I remembered my feelings before the interview. Looking back, they seemed as foreign as if they belonged to a stranger. All I wanted was to live there with David. It was the only way I could imagine feeling safe when leaving Barcroft. No matter what Cubby said.

We stood there, his arms around me.

"Columbia was my first choice," I said. "But it was a huge long shot to begin with. There are other schools in New York. NYU, The New School . . . or if I want to do architecture, somewhere like Pratt or Parsons. I've been looking into them. It'll all work out. I'll end up where I'm meant to be."

"Just as long as it's in New York, I don't care about anything else," David said, pulling back a bit. "Hey, now that I know you don't want to get rid of me, I need to ask you something. Sunday the seventeenth is my mom's fiftieth birthday. She's having a big party at the house—kind of like a family reunion. Would you come with me and Celeste?"

Celeste. Bruises. The sincerity in David's eyes. Why did there always have to be *something* about Celeste hanging over me?

I tried to smile. "I'd love to."

STUDENTS ENTERING THE CHAPEL later that afternoon filled the cavernous space with shouts and laughter, waved at each other, and rushed to get seats near friends. More than one person had blue face-paint on; Barcroft apparel was ubiquitous. Stupidly, I'd worn a red sweater. After my talk with David, the last thing on my mind was Barcroft-Edgerton weekend. Now I looked like a Red Sox fan in a room full of Yankees.

Instead of letting my eyes stray in the direction of the left-side balcony, where I used to sit with Viv and Abby, I watched the hundreds of bodies milling around the oak pews on the main level. Too short, too pale, too heavy—no one matched my David blueprint. He'd had an appointment with his advisor right before this. Maybe she'd kept him late.

I randomly followed a group down the center aisle, now searching the pews for anyone to sit with. I was about to give up and sit alone when I saw a familiar green beret.

"Hey," I said. "Are you saving that seat?"

Celeste followed my eyes to the spot next to her. "Nope."

I stepped over her crutches and sat on the hard, wooden bench. Almost none of Celeste's skin was showing. She had on a velvet blazer, a high-necked, Victorian-style blouse, and men's khakis, slit up the leg to accommodate her cast—an interesting change from her usual style.

Someone tapped me on the shoulder.

I craned my head around and saw peer-counselor Toby's dark hair and silver glasses. "Hey, Toby."

"We miss you," he said.

"Of course you do." I smiled. "Can't say it's mutual. I'd forgotten how nice it is to have free time."

He laughed thinly. We both knew I was lying.

I turned back around, bumping my elbow lightly against the pew, reigniting the pain. I rubbed it as I studied the assembly program and tried to decide what to say to Celeste. My eyes caught on a familiar name.

I nudged Celeste and held the program out in front of her. "Did you know Whip's father and grandfather are speaking? Telling stories about fifty years of blue-red rivalry?"

"Of course," she said. "I'm having dinner with them."

She was? "So you're still hanging out with Whip? I haven't seen him around the dorm."

"I wouldn't bring him there," she said. She tipped her face toward the chapel's soaring windows. The light brought out the thin lines on her chapped lips.

"Is everything okay, Celeste?" I asked in a lower voice.

"Yeah, fine."

"Well, is there some reason you haven't been using our bathroom?" I felt like I was walking on hummingbird eggshells. "If something's wrong with the water pressure, or whatever, I can figure it out. I'm good with that stuff."

A low, rhythmic thumping crept into my ears from behind us.

"No. No reason."

"I know you're not using it," I said. "There must be something wrong. You didn't burn yourself again, did you?"

She gave an exaggerated sigh. "I'm showering at the gym after physical-therapy sessions. The tub is too slippery with my cast."

"Really? That's it?" I said. The thumping had gotten louder. Now I could feel it under my feet.

Celeste turned to face me and smiled. "Somehow you know that little redhead saw me in the locker room, and now you're trying to find out why I'm all beat-up looking. Right?"

"Well?"

She began to make quick, precise folds in her program, like origami. "I'm fine," she finally said. "I'm handling it."

"There's no reason you should have to handle it on your own," I said.

"If I needed to talk about something, I would. Okay?" Her program had turned into an origami crane. She balanced it on the back of the pew in front of us. It trembled from the vibrations coming up from the floor.

"It's weird, Celeste. Being covered in bruises. I don't want to lie to David if he asks how you're doing."

"Don't tell him anything," she said. "I mean it." Her sharp jaw clamped together and appeared even more angular than usual.

The thumping was now thunderous, hundreds of students slamming their feet down in unison. The energy made my face hot. I had to raise my voice.

"I only would because we worry about you. If you're being hurt in some way . . ."

"Shh! I'm not." Her eyes bored into mine. "If I tell you, will you shut up about it already? You're as bad as my smothering brother."

"Okay," I said.

Thump, thump, thump, thump.

Celeste stared up at the organ pipes behind the dais. "I'm getting my blood tested to make sure there's nothing wrong, like some sort of condition that's making me bruise easily."

"What do we eat? What do we eat?" The cry came from a group of senior football players at the back of the chapel.

"Condition? Like what?" I said.

"Red meat! Red meat!" the rest of the student body answered, shouting.

She shrugged.

Bruises. Blood test. "Like . . . like leukemia?" I said. My stomach rolled.

"What do we eat? What do we eat?" Louder this time.

"That's just the worst possibility," Celeste said. "It's probably not that."

"Red meat!! Red meat!!"

Probably? "Celeste, aren't you worried? Don't you want to tell David? I'm sure he'd go with you to the doctor."

"No!" she snapped. "Don't tell David anything."

"What do we eat? What do we eat?" Full-throated hollers now.

"But—"

"Don't tell David anything," Celeste said, "and I won't have to tell him about your little pill problem."

The rows of heads filling the pews swam in and out of focus. A wave of nausea passed through me.

"Red meat!!! Red meat!!!" everyone screamed.

"My pill problem?" Toby's laughter behind me reminded me he was there. Could he have heard any of this over the commotion in the chapel? I lowered my voice again. "You must be kidding. I don't have a problem."

"How do we like it?" the seniors bellowed.

"I could convince David you do," Celeste said. "You know he'd believe me. I've *seen* what's in your owl, Leena."

"RAW!!!!!!"

33

DESPITE THE COLD PANIC in my chest and the flashes of heat on my skin, somehow I made it through the assembly. The walk home blurred by as I stared at my feet and told myself that everything was under control, that Celeste wouldn't tell David. I wasn't doing anything wrong by having medications, of course, but I didn't trust that he'd understand my explanation—especially not if he asked where I got them all from.

Back at the dorm, I snagged Cubby off the window-sill and a plastic bag out of the trash can—appropriately one from Barcroft Drugs. I opened Cubby and let the small baggies of pills tumble into the bigger bag, tied the handles in a knot with shaking hands, then stashed it in the closet, snug between the foam mattress and the wall. If Celeste did tell, I could at least make sure she didn't have any evidence. Sweat trickled down my spine; chills ran through me. A sharp pain stabbed at my temples and sent my brain spinning.

I shut the closet door and locked it from the inside, curled up in the corner, and wrapped my arms around myself, not sure if I was trembling from nerves or from cold. *Should I take a pill?* I wondered. No. This wasn't that big a deal. Everything was fine. Being inside here, quiet and safe, was enough. My headache and chills didn't lessen, but, slowly, I did feel calmer. As if warm milk had been infused into my veins.

If I could stay in here all the time, I wouldn't need any pills.

Being out of panic mode, though, didn't mean my worry was erased. Certainly not about Celeste's bruises. I found it hard to believe that she wouldn't tell David if she thought she had a blood disorder. As much as she fought against it, I still knew she loved to have as much of his attention as possible. Why wouldn't she want him to know she might be sick?

And even if she did have some condition that made her bruise easily, would the bruises be so prominent that they freaked out Nicole? Was any of this related to Celeste's broken leg? Or her burn? Maybe she was hurting herself on purpose, like she used to cut, and that's why she didn't want David to know. I felt around the mattress until I found Cubby, then held her in both hands and wished for her wisdom. If Celeste was hurting herself, I'd have to do something.

Or is someone else doing it to her?

A possibility, of course. One almost more disturbing than the alternatives. But Whip wasn't there when she broke her leg, and who else—

Don't you know?

An idea was scrabbling to get in my brain. I didn't want it.

Someone who needs her to feel vulnerable. So he can take care of her.

Nausea gripped my body. I threw Cubby away from me and pressed into the corner, away from my thoughts and her voice. How could I have even let myself think that? Where had that come from? Still, as I pressed back and tried to shut out more words, they came again.

You won't let yourself think it; it feels too true.

My gut surged upward. I was actually going to be sick. One hand covered my mouth, the other fumbled for the slide lock.

I made it to the toilet just in time. The tile floor pressed rocklike and cold under my knees. A convulsive wave ripped through me. I grasped at the edges of the seat and heaved. Acid burned a path through my throat. This happened over and over, until the chilly floor held my empty, outer shell as I shook and cried.

34

I ALTERNATED BETWEEN HUNCHING over the toilet, sleeping on the inhospitable but convenient tiles, and curling up in the closet, shivering, sweating, drifting off into half sleeps, feeling so weak I couldn't even reach up to lock the door. My limbs were glued to the ground until a subtle movement in my gut gave me the adrenaline to somehow make it to the bathroom for the next round. My head pounded and I imagined a construction worker slamming his hammer into it, over and over.

I think David called. I think I told him not to come by. Celeste offered to help when she heard me puking, but I told her to leave me alone. What could they have done, anyway?

After a spell in the bathroom sometime on Saturday, I

dragged myself on hands and sore knees into the hall and back into my room. I couldn't even walk.

"Leen? Are you okay?"

My neck ached as I moved my heavy head to look at the shadowy figure sitting on my bed. Viv.

"Mm." A bleat was all I could manage. My throat screamed. My mouth was dry as salt. Even my lips hurt.

She materialized next to me, kneeling, touching my hair. "I heard you when I was coming in. How long have you been sick?"

"Mm."

The cool, soft skin of the back of her hand rested on my forehead.

"You're burning. We've got to go to the infirmary. Can you make it?"

"Mm."

"Can you stand up?"

An arm wrapped around me. I pressed into the floor.

Light slipped away.

In the dark, my mother came. Ice slid down my neck. I shivered. "Here," my mother said. The blanket was too heavy, too hot. Where was Cubby? A rumble beneath me jostled my bones. Like driving on a cobblestone street. White light split open my head. My mother stood in the beam, holding Cubby.

"Don't take her," I said.

"I'm here," my mother said. "You don't need it." She

301

moved Cubby behind her back.

"You're always taking things from me."

She brought her hands in front again. Cubby was gone. Disappeared. "Don't you see?" she said.

I tried to reach. To find, to touch her. The light flickered off.

I spent days in the infirmary, recovering from the virus and severe dehydration. It took a while before I was able to eat even a cracker without bringing it back up. My head ached all the time. I'd imagined my mother's presence, of course. But even though the dream hadn't been a good one, I wanted her so badly that I called her several times. I couldn't ever talk long, and later I couldn't even remember the conversations, but in my weakened state even hearing her say my name helped. I knew I was acting like a baby. That's what I felt like.

Complicated, confusing thoughts unraveled as I grew stronger, became more coherent. It comforted me to know that I had been sick physically, when I'd come up with the suspicion that David was hurting Celeste. When my mind felt clearer—*cleaner*—I knew that wasn't true. *Couldn't* be true. Usually, the thoughts I had in Frost House, in the closet, felt like moments of insight. But this time . . . it must have been my sickness talking.

As for Celeste's bruises, though, I didn't feel any clearer about whether or not to believe it was a medical condition.

And I worried all the time that she had decided to make good on her threat to tell David about me. But whenever David visited or wrote or called, everything seemed fine. In fact, he made a point of visiting twice a day, and bringing me little things he thought would cheer me up—the apartments-for-rent section of the *New York Times*, Life Savers, the miniature metal wrench from an abandoned Clue game. 'It made me think of you," he said. "Miss Fix-it."

And, best of all, one of his spoons. He said it was a special, chicken-soup spoon. I slept with it under my pillow.

The day they finally deemed me strong enough to go home, I walked back to Frost House slowly and carefully, still getting my sea legs. It was the middle of a class period; campus was eerily still. And even though I'd only been in the infirmary for a few days, the season seemed to have jumped forward. So many more trees were bare than I remembered. Silver trunks stretched up to skinny, naked branches.

Then I saw Frost House. Waiting for me. The evergreen bushes surrounding her made sure she wasn't too exposed. She looked just as cozy as she had the day I'd moved in. Just as welcoming as the first day I'd seen her, when I knew I had to live there. And, like that day, I could almost hear her calling out to me.

The door to my room was unlocked, not surprisingly. I'd hardly been in a state to lock it when I left. I opened it and for a moment felt as if I was coming upon the room as a stranger. Look at how beautiful it was! Full of light and color and warmth. Not very neat, but still . . . God, I'd missed it.

My plants didn't seem to be thirsty. Pressing a finger into the soil confirmed they'd been watered recently. And—wait. They'd gotten sun, too. The window shades were all rolled up. My pulse quickened. I'd kept the shades down when I was sick, to block the painful light. Someone had been in here. Someone had been in my room.

What else? What else had been touched?

Cubby. She wasn't on the windowsill. Where was she? I went into the closet. Shelf—no. Floor—no. Wait. Yes. In the corner. I grabbed her and brought her to me, noticing her lightness, and how nothing inside her shifted with the movement.

Then I remembered.

My hand searched in the crack between mattress and wall. Only when I felt the plastic bag did I release my breath. I brought the pills out into the light of the bedroom to make sure they were all there. As far as I could tell they were. But the paper . . . my sheet of paper was gone.

I knelt down again, feeling all the way around the mattress. Nothing.

I'd look insane if anyone saw that page of notes. Celeste knew about it—she'd seen it that time she'd discovered I kept my meds there. Maybe she took it to show David? He'd seemed fine when he visited. Maybe she was holding on to it. For now. Biding her time.

I sat on the bed and tried to remember the afternoon when I'd gotten sick, but it was all scrambled. My mind had been so messed up. I glanced around the room for clues. A pile of clothes sat on my dresser. Red sweater. Right—the clothes I'd thrown up on that first day. But they were all folded and clean, now.

I was still staring at them when my phone rang. David, wanting to know if I was up to dinner in Commons. His voice sounded normal, happy I was home.

"Not really," I said. "Could you bring something by when you're done?"

"I wish I could," he said. "But I have to rush to a movie screening for English. Do you want me to come visit later? Like nine or so?"

"Thanks," I said. "I think I'll be too tired, though."

"Do you think you'll be well enough to come on Sunday?"

"Sunday?"

"My mom's party. Did you forget?"

"Oh, right," I said, and then after a pause, "Will Celeste be there?"

"Of course. She and I are going home on Saturday. My mom really wants to meet you."

"I want to meet her, too," I said. "I'm sure I'll be able to go."

A knock on the door startled me awake. How long had I been asleep? I put on my glasses and saw it was a couple of hours later. My stomach grumbled. The knock came again.

"Come in."

The open door revealed Viv, standing with a red-and-white-checked cardboard take-out box from Commons in her hands.

"I ran into David at dinner," she said. "He thought you might appreciate this." She extended her arms.

"Oh, thanks, Viv." I sat up straighter in bed.

She crossed the room and handed it to me, along with a fork and napkins. "I wasn't sure what would agree with your stomach."

I rested the heavy box on my lap; warmth spread through my thighs. Inside was probably everything Commons had offered tonight: spaghetti, chicken, potatoes, sautéed veggies, bread, cake.

"This is great," I said. "I'm starving. I just wasn't up to trekking over there."

Viv sat down next to me. "I don't blame you. I can't believe how sick you were. I was really scared when I found you."

"Thanks again for helping me." I tasted a bite of buttery mashed potatoes. So much better than the infirmary food. Actual flavor.

"Viv?" I said. "Not to sound all second grade, or anything, but does this mean we're okay? Because you know, I'm really, really sorry about Cameron. About the whole thing. More sorry than I could ever say. I feel as awful about it as I have about anything, ever."

Viv stared at her lap. "I love you, Leen," she finally said. "And it's so not Buddhist of me to stay angry. But . . . the thing is, I can't help getting mad, still, whenever I miss Cam. Not to mention getting mad about what this has done to him. But at the same time, I also miss *you*."

"I miss you, too," I said. "So much. And Abby."

"Abby's a different story," she said. "That's another reason it'll be hard for us to really be friends, like before. At least for now."

"Oh." I took another bite; the chicken tasted like dust.

"But we can try, a bit," she said. "You know, start slow?" I nodded.

"So . . ." Viv smoothed out the wrinkles on the quilt next to her. "I watered your plants. And opened the blinds, to give them sun. And washed the puke out of your clothes."

"It was you? Thanks, Viv. That was so sweet."

She kept her eyes on the bed, pressed her lips together, and smoothed the quilt over and over as if she'd developed OCD while I'd been gone. "I, uh, I saw something while I was in here," she said. "I . . . wanted to ask you about it."

Oh, God. "It's not as weird as it seems, Viv." How wasn't a piece of paper with info about ten or so psychotropic meds not as weird as it seems? Maybe I was studying for a test, in psych? About medications?

"Really?" she said. "What do you do in there?"

"In there?"

"The closet. I saw that whole mattress thing you have set up, the pillows. Do you, like, sleep in there or something?"

The closet. She knew about the closet. My chest tightened. But, then again, she didn't know about my conversations.

"No, I don't sleep in there." I drew crisscrosses in my potatoes and searched my brain for a plausible explanation.

"So, you . . . ?"

"I . . . I meditate."

Viv raised her eyebrows. "You? Meditate? How come I didn't know this?"

"Well, it's not like we've been close enough recently for you to notice." As I spoke, I realized that the dreamlike state I went into in the closet *was* kind of what I imagined meditation to be like. An alternate consciousness. "It's helped me be less stressed."

"You do this in a closet?"

"It blocks out the distractions, being in there."

"Gosh, Leen. I'd never have pictured you meditating. Did you, like, learn it somewhere? Or just figure it out on your own?" There wasn't an ounce of humor in Viv's eyes. Just genuine interest.

What would she say if I told her the truth? Viv, of all people, might understand, after all. She was open-minded about these things. She'd probably love the fact that I'd been coming to terms with suppressed feelings. Could I . . . ?

"Well, it's not really traditional. I have my own way."

"You should come to the meditation center with me

sometime," she said. "In the Berkshires."

"I'd love to," I said. "But, there's . . . there's something different about . . . about the way—"

One minute, I was speaking, then—my throat. Swollen shut. Hands on my neck—tightening. My hands? I loosened my grip. Still, something pressed my throat closed. No air. No breath. Viv leaned toward me. "Are you okay?" Blood rushed to my face. Eyes watered. No breath.

"Should I do the . . . that thing? Whatever it's called? Leena?"

Don't know. Oh my God. Jesus. Can't breathe. Something's pressing, pressing . . . I need air need air need—

Air.

A shift. A release. Yes, finally, a cough. Oh, Jesus. Tears swam in my eyes.

The cough hurt. Ripped my esophagus. My chest heaved, sucking in all the air, all the air from the room. Oh. Thank God.

"Leen, are you okay?"

I nodded, still trying to right my breathing. I coughed again. Tasted blood. I wiped the tears that had spilled onto my cheeks.

"What was that?" Viv said. "Did you choke on the food?"

Did I? The spaghetti-chicken-potatoes lay in the box on my lap.

"I guess so." My voice rasped.

"Are you sure you're okay?"

Was I? I could breathe. "Yeah. Sorry for scaring you. I'm fine."

The food swam into an unappealing swirl of colors and textures. I set the box aside. I was exhausted. "I think I might need to sleep a bit more."

Viv stood up. "Of course. Let me know if you need anything else. Okay?"

Left alone, I touched a hand to my neck. I lay down and tried to convince my lungs that there was enough air in the room. Something wasn't right, though. The episode had spurred my nervous system to go into high alert. My breaths were too fast. My lips quivered. My skin crawled.

I needed the closet.

As I shut the door behind me, I realized that as unpleasant as the choking fit had been, it was probably fortuitous—it had stopped me from telling Viv something she really didn't need to know.

35

SUNDAY MORNING THE TEMPERATURE had plunged to what felt like a midwinter low. Probably not the best day for someone recovering from an illness to be out, but I had no choice. As I sat in the car, my breath fogged up the side window, romanticizing the view of 67 Plainville Road. The house needed all the help it could get—Plainville was an apt name. A recent faux-Colonial. Pale gray aluminum siding. Four thin columns with no structural purpose. Spindly trees out front; the mark of a new development. It looked just like the house next door. Not at all what I expected for the family that produced David and Celeste Lazar.

I forced myself to take the key out of the ignition and unbuckle my seat belt. Consciously procrastinating, I searched the glove compartment until I found the butt of a pack of Life Savers and slipped one into my mouth. My throat had been raw ever since the choking episode. My neck had been sore, too, from where my fingers had tightened on it, I guess.

I wrapped a hand around the crinkly paper covering the bouquet of dahlias I'd spent so much time choosing and stepped into the bitter chill. For the hundredth time I tried to ignore the ridiculous thought that I might be meeting my future mother-in-law. Logically, I knew that was a totally far-fetched idea.

Within a second of my bell ring, a salt-and-pepper-haired woman wearing a gray velour track suit and sneakers answered the door. She was thin almost to the point of concavity. Sharp cheekbones, high-bridged nose. Gray like the house. Beautiful once. Now, a little drained.

"Leena!" she said in a tone that was on the brighter side of the color spectrum. "It's so wonderful to finally meet you. I'm Phillipa Lazar."

"Nice to meet you, Mrs. Lazar." I extended a hand but she ignored it, saying, "Call me Phippy, please," and gave me a bony hug. My hand holding the flowers flailed out to the side.

"Thanks for having me," I said into her shirt. "And happy birthday."

"It is a happy birthday," she said, releasing me from the embrace. "With the kids here, and George, and meeting you.

I'm glad you could come early, before the gang."

George? Frigid wind tickled my ears. "Could I come in?"

"Oh, of course." Mrs. Lazar laughed and backed into the house. Warmth and rich cooking smells spilled out. "Unusually chilly for this time of year."

I handed her the dahlias. When I bought them, I almost chose tulips, instead, before remembering the ones that had strangely died the day Celeste arrived at Frost House.

"How lovely!" Mrs. Lazar said, sniffing the magenta blooms. "As are you. I hear you've been under the weather. You don't look it at all."

"Thanks." I unwound my scarf. We stood in a spacious entryway, mostly blond wood. A decorative niche in the wall held a delicate sculpture made of birds' nests and wire— Celeste's, no doubt. "I'm still exhausted. Not contagious, though."

Quick thuds of sock feet on wood came from a nearby staircase.

"David says you're a strong one," Mrs. Lazar said. "Not easily—"

"Hey!" David jumped the last three steps and slid across the floor to where I was standing. "You made it! Take off your coat. Didn't you ask her to take it off, Mom?"

David's hand rumpling my hair and his "so happy to see you" smile made it clear Celeste hadn't said anything about me.

"Where's Celeste?" I asked, shedding my puffer.

"Resting," David said. "She's been kind of out of it. I hope it's not the start of what you had. If it hit you that bad, I can't imagine what it would do to Celeste."

Was this part of whatever was wrong with her? Maybe it really was a blood disease or other serious illness. I hated the responsibility of knowing something David didn't. Not that there was anything he could do. He wasn't a doctor, and Celeste already had an appointment with one. Or maybe she had already gone. I hadn't seen her to ask.

"I hope she's okay," I said.

"Where's Dad?" David asked his mother.

I felt my jaw open slightly.

"The living room," Mrs. Lazar said. "Best to introduce Leena now. He's feeling okay." She rested a hand on my arm. "This is a momentous occasion, you know."

"Oh, right," I stammered through my surprise. "Fifty is a big one."

"No, no," she said. "Fifty is just an excuse for a party. Momentous because this is the first time David has brought someone home to meet us. Celeste has been falling in love since kindergarten, but not this guy."

"Mom." David sounded like an annoyed little kid as he grasped my hand. "Come on, Leen."

My pleasure at being the first formal Lazar girlfriend was way overshadowed by the realization I'd be meeting his father. Why had I assumed that Mr. Lazar wouldn't be here? It was his wife's party, after all, and I would think he could come and go from the facility he was in; it's not like he was a prisoner. I just hadn't thought about it, among all of the other issues crowding my brain for attention. I hated to admit it, but I was scared.

In the living room—more like a library, there were so many books piled around—a man sat folded into a large armchair. His face held none of the sharpness of David's and Celeste's. Like in the family photo, it seemed almost blurry, even though he was sitting perfectly still. He was mostly bald on top, except for a thin but longish section that was awkwardly combed to one side. He stared out a window. Classical music—a piano concerto—played softly.

"Dad, this is my friend Leena," David said. "This is my father, George Lazar."

"Hi," I said. "It's so nice to meet you." I stood next to his chair, my hands dangling uselessly. I clasped them behind my back.

"Nice to meet you." His eyes strayed up to me, and then back to the window.

"You feeling okay, Dad?" David asked.

Pushing with one arm and then the other, Mr. Lazar shifted himself up to stand. Although his face wasn't too heavy, his body filled his sweatpants and sweatshirt and then some. He walked with stiff legs over to the window. Side effects of his medicine, probably—weight gain, movement difficulties. And I shouldn't take it personally that he wasn't interested in meeting me.

"Did the mail come yet?" he asked, then moved over to the next window. "I should probably wait outside. Until it comes."

"No mail today," David said. "It's Sunday."

I studied the books on the shelves, the wallpaper's light brown bamboo pattern. Flat affect—that's what it was called, the way his voice just slid out like a robot's, no expression.

"I should wait outside," he said. "Sometimes they bring something on Sunday. I ordered something for your mother."

"Stay inside, Dad." Celeste's voice came from the doorway leading into the hall. "It's cold out." She hunched over her crutches, wearing the very un-Celeste outfit of a denim skirt and an oversize Hooters T-shirt. Long sleeved, of course.

"Hi, Celeste," I said.

"How's it coming?" David asked. He turned to me. "She wasn't really resting upstairs. She's making this incredible thing for the party—one of those painted caricatures where you stick your face in and get your picture taken."

"Fine," she said. She looked like she *should* have been resting. The circles under her eyes were now dark like plums.

"Let's go upstairs, Dad," Celeste said. "We can decide what you want to wear for the party. Mom and I bought you some new shirts yesterday."

"I'm not going to the party," Mr. Lazar said. He leaned forward so that his face was practically touching the windowpane.

"That's okay," Celeste said. "We still need to get you cleaned up and dressed."

"Can't you do that in a bit?" David said. "Leena just met him."

"Don't you have to go finish cooking or something?" Celeste replied. "People will be here in a couple of hours."

I hooked a finger in one of David's belt loops. "I can see your father later. What can I do to help out?"

"Anything Leena can do?" David said. "To help with your project?"

"I don't give a fuck what Leena does," Celeste said.

"Jesus," David said. "What's your problem?"

I had to blink away the threat of shocked tears, even though I knew better.

"Nothing," she said. "Sorry. I have a terrible headache." She clamped the bridge of her nose between her thumb and index finger.

"Do you want something for it?" I asked.

"No."

"I know you don't like taking stuff. But it will—"

"*Nothing* will make it better."

After Celeste's outburst and meeting Mr. Lazar, I slipped away to a downstairs half bath and used one of the pills I'd brought with me to take the edge off. I hadn't wanted to medicate today, mostly because of Celeste's theory that I had a problem with it. But my first day at the Lazars' house didn't seem to be a good time to prove I was fine without them. Not to mention, who cared if I wasn't fine without them? They weren't harmful, like alcohol or whatever. They were a valid way of dealing with a stressful situation. If David didn't have such a harsh view of meds, I wouldn't have cared at all if Celeste told him.

Ironically, though, after the initial bumps, the day became surprisingly enjoyable. Mrs. Lazar—*Phippy*—had plenty of things for me to do around the house while we were waiting for people to come, and David needed help in the kitchen. Once everyone arrived, you'd have thought I'd been coming to Lazar functions since birth. Everyone was nice and funny and easy to talk to. And not one person asked me where I was applying to college. That had to be some sort of record for a high school senior at a social event with adults. Most of the time was spent talking about food.

"This pea-pod thing is amazing! Did you try one, Leena, hon?" David's aunt Jill said. "Davey's incredible, isn't he? And do you know he's like a genius? He was doing multiplication at two or something. Ask Phippy about it."

I'd definitely learned that the female members of the family thought I'd snagged quite a catch.

"What about the bruschetta?" her daughter, Meg, said. "God. And where did you get that dress, Leena? It's really cute."

"Thanks. Anthropologie." A sticky warmth embraced my hand. One or another small cousin had grabbed it.

318

Which one was the towhead?

"I show you somefing," he said. Gabe. That was his name.

"Leena's having some food now, hon," Jill said. "Later you can show her."

"Actually, I show now." He tugged.

Tiny Gabe had an easier time than I did worming through the clumps of people, most of whom were holding plates and glasses. I tried to keep up, so that he wouldn't rip my arm out of its socket. "Sorry!" I kept saying as I bumped into most of them. Where was David? I had barely seen him.

"Joan Fontaine," a white-haired man I'd met earlier said as I pushed by. He tapped my shoulder repeatedly. "That's it. You look like a young Joan Fontaine. I'm sure someone's told you that."

"Nope," I said. I wasn't quite sure who Joan Fontaine was. An old actress, I thought. My arm was still moving so I couldn't even stop to find out.

Gabe pulled me to the bottom of the staircase then let go of my hand and scrambled up the stairs like a spider.

"Gabe," I said, "let's stay downstairs." But by the time I said it he was around the landing and up the next flight. I followed.

At the top of the stairs he pushed open a door into a dim room—curtains drawn, a big bed over to one side covered with a mess of burgundy paisley sheets and comforter. Clothes strewn around. The master bedroom. I'd been shown David's and Celeste's rooms, but not this one.

Gabe pushed open another door, put a hand to his mouth, and gave a guilty little smile. A big bathroom stood in front of us. He giggled.

"What did you want to show me?" I said. "We shouldn't really be in here." As if he cared.

He pointed. "Dey've got a potty."

"Yes," I said. "They do have a potty."

"I wear big-boy underpants."

"Gabe?" The woman's voice came from out in the hallway. She stuck her face in. "I thought I saw you racing up here."

Gabe ran over to her.

"He was just showing me the potty," I said.

"He's big on potties," she said. "Do you have to go, Gabey?"

"No!" Gabe shouted, and ran off down the hall. His mother gave me a quick, tired smile and followed him.

I was reaching to pull the bathroom door closed the way we found it, when it occurred to me that as long as I was here, I might as well pee.

The toilet seat had a disconcerting, squishy plastic cover on it. Instead of making me feel comfortable, it made me think of the other thighs, the other skin, that had pressed on it over the years. The thought made me shiver.

I washed my hands quickly and was about to slip out when I noticed a piece of sundried tomato snagged between my front teeth. Crap. How long had it been there? I leaned forward and picked at it with my pinky nail. Did I have crumbs in my hair, too? As I checked, out of the corner of my eye I glimpsed a largish metal bracket on one side of the medicine cabinet. Huh. A lock? I pulled at the mirrored door. Yup. It made sense, if this was Mr. Lazar's room. My hand automatically reached up and swept across the cabinet's top. Sure enough, a blip in the surface turned out to be a small key.

I had been expecting *something*, of course, otherwise the cabinet wouldn't have been locked, but not what I saw. Rows and rows of little orange-and-white bottles, interspersed with more mundane items, but still filling up the majority of the shelf space.

I began adjusting the bottles to read their labels. They were outdated prescriptions, for almost every psychotropic drug I'd ever heard of: antipsychotics, antianxiety, antidepressives, sleeping pills. . . .

I stared in amazement. Then, realizing I shouldn't stay too long, I began fumbling with the caps and with the tiny tablets and not-so-tiny tablets, wrapping each group in separate wads of tissue, writing on the outside in an eyeliner pencil what each group was. Not all the bottles, of course. I picked five. My bag was downstairs, and I didn't have any pockets. How was I going to carry them? I shoved a couple of packets down the sides of my high leather boots, a couple in my bra, one in my tights.

A noise came from outside the door. I turned on the

tap, praying the running water would mask the sounds as I carefully put the bottles back in the cabinet. Damn—I was taking too long.

I flushed the toilet, opened the bathroom door slowly.

Celeste and her father sat on the bed. "What are you doing here?" Celeste asked.

"Sorry," I said. "Gabe took me up here and then I needed to pee so I used this bathroom. I hope that's okay."

"Raiding the medicine cabinet?" she said.

My heart stopped. "No, I —"

"You really shouldn't be here," Mr. Lazar said to the floor. "Why would you be here? Did someone tell you to be here?"

"I . . ."

"It's okay, Dad," Celeste said. "Leena is my friend. She was just using the bathroom."

Mr. Lazar shook his head from side to side. "No one should be here. You told me that no one would be here. There are so many people." His voice had become inappropriately loud.

"I'm sorry," I said, moving as quickly as possible toward the door. "I didn't know."

"Why are you here?" Mr. Lazar continued. "No one knows you. You shouldn't be here."

"Sorry," I said again to Celeste as I finally made it out to the hallway.

I hurried down the stairs, almost tripping on the way.

Once in the crowd of people, I looked all around. Faces that had taken on a familiar note before now were just strangers, again. I *didn't* know these people. What *was* I doing here? All of my muscles were tense. I needed to get the pills into my bag. Which room was it in? Or better yet, I needed to leave. I needed to leave right now.

"Leena, hon? Everything okay?" Mrs. Lazar rested a hand on my shoulder.

I tried to relax, unclenched my fists. "I'm fine," I said. "I upset your husband. I didn't mean to." My fists. Shit. Something was in my right hand. The key.

"Ah," she said. "Don't worry about it. Please. This was a hard day for him, all the people. You'll have to come back and see him some other time. Just you and David." She gave my shoulder a gentle squeeze.

"Sure, yeah. That would be great." I needed to return the key, but I couldn't go back upstairs while Mr. Lazar was there.

"Where's that David kid hiding?" she said.

"I don't know. Maybe the kitchen?"

Mrs. Lazar reached for my elbow and began leading me in that direction, down a hall that was empty of people.

"He takes so much on, with his father and sister. It's wonderful for him to have a . . . a friend like you who isn't so mercurial, who is so . . . so . . ."

"Grounded?" I said. The tiny key weighed heavily in my sweaty hand. The tissue wad in my bra was itchy.

"Yes, right," she said. "I was going to say normal, but

323

then, what is normal? And what kind of mother calls her daughter abnormal?" She laughed. "Celeste is a rare bird. I feel very lucky to have her. But no one would identify stability as her cardinal trait."

"I guess not."

"I hear you're going to New York over the break," she said. "Why don't you come here for Thanksgiving, too? Unless you've got family plans?"

"No," I said. "I don't."

"Invite your parents, as well."

"Oh, I don't think—"

We'd reached the kitchen. David was beside me. "That's a good idea," he said. He looked at me hopefully.

"Well," I said, "my mom will be in LA. I suppose I could invite my dad, though. David, do you remember where I put my bag? I need something out of it."

After finding my bag in the mudroom, I hid out in the downstairs bath and transferred the pills into it. I still needed to return the key, though. As far as I could tell, Celeste and Mr. Lazar had never emerged from his room. I was biding my time, talking to the older man who thought I looked like the movie star, when David tapped me on the shoulder.

"I'm going to head out for a bit to drive my dad back to Riverside. Is that okay?"

"Of course," I said. *Yes! Take him!* "Do you want to borrow my car?"

"No, no," he said. "I'll take Mom's. It's about ten minutes away so I won't be long. I'd ask you to come, but it's probably better—"

"That's totally okay," I said. "I can fend for myself."

I stood by a window in the living room, watching until the car rolled out of the driveway and down the street. I checked around the party rooms for Celeste. No sign of her. I casually walked back up the stairs. The door to the Lazars' room was shut. I knocked lightly. No answer. "Celeste?" I said. Nothing.

I slipped inside and shut the door behind me. Get in, get out. No problem. Just walk through. Don't look around. My armpits were sweaty. I made it across the room, gripped the bathroom door handle.

Then I heard it. The slightest shifting of fabric. I turned. My eyes fumbled to make out shapes in the gloom. There. Subtle movement underneath a large desk. Shit.

"Hello?" I said tentatively.

No answer.

"Are you okay?"

"Leave me alone, Leena." The voice was Celeste's. But it was rough and strained. She'd been crying.

I took slow steps toward her and lowered myself down so I was kneeling next to the desk.

"What's wrong?" I said.

Her thin arms wrapped around one knee. Her whole body shook.

"Are you sick?"

"No." She began sobbing so hard she could barely speak. Noises from the party floated up the stairs. She rocked back and forth.

"What can I do?" I said. "Tell me. Do you want me to get David?" I remembered he was gone. "Or your mother?"

"No!" she said. "I'm . . . I'm . . . I'm just too tired to fight it anymore." Her words were forced out between sobs and gulps for air. "I'm so, so tired."

"Fight what?" I said.

"How can you not know?" She gripped a leg of the desk, as if to steady herself. "How can you not know?"

"Celeste, I'm not sure what you're talking about." My pulse had quickened. The tone of her words, her body language, her incoherence—it all made me worry I was in over my head. "Can you come out and sit on the bed? It would be easier to talk."

She maneuvered out from under the desk. She was visibly shaking, and on top of that, her body still heaved with sobs. I stood up and grabbed a soft blanket that was piled at the end of the bed. I wrapped it around her shoulders and led her to sit down. I sat next to her.

"Can you tell me?" I said.

"No." She shook, her head and her body. "I can't tell you. I can't tell anyone."

"If you're too tired to fight it alone," I said, "you need someone to help you. Right?"

"I can't," she said. "And not you. Before, before . . . maybe. But not now. I can't tell anyone. Don't you see?"

"How can I see, Celeste, since I have no idea what you're talking about? Well, I mean, I have some idea, but . . ." Either she knew she had some blood disease, someone was hurting her, or she was hurting herself. That much I knew.

"You do?" She gripped my sleeve with a hand that glowed white and skeletal in the darkened room. "It's happening to you, too?"

It's happening to you, too. Oh, God. Was she talking about David? My head began to spin.

"Maybe," I said. "Tell me."

"What is it?" she said. "What's happening?"

She wasn't making any sense. "What do you think it is?" I said.

"There's . . . there's something there. Right?"

Not about David. *Breathe, Leena.*

"Something there?" I said. "Where?"

"What do you mean? Frost House. Isn't that . . . Don't you know what I mean? Frost House."

Frost House? I thought of the closet. She wasn't talking about that, though. That was mine.

"I'm not sure what you're talking about." I spoke as gently as possible. "But you need someone to help you. To help you fight it. So tell me." If I used her words, maybe she'd trust me more.

"How can you not know?" she said. "How can you live

there? It's . . . There's no word for it. There's something there. There's someone. It's . . . evil. There's something that's trying to kill me."

Sweat clammed up my hands.

"You mean, it's haunted? Something like that?"

"That word sounds so stupid," she said. "This isn't a fucking Halloween prank."

"Have you told anyone else this?" I asked.

"Of course not! How could I ever tell anyone? They'll just think I'm crazy. But I'm not, Leena, I'm not!" She grabbed my sleeve. "Don't you feel it in there? Your room is the worst. That's why I moved, you know." Her words were coming quickly, one on top of the next. "It used to just do things to my stuff. But then it got stronger, it's seeping over. It's in the bathroom. It burned me that day. I wasn't sure at the time, but now I am. And it's tried to push me under, drown me. It hurts me while I try to sleep. Presses on my chest so I can't breathe. I can't get away from it. I'm so scared it's going to kill me. I don't know what to do. I can't tell anyone. I shouldn't have even told you. But you believe me, don't you? You know I'm not crazy?"

What could I say? Of course I didn't believe her. Of course I thought she was crazy.

"I just want to help you," I said. "I hate for you to be so upset."

"I think I know what it is, too. I talked to Whip's grandfather, when I had dinner with him after that assembly. And that girl, that girl Whip told us about. She died there, in Frost House."

"What girl?"

"You know, that one Whip told us about. The one who lived there, before it was a dorm."

God, she'd worked up a whole thing in her mind. "Celeste, that was just a stupid rumor."

"No. No, it's not. He told me. She went crazy, after having a baby. And she was locked back there, where we live, and she died. And now she's there . . . sort of. Trying to kill me. I don't see her. I don't hallucinate, Leena. It's all physical. My bruises, Leena, that's what they're from. She's hurting me." She gripped my arm, dug fingernails into my flesh. "You believe me, don't you? My bruises are proof. You have to believe me."

Her bruises—she thought they were from a ghost? What did that mean? Was she doing it to herself? "How long have you been feeling this way?" I said.

"It's never been right in there," she said. "All of the stuff that happened. All of it. It's this . . . it's this . . . thing. It's gotten stronger and stronger and I can't tell anyone and I can't keep fighting it. I tried . . . I tried to make peace. I tried to talk to her—to contact her—so many times. You know, how you're supposed to. But that's probably all bullshit, talking to them. She just wants what she wants."

Jesus. That's probably what Celeste had been burning those big white candles for. Some sort of . . . séance.

"Celeste, why wouldn't . . . why would it only do this stuff to you? Why haven't I felt anything?"

"Maybe you have," she said. "You're . . . Look at what you do all day. You take your pills and you don't have any friends—it's ruining you, too."

"No!" I said. "That's not . . . that's all just from stress. Frost House . . . I love Frost House. It's not—"

A quick knock came at the door and before either of us could answer it opened and David was there.

"Here you guys are. I just got back and couldn't— Hey. What's wrong?" He came over and knelt next to Celeste.

She wiped at her eyes, pushed her hair behind her ears. My heart hurt, it was beating so hard. I couldn't believe any of this was happening.

"Nothing," she said, remarkably pulled together all of a sudden. "Just, it's difficult to see Dad, you know?"

"He did pretty well tonight," David said. His brow wrinkled. "Don't you think?"

"I guess," Celeste said.

David looked at me. I didn't know what expression I wanted my eyes to telegraph. Desperation? Panic? Calm?

"Do you want us to stay up here with you?" he asked.

Celeste wiped her nose with the cuff of her blouse. "No. I'm fine. Let me just rinse my face and we can go back down. I need to say one last thing to Leena, though."

"Okay. If you're sure." David stood slowly and started out of the room, turning back to look at us several times. I could

330

feel his reluctance as he disappeared into the hallway.

Celeste stared at me with a fierce, completely composed expression. "Telling David is not the way to help me," she said. "What I need is your help to get rid of this thing so I can make it through the next few weeks. Okay? When I don't live there anymore, I'll be fine. I just need to find a way to live. Okay?"

I swallowed hard. Nodded.

"If you tell David, I'll make sure you regret it. Understand?"

"Okay," I said. "I understand."

She lay back on the bed, an arm over her face.

I stood and made my way to the bathroom, splashed water on my cheeks and returned the key to the top of the cabinet, although it didn't seem urgent anymore. Before, when she had threatened to tell David about my pill stash, it had scared me. Now, her threat just made me sad. Like I was witnessing her last, desperate attempt to hang on to power. Power her illness would completely strip away.

We drove onto Barcroft's campus ten minutes before sign-in, giving me no time to talk to David alone. After Celeste and I dropped him off, the claustrophobic space in the car was filled with a silence more haunted than any house could be.

"You don't believe me," Celeste finally said as I parked in the driveway. Her voice was calm now. Frost House crouched in front of us, shrouded by layers of branches and the darkness. Warm orange light glowed in the upstairs windows of Viv's bedroom. How had this all happened? How was it that I was here in this car, as scared as if I'd fallen into someone else's open grave, rather than up there, with my friends?

"I don't think you're lying," I said.

"Tactful. You don't think I'm lying. You just think I'm psychotic."

Silence returned as I helped her with her bags and crutches. I resisted the urge to run down the path to my room and into the house, resisted the urge to find calm and sanity in my closet as quickly as possible. Instead, I matched my steps to hers, and held open the door when we reached the entrance. Celeste hesitated for a moment. It must have taken all her courage to return to Frost House. She obviously believed she was in danger, regardless of the fact it wasn't true. To her, it *was* true.

In the hallway outside our rooms I said, "Do you want me to stay in there with you tonight?" It didn't feel responsible to let her sleep alone.

"No," she said. "It didn't make a difference before. When we were in the same room. It was just as bad."

"Why haven't you asked, you know, to be moved somewhere else?"

"What would I say? People don't just switch dorms with a month left in the semester. What could I possibly say?" Her voice was so tired.

"I don't know," I said. "You're positive you don't want me to stay with you?" If she were causing the bruises herself, somehow, maybe my presence would deter it.

"I've got work to do, anyway. I'll pull an all-nighter in the common room—it hasn't touched me in there. Yet." She reached for her doorknob, then looked back at me. "What are you going to do?"

"Right now?"

"No. Are you going to help me, Leena?"

I smoothed down a flake of paint curling off the wall. "Did you . . . did you think you might be imagining it? At the beginning?"

"Of course," she said. "You think it struck me as totally normal to be living in a place like this? To have all this stuff happen? Of course I thought I was crazy. I didn't know that something like this was possible. I thought . . . you know, it was made up, in books and movies."

"And why—I mean, how—did you decide, you know, that it's really happening?"

"I don't know," she said. "I can just tell. It's real, Leena. Don't you know when something is real?"

How could she be so blind, after seeing her father today? Real was walls and flesh and DNA and brain chemistry. How could she not know that?

I shut and locked the door to my bedroom, went into the closet, and shut and locked that door, too. I sank down on the cushion, opened my cell, and pressed the glowing green buttons. The phone looked like something from outer space, some alien tool. But it wasn't. It was a cell phone, made in China, with LED lights that lit up the buttons so I could see them here in the dark. Real.

"Miss me already?" David said.

His voice brought everything else about him—his eyes, his goofy laugh, the smell of his skin. . . . The way he takes care of his family. What was I thinking, doing this over the phone?

"Leena? You there?"

"Yeah, I . . . I just wanted to say thanks. For inviting me."

"Everyone loved you," he said. "And thanks for being so patient with Celeste. I'm surprised she was so upset. Dad was pretty good, all things considered."

I tipped my head back against the wall. "I'm glad I got a chance to meet him. And your mother. She seems wonderful. Your whole family does. Anyway, I have to go. I just wanted to thank you for including me. It meant a lot."

"I hope you didn't think I was too pushy," he said, "telling you to invite your dad to Thanksgiving."

I hadn't even remembered that. "Oh, right. I'll think about it."

"Because at the risk of sounding like an after-school special," David said, "you're really lucky you have two . . . healthy parents. And I think, someday, you might regret not . . . not trying harder."

334

I breathed deeply.

"I'd love to get to know your family," he said. "They couldn't be all that bad if they made you."

I smiled. "Thanks. And I'll definitely think about it."

After saying good night to David, I picked up Cubby, thinking I should put the new pills in her now. Then I remembered my pills weren't in her anymore, and reached for the plastic bag. As I did, her voice rang in my head.

He doesn't know what he's talking about.

More and more, the voice came on its own, without me asking any question. Like a muscle, maybe, my subconscious was getting stronger. This time, I didn't understand what she—what *I*—meant.

You're not the one who should try.

With my family. But . . . why? Maybe inviting my dad would be a good thing.

Stupid. Weak. Believing what David says. He doesn't know you.

I'd do it if it made him happy. Did that make me weak?

David's happiness. What would even be going on in his life at Thanksgiving? Where would Celeste be?

"Hello, spirit," I said. "Are you there?" I felt like a total idiot the minute the words were out.

No answer, of course. I almost wished there had been— a diaphanous figure appearing next to me, saying, "You called?" Then I could have just convinced it to leave Celeste alone, and I wouldn't have had to worry.

There was no ghost, though. Not now. Not ever. The

whole idea of Frost House as evil was . . . unthinkable. If there was such a thing as a haunted house, it would be the type of place people write about—where you feel uneasy and scared to turn out the lights. I'd never felt anything but safe and wanted in here. It was that type of house—I'd seen it right away—the type of house that welcomes and protects. You could tell just by looking.

That much I was sure of. And while I certainly didn't think believing in ghosts meant you were crazy, thinking one was trying to kill you, well . . . that took it to a whole other level.

I pressed my hand against the wall. I moved it slowly, as if feeling for a pulse. Or reassuring it. Good house. Good, strong house.

Celeste didn't realize it's what's inside us that's most scary. Nothing in the real world could match what our brains and bodies come up with. It's all a matter of degrees, what we create as our demons. Some minds create scarier ones. Poor Celeste. And poor David. That sadness in his voice when he talked about losing his father. . . . Once I spoke to him, he would know perfectly well that he was losing his sister, too.

36

I WAS TOO ANXIOUS TO SLEEP WELL, felt every spring of the bed frame through the mattress. Even the Tylenol PM didn't keep me from falling in and out of bad dreams and stretches of lying awake, obsessing over what I was going to say. And in that sort of delirious half sleep, a new worry occurred to me. What if Celeste twisted the story around? What if she told David I was making it all up, that *I* was the unstable one? She could use the pill stash as proof. If she had that missing paper, maybe he would believe her.

And something else, new and confusing: if Celeste was a physical danger to herself, was she a danger to me? When she found out what I'd done, would she . . . hurt me?

At 5:15 a.m. I gave up and turned on the lights. I slipped

into sweats and sneakers, before realizing that I didn't know what time it was actually legal to leave your dorm. We had to sign in by ten, and you couldn't leave in the middle of the night. But when was it officially "morning"? The last thing I needed was to be kicked out of school because of an early morning walk.

Instead of risking the world's stupidest expulsion, I booted up my laptop and did research, any topic that related to anything Celeste had said. I searched for a site on hauntings that struck me as authoritative and scientific. But all they did was confirm my opinion. Photos of fuzzy shadows on staircases, presented as proof. Please! I also googled the town of Barcroft and hauntings, to see if there were any accounts of the story Celeste had mentioned. None, of course.

And students had been living in Frost House for generations. Wouldn't there be more stories going around about it, other than those old, tepid ones of Whip's?

If there was an infinitesimal part of my brain that wanted an explanation for all those things that Celeste mentioned—the vase, the burn, the nests—before closing the door on what I knew wasn't true, I got it, moments before I was about to put my computer to sleep. I stumbled on one last site, after searching a new combination of terms. Finally, a rational site, that offered legitimate explanations for what lay behind some "hauntings." What I read on it made me feel both a rush of relief and a slow creep of horror. Because it all

338

fit together. And I was more sure than ever about what I had to tell David.

By seven a.m., I sat waiting for him on the steps of his dorm. I tore up dried leaves into little pieces and considered my approach, as if there was a good way to tell him his sister might be heading down the same path as his sick father. I'd also decided I needed to come clean about everything, just to be safe. So Celeste couldn't manipulate the situation. I was trying not to be too nervous, but I still had the jitters. There was no telling how he would react.

Guys straggled out of the dorm, in pairs and alone, fuzzy, not-quite-awake expressions on their faces. I sat off to the side, inconspicuous. David glided right by me with his hands in his pockets, a brown-striped scarf around his neck and his black wool hat on his head. I waited, appreciating this moment in which he looked like a typical prep-school student, headed off for a normal day of classes and sports and friends on one of the most beautiful campuses during New England fall.

"Hey," I called. "David."

The bench on the steps of the chapel was bathed in the slanted rays of morning sunshine. We held steaming cups of Commons coffee in our hands. I'd delayed as long as I could. My pulse felt too quick and erratic, despite having taken a small dose of something to calm me. I remembered how angry he'd been when he'd found out about my Columbia interview. How was he going to react now?

"There are a couple of things—hard things—I need to tell you," I said.

"That doesn't sound good."

A V of geese flapped and honked overhead in the pale blue sky.

"First," I said, "is about me."

I kept my eyes on the birds as they receded into the distance.

"Ever since my parents split up, I've been on meds. You know, psychotropic."

I paused, took a sip of coffee. The steam fogged up my glasses.

"It started as a regular prescription thing. But then my doctor said it was time for me to stop. So, I got in the habit of finding other ways to get pills. From my parents, other people. I don't use them every day. Just when I'm stressed, or anxious. I know it's not ideal, but I'm really careful. And . . . I know it's wrong, how I get them. I do feel bad about that."

I rolled the warmth of my cup between my hands.

"I didn't want you to find out," I continued, "because I know you don't like meds, and I thought you might think it's a problem for me. But it's really not. I'm not addicted or anything. Not at all. They just, they just make things easier. Like, emotional aspirin." I bit the inside of my lip. "I know you might not think of me this way, but I can be really . . .

unproductively emotional. Like, when my parents split. And other times . . . It scares me."

Silence. Heart hammering, I forced myself to meet his eyes but couldn't read their expression.

"Is this what that chart you made is about?" he said.

"You saw it?" I said, surprised.

"I found it on the floor of your room, when you were sick. With so much else going on, I haven't asked you about it."

David had the paper this whole time? I couldn't believe it. "I know you probably think it's really irresponsible," I said. "But I always do research. About dosages, drug interactions. That's what the chart is for."

His gaze moved to his coffee cup. "The thing that makes me sad," he said, "is that you feel you need to do it." He paused. "And, I guess, it makes me wonder if I know the real Leena."

"Of course you do," I said. "I only take really low doses. Just to even out. It's not like I walk around in a haze. And I only use them when I need to, like I said." My chest was beginning to hurt. "You do know me, David. You do."

Sun brought out the reddish strands in his dark hair. He was quiet. I hated that I couldn't tell what he was thinking.

"Are you mad?" I finally said.

"Mad? Of course not. I think you should stop. I think maybe you have some stuff you need to work out. But I'm not mad." He reached over and stroked my cheek with the back of his hand. Then he smiled. "Let me be your antidepressant, baby. How's that for a song lyric?"

"Incredibly cheesy." I leaned forward to kiss him on his cheek, overwhelmed by how well he'd taken it. I'd underestimated him.

"Was there something else?" he said. "'Cause we've got class in about ten minutes."

Something else. Right. I took a sip of coffee as a momentary delay. Then began.

"This is the much, much more serious thing," I said. "It's Celeste. She wasn't upset about your father yesterday."

"Did she give you a hard time about being there?" he said. "I thought she was being more mature about—"

"No. David, I . . ." It was difficult to talk past the brick in my throat. "I'm really worried about her. More than just worried."

"Worried?"

"You know how she's always acted weird about the dorm? And how she switched rooms. And now she won't use the bathtub either."

"I know," he said. "She told me that tub is dangerous, with her cast."

"That's what she told me, too, at first. But that's not it." I reached over and took one of his bare hands between my mittened ones. "Okay. There's no easy way to say this, so I'm just going to say it. She thinks . . . she thinks the dorm is haunted."

David's mouth curled into a questioning smile. "What?"

"She thinks it's haunted, and that there's some sort of evil spirit trying to hurt—trying to kill her."

"Wait." David pulled back his hand into his lap, tilted his chin down, and looked up at me, eyebrows raised. *"What?"*

I went on and told David the whole story—everything she blamed on the ghost, from the ripped skirt to the bruises.

"I did a little research, and it's possible most of the things were caused by her," I said. "I mean, not on purpose. Subconsciously. These poltergeist-type things tend to happen in houses with intense girls living there. So she really doesn't realize that it's in her head, because it's actually happening. But it's being caused by her in some way. I don't know how this all would tie into delusions and hallucinations. I actually don't think she has hallucinations, unless the feeling that she's being physically hurt or whatever, unless that's some sort of physical hallucination. But the bruises could definitely be self-inflicted. There's a correlation between . . . between mental illness and self-harm."

David's left cheek twitched as I spoke. Maybe I should have printed out some of the articles I read. It's what had affected me most—the idea that Celeste could have unknowingly done these things herself. It's what had filled me with that strange combination of relief and terror.

"I know this is a lot to hear," I said. "I felt sick all night, knowing I had to tell you. Well, that and worrying about her." I reached for my coffee cup, but the heat had drained away.

"Why didn't she tell me herself?" he said. "Why did she tell you?"

"I think . . . well, she knows how much you worry about her. That scares her. She assumed you'd think she was . . . you know. Sick. She thought I might believe her."

David shook his head. "No," he said. "I'd know if she was sick." He rubbed his palms back and forth on his knees.

I took a minute to consider his choice of words. "What do you mean?"

"I'd know if she was sick," he said. "I'd be able to tell."

"Oh-kaay," I said. "But you haven't talked to her about this stuff. You haven't heard the way she talks about it."

"No. But still."

"So, then . . . what's the alternative?" I said. "If she's not imagining stuff?"

"I don't know. Maybe there really is something . . . weird in there."

"Like, something evil?" I said. "Something trying to hurt Celeste? Is that what you mean?" He couldn't.

"I don't know. Do you really think we can understand everything about this stuff?"

"No, I guess not. But—"

"There are plenty of documented stories of hauntings."

"David. Are you serious?" I studied his face. His stubble-covered jaw was set.

"Well, there are," he said.

"Maybe," I said to avoid arguing over that side issue. "But

you have a history of psychosis in the family. And Celeste has the paranoid impression that someone—something—is trying to kill her. I mean, statistically—"

"I'd know if she was sick, Leena."

I pushed my glasses up my nose. He was a mathematician; how could he be so illogical?

"Are you really saying it's more likely that the dorm is haunted than that she's had a psychotic break, something she's genetically predisposed to have?" Now I couldn't take my eyes off his profile, waiting for some sign that I wasn't hearing what I thought I was.

"You make it sound as if having a father like ours means it will happen," he said. "It's a pretty low percentage, you know."

"But, David. Are you seriously listening to yourself? Haunted. You believe the dorm is haunted."

"I don't know. But I'm not going to assume that she's lost it. She would tell me if she felt not right, mentally. We have a pact."

"People don't know!" I was having trouble keeping the frustration out of my voice. I needed to remember how hard all of this would be for him to hear. It shouldn't have surprised me that his first response would be denial. "Don't you see? It all seems real to her because her brain is perceiving it as being real. People don't know when they're delusional. I live there, David. That house is not . . . haunted. If such a thing even existed."

"Since you don't believe it *can* be, maybe you're just not open to seeing it."

"David!" I said too loudly. "I'd know if there was something wrong in the house. I'd certainly know if something was trying to kill me. And nothing bad has happened to any of my stuff, you know. Nothing." I paused. "We have to tell the dean about this. Or maybe not the dean first. Maybe your mom. Would that be better? It should be your decision."

He finally turned to face me. The blue of his eyes glowed radioactive in the strong sun. "And then what? They send her to some horrible place and shove her full of meds?"

So now he was throwing that back at me?

"Well, somewhere she can get help," I said. "Of course. And yes, meds can help."

"God! You're not a doctor yet, Leena. Even if you treat yourself. How many psychotics have you even met? My father was probably the first, right? And he wasn't even having an episode."

"Yeah, but—"

"But what? I *know* psychosis. I've lived with it. Celeste is not acting at all like my father ever acted. I'd be able to tell."

This conversation had strayed so far from what I had anticipated. I had no idea what to say anymore. "But, David. If you listen to what Celeste is saying—"

"Celeste is rational. She doesn't have any other symptoms." He held out his hand and counted off on his fingers. "She's doing her schoolwork. She's already got all of her college apps in—did you know that? She has good personal hygiene. She hasn't withdrawn—"

"Of course she has," I said. "We barely ever see her anymore."

David shook his head. "That's because of us, because she doesn't know how to deal with our relationship. And I see her on my own, when you're not around."

"I can't believe we're arguing over this," I said. "If she's not sick, then it won't hurt to tell someone, right?"

"Leena. I'm going to talk to Celeste. Until then, don't do anything. Anyway, waiting won't make a difference. If you are right, if she's sick, what'll it matter? A few days won't change anything. Right?"

"It's just, if she's sick—"

"If you are right," he interrupted, "if she's sick, then I promise, a day or two won't make any difference. Nothing will change the fact that Celeste, the Celeste I know, is gone."

37

GOING TO MY CLASSES WAS NOT AN OPTION. David's completely irrational view of the facts had thrown me for almost as big a loop as Celeste's revelation. There was only one place I could safely process the information.

I fumbled a round yellow pill into my mouth. I needed clarity. Too much emotion and confusion battled in my brain. I breathed in the closet's comforting smell, traced my finger over Cubby's feathers, and tried to think.

Was the power of denial so strong that it could completely prevent David from seeing the truth? Maybe the drive for self-protection trumped logic, rationality. When David talked to Celeste, though, when he heard the paranoia in her voice, he'd have to come to terms with what was really happening. He just needed some time to let it sink in.

And where would that leave us? The loneliness that lay ahead of him made my chest ache. It made me want to tell him that I'd be there, in whatever way he needed. Did he know that? I couldn't believe how strongly attached I'd grown to him in such a short time.

You know that can only hurt you. Once he doesn't want you.

"No," I said. "He's going to need me. He's not going to have Celeste anymore. He'll need me." I rubbed my temples. More and more I'd been getting these deep, throbbing headaches.

Don't you see? He's sick, too. He'll never want you the way he wants her.

"Why do you say that? That's awful."

In here is the only place you get the truth.

I'd had enough of the truth these past couple of days. I was exhausted from it all—the revelations, confrontations. And though usually I loved the way I felt in here, right now, I couldn't handle any more insights into my sometimes ugly subconscious.

It took an enormous amount of energy to push myself up and out into the blinding light of my room. And the minute I was out there, I almost went back in. Somehow the open space of the room was overwhelming. Not contained enough. I needed an activity. Something to occupy me until David got in touch. Something physical—there was no way I could concentrate on homework. The furniture was happy in its arrangement. No space on the walls to hang more pictures. Maybe the garden needed something.

I crossed the room to look outside. The angle of the light coming through the window brought out the layers of dirt that had built up on the pane. Ugh. How had I not noticed this before? I ran a finger down the cold glass. Dirt stuck to the tip.

I got a pile of newspapers from the common room and the Windex from under the bathroom sink. I started at the far right window—just as dirty as the other. I sprayed the cleaner and began wiping with a wadded-up clump of newspaper.

I breathed in and out with the strokes of my arm. Okay. I didn't need to think about David's part in this. About his strange reaction. Or what was going to happen to us. No good could come from dwelling on the possibility of losing him, the way I always seemed to do in the closet.

I rubbed circles of streaky liquid round and round the next pane. My wad of newspaper bumped up against the wood frame that had splintered when I'd been hanging the blinds with David. It had been ready to fall apart, that piece of rotten wood. But it took me drilling into it for the large chunk to splinter off. What had happened to Celeste, to make her mind splinter like it had?

I thought back to the beginning of the semester, to the bad things that happened to her right off the bat—the ripped skirt, the broken vase. One possibility, of course, was that she had unknowingly caused these things to happen herself. But maybe she hadn't. Maybe someone else had done these things, and that had been part of what had instigated Celeste's paranoia. She thought someone was out to get her because, in a way, someone *was* out to get her. Was it possible that a mental disorder could be set off by something like that? Or had the mental disorder itself caused the things to happen? Which came first, the chicken or the egg?

I didn't hear from David until late that afternoon. I was about to lose it, wondering whether he had talked to Celeste yet, when my phone finally flashed his name.

"Can you have dinner at Tonio's?" he said.

"Tonio's? Sure, why?"

"I'm hungry." I thought I heard laughter in the background.

"Okay," I said. "I'll pick you up in half an hour."

I was surprised that David was hungry at all, let alone in the mood to go to a romantic, off-campus restaurant. I was even more surprised when I picked him up at his dorm and found Celeste there with him. He slid in the front, Celeste and her crutches in the back.

"Where should I drop you off?" I asked her.

"I'm coming to dinner," she said. Even in the small reflection in the rearview mirror, I could see that despite the dark bags, her eyes sparkled like they hadn't before. Her whole expression was entirely different from yesterday's.

David's face was more serious than hers, but not nearly as morose as when I'd left him. A disturbing new idea wiggled its way into my brain. Was it possible—at all possible—that this whole thing had been a joke? Or some kind of sick Lazar family test? Well, if it was, there was no question—I was done with both of them.

I got no clues from their conversation on the drive to Tonio's. Celeste spent the whole time talking about the upcoming student exhibition her photos were going to be in, and soliciting our opinions about what she should wear to the opening. If this wasn't a joke, had David even talked to her?

At Tonio's, the maître d' gave us the polite but tired smile Barcroft students always get and led us to a small, velvet-upholstered booth at the back of the dark restaurant.

Celeste immediately grabbed a breadstick from a ceramic jar. David opened the stiff, gold-embossed cover of his menu.

I opened mine, but the words didn't coalesce into meaningful phrases. I shut it. "So, why are we here?" I said. "It's not your birthday, is it? That's in a couple weeks." A ludicrous guess; of course this wasn't a birthday party.

"We wanted somewhere private," David said.

"Aren't these booths great?" Celeste ran a hand over the tufted, burgundy velvet. "Old-school glamour. I'd like to have one in my house."

A waiter in black pants and a white button-down appeared at our table. "My name is Cliff and I'll be your server this evening. May I take your drink order?"

"Diet Coke, please," I said, then added, "Actually, just water." I didn't need any caffeine.

"Club soda," Celeste said. "With one maraschino cherry, and a slice of lime."

"Sam Adams," David said.

"May I see some ID, sir?" Cliff said.

David looked surprised, then embarrassed. He began patting his pockets. "Oh, sorry, I don't think I brought . . . That's okay. I'll just have a Coke."

"Why somewhere private?" I said, once we were alone again.

"We have a plan," David said. "Well, the start of one."

"Okay . . ."

David placed both palms on the table and leaned forward. "Here's what we do. We convince the school that Frost House isn't safe to live in. That way, you all get to move out, no one knowing the real reason you need to."

"What do you mean, 'isn't safe'?" I said. "You're going to tell them there's something evil in the house?"

"Of course not," David said. "We prove that it's physically unstable. I don't know, like the roof might collapse or whatever. Maybe we could start a fire or something, just a small one."

I sat there, looking back and forth between the two of them. Their expressions were anxious, but in an excited, not-nervous way. Kids listening for Santa's sleigh on the roof.

The waiter placed our drinks on the table. "Would you like to hear this evening's specials?" he said.

Specials? Who could think about food? I couldn't even conceive of reading through the menu with David's words hanging in the air. A fire? Was he kidding?

"I don't need to hear specials," I said, just to say something. "I'll have the fettuccini Alfredo, please."

"Steak for me," David said. "Rare."

"Ooh, me too." Celeste was almost giddy. "Listen," she said to the waiter, "do you think the restaurant is going to get new seating anytime soon? Because if they do, I'd be interested in buying one of these booths."

Cliff stifled a smile. "I don't think so. I'll check, though." He chuckled as he walked away.

"You're joking, right?" I said to David.

"I know it sounds extreme," he said. "But think about it."

"Burning down the haunted house," I said. "Like in a cheesy horror movie? Are you crazy?" Right away I knew it was a bad choice of words.

"David and I are both crazy," Celeste said in a woo-woo, exaggeratedly eerie voice. She wiggled her fingers in the air. "And we're going to make you crazy, too."

"No, we're not," David said. "I don't necessarily mean a fire. Just something to make the house unlivable. You know all about house construction. What could we do to make it unlivable? Like, a major plumbing leak or something that ruins some stuff."

"I don't want it to be unlivable," I said. "In case you've forgotten, I live there!"

"So you'll move into an empty room somewhere else." David pulled out a breadstick and snapped it in half.

"No. This is a ridiculous idea."

"Leena," David said. "Celeste can't keep living there. And any other solution involves making her look sick. Unless you want us to make up some story about how you guys are mean to her. We'll tell the dean she's too miserable to stay there."

"No way," I said. "Absolutely not." Aside from the fact I'd be mortified for them to do that, this whole plan was predicated on the fact that Celeste would be okay if she moved out. Could David honestly believe that?

"Come on," David said, cajoling, as if he was trying to convince me to take a breadstick or something equally trivial. "Next year we'll have a nice place in the city. You can handle living in some other dorm until then. What's the big deal about you staying there?"

The big deal? He knew how I felt about my room. How could he even ask? And how could they be so casual, so . . . so . . . so goddamn cheery? I stared at my fork. "I don't want to move out." My voice was tight.

"It's a good plan," Celeste said to me. "We know it's kind of weird, but not so much if you think about it."

"It's kind of impractical, to put it mildly," I said. "And what about Viv and Abby and Ms. Martin? You're going to make all of them move out, too? And Kate is supposed to move in next semester. What about her? We're all supposed to live there."

"Do you have a better idea?" David said.

I couldn't believe he was putting me in this position in front of Celeste. He knew what I thought.

"A problem with the wiring," he said. "Don't old houses have dangerous electrical problems sometimes?"

"The dangerous wiring isn't in the house," I muttered.

"What?" David leaned toward me.

"Nothing. I mean, yes, of course there could be dangerous wiring. But we wouldn't know."

"What if we just scorched the wall?" he said. "Not a full-fledged fire. Just enough to make them nervous. You know, a big, scorched area around an outlet. Would that be enough for them to move you?"

With no warning, Celeste stood up, jiggling the table and sloshing our drinks. She lifted her glass. "A toast," she said.

"What?" I said.

"I can't even tell you how good this feels," she said. "Even just knowing that you guys know, and that we're going to do something about it. I have been so fucking scared and so fucking alone. I would like to toast our new coalition. Formed out of a betrayal, yes," she said, looking me in the eye, "but formed nonetheless."

"Celeste," David said. "Leena did the right thing, telling

me. We wouldn't be here if she hadn't." He lifted his Coke. "We should be toasting her."

"Fine. To Leena," Celeste said.

Their eyes pinned me against the back of the booth. At that moment, I couldn't see how not to do what they wanted. I lifted my glass.

38

"How can I do it?" I said. "How can I help Celeste without losing David?" Please *be wise*, I thought. *Please, I need help. I need wisdom.* Cubby's eyes stared back at me in the light from the camping lantern. I'd taken a pill to calm down, but what I really needed was answers.

You can't.

I shivered. "I don't understand how he can be so blind."

He's not blind. He's sick.

"No." I shook my head. "He just wants her to be okay."

He wants her to be crazy. He likes it.

No. I knew that he wanted to take care of her, but he would rather he didn't have to. I knew that. He wasn't sick.

And now he's going to take away Frost House.

"No."

Someone was knocking on the bedroom door. Loudly. My room light was on; I couldn't pretend to be asleep.

I emerged from the closet, unlocked and opened it.

Celeste stood with a manila envelope in her hand.

"Okay," she said. "I told you not to tell David. Right?"

I swallowed. "Right."

"But, I've decided, there's no reason for me to be mad, really, since David is being so great. I actually . . . I want you to have this," she said, handing me the envelope. "As a kind of thanks. You know, I see that you were really just freaked out. And how can I blame you after the way I was acting at the party? That was too much to expect you to deal with."

I ran my finger along the sharp edge of the manila flap. I had visions of finding something inside that she could use to blackmail me. "Should I open it?"

"Of course."

I eased out an eight-by-ten color photograph. In it, a cockroach wearing a tiny white dress and gold wings appeared to be flying in front of what was obviously a painted sky and green mountains—like the flats from a miniature stage set. It was delicate and strangely beautiful.

"You made this?"

She nodded.

"This is what you do with the roaches?"

Celeste leaned forward on her crutches so she could look at the picture. "Well, basically. But this is the only one that's of an angel. I have a whole bunch of different painted sets that I photograph them in front of. I have so many roaches because I ruin a lot in the process. It's hard to get it all perfect. I don't like correcting stuff in Photoshop. I like it to be all . . . real."

"It's really strange. In a good way," I said. I slid it back in the envelope. "I like it. Thanks so much."

"Sure," she said. "Well, like I said, I realized you were trying to help. And as it happens, you ended up doing the right thing. David and I will owe you after this is all over. I'm sure he feels that way, too. I'm sure this will, you know, bring you guys closer together. All of us. Like, now it's the three of us in on it. Right?"

"Sure," I said. But I must have hesitated just a second too long.

"You still think I'm sick. Don't you?" she said.

My big toe followed a crack between two floorboards. She wouldn't hurt me, would she? I didn't think so. Her violent tendencies were toward herself.

"It's okay," she said. "As long as you give me a chance to show that I'm not. You'll see. It'll be better for you, too. David'll see how much he can trust you." She reached up and brushed something off her cheek. The sleeve of her leopard-print vintage sweater crept up a bit. A bruise I'd never noticed before circled her wrist. "It bothered me a bit," she said, "when you and David got together. Partly, you know, I already felt lonely because of this . . . this house stuff.

360

But also, I think, as much as I hated how protective he was, I got nervous that I needed him. But now I'm glad you're, like, in love. I'm sorry if I made it hard. I should've realized it didn't have to be you or me. And that I'm stronger than I thought."

I lay down on my bed and stared at the cockroach angel in Celeste's photograph. I pictured that bruise on her tiny wrist, a bizarre bracelet. I couldn't do what they wanted me to do. But maybe . . . maybe there was a way. A way I could take care of Celeste without losing David. Or Frost House. Because if I lost them, what would I have left?

39

M OST FRESHMEN EAT IN L OWER R IGHT, at least the ones who haven't made varsity teams or gotten leads in plays. Sure enough, the next morning I found Nicole there, eating breakfast with her friend, Sera.

"Can I talk to you, Nicole?" I said. "Alone?"

Sera stood and picked up her tray. "I was leaving anyway. FYI, Nicki, danger at ten o'clock." She giggled. "See you later, lovebird."

I followed Nicole's eyes toward ten o'clock where a guy in an oversize Barcroft hoodie sat. Nicole jerked her gaze down to her plate. "Shoot. Did he see me?"

"I have no idea," I said, sliding into the seat Sera had vacated. If only my main worry was running into some guy in Commons. "I need your help, Nicole. The situation is more complicated than I thought."

"What situation?" Nicole's eyes flicked back toward the guy. She smoothed her hair behind her ears.

"The thing with the girl in the locker room. I'm hoping you'll do me a favor."

Now she focused on me. "What can I do? I don't even know her."

"It's not a big deal," I said. "Just tell Dean Shepherd what you saw. You know, the bruises. Don't mention my name. Tell the dean like she's the only person you've told."

"Why? Dean Shepherd hates me. Can't you tell her?"

I shook my head, antagonizing the terrible headache I'd had since last night. I'd thrown up this morning, too. Nerves. "Like I said, it's complicated. You don't have to have a long thing with the dean. Just go in, tell her what you saw. That's it."

"Couldn't it just be an anonymous tip?"

"Nicole," I said. "You owe me."

She bit her bottom lip and scraped her fork across her plate, through clumps of scrambled eggs.

"Okay," she finally said. "I guess it's not a big deal. I'll do it."

"Thanks." I smiled with relief. One hurdle cleared. "Dean Shepherd usually gets to her office at seven thirty, so maybe you could stop by on your way to your first class."

Nicole watched as I stood up to leave. "What's going on

with that girl, anyway?" she said. "Someone told me she's going out with Whip Windham. Is it, like, an abusive relationship?" I could see in Nicole's eyes that she'd be on the phone the minute I left, telling Sera what had just happened.

"No," I said. "It's nothing to do with that." The last thing Celeste needed was to be the grist of the Barcroft rumor mill.

Although, I supposed that was the least of her problems.

There was a time bomb ticking. I could hear it counting off with every one of my shallow, accelerated breaths that morning. After bio, I wandered down the crowded hall, wondering if Nicole had done what I'd asked, if Celeste had been called to the office, if David knew. Silas Williams, from my Calculus class, stopped and asked me if I'd finished the homework. I couldn't remember. Saturday, the day I'd last done homework, seemed so far away and fuzzy. I was about to tell him no when I felt a tug on my wrist. I turned.

"Leena," Celeste said. "Come here." My heart leapt into my throat. I followed her off to the side of the crowd, into an open space underneath the main staircase.

She stood so our faces were only inches apart and spoke in a whisper. "She told. The little redhead. She told Dean Shepherd."

"She did?" I said. Celeste's eyes betrayed no emotion. I hoped mine were just as unreadable.

"Yes! Can you believe it? She already snitched to you. Why would she tell the dean?"

"I guess she was worried," I said. "So, are you okay? What's going to happen?" Honestly, I was surprised she was in the classroom building. And that she seemed relatively calm.

"Nothing," Celeste said. "Thank God. It's just a pain in the ass."

"Nothing?" That couldn't be right.

Celeste brought out a tube of Blistex. I bit the insides of my cheeks to keep from asking more questions as she ran it over her lips. "I saw the dean a few minutes ago," she finally said. "I gave her the whole blood-disorder song and dance, told her about my doctor's appointment, blah, blah, blah. . . ."

"Oh," I said. "Right." All of my muscles tightened. I had known Nicole would only tell Dean Shepherd about the bruises, of course. Why had I assumed that would lead to the dean finding out everything else?

Instead, it had led nowhere.

"The good news is I think David figured out a plan," Celeste said. "Like we discussed."

The tightness in my chest was keeping me from breathing. "Already?"

"Of course already. The sooner the better. You want me to die in there?"

"What is it? He's not going to do anything too extreme, is he?"

"He hasn't told me," she said. "He sent a text that says, 'Got it.'"

"'Got it'? That could mean anything."

"No way. It means he's got a plan."

As much as I wanted to believe otherwise, I knew she was right.

This couldn't happen. I couldn't let David do something horrible to Frost House. I couldn't go along with this fantasy that Celeste wasn't sick. And if I waited any longer, it would be too late.

"Can Dean Shepherd see me?" I asked Marcia. "It's an emergency."

I stood in front of Marcia's desk, scrunching and unscrunching my toes in my boots, telling myself that this was the right thing to do. That whatever happened with David, I had no choice. I couldn't jeopardize Celeste's life just to hold on to him. I checked my phone about a hundred times to make sure I hadn't missed a call or text. I'd left David a message that he shouldn't do anything until we spoke. I was reaching in my bag to check it again when Marcia motioned me to go into the office.

Dean Shepherd was wiping the sleeve of her blouse with a paper towel. "Coffee spill," she said. "Have a seat, Leena."

I sat down and laced my fingers together tightly in my lap to keep my hands still.

The dean set aside the paper towel and gave me a small smile. "So," she said. "Judging from the morning I've had, I'll guess this is about Celeste?"

I started at the beginning, with the ripped skirt, the

broken vase, the ruined nests. "I thought she believed Ms. Martin's cat had done everything," I said. "I didn't realize she was connecting it to this other stuff." I explained about Celeste's fear she was being watched, the knocking noises, everything Celeste had told me, how she'd built it all up into this final paranoid delusion.

Dean Shepherd listened with a furrowed brow, absent-mindedly running her fingers over her chin. "Are you sure this isn't a joke?" she said when I'd finished. "Maybe she's upset about you and David, trying to get back at you. Isn't that what you told me before?"

"No," I said. "She's serious."

"And the bruises? They're part of this?"

I repeated what I'd told David, about how she might not realize she's hurting herself. The way she might not have realized she was causing the other things to happen, as well.

"It sounds like there's been a lot of trouble in the dorm I didn't know about," Dean Shepherd said. "I can't help feeling that maybe it could have been noticed earlier that something was wrong."

"Noticed by me, you mean."

Most people might have missed the look that flitted across her face, but I didn't. Just a twitch of her lips that let me know that's exactly what she'd meant. That it was my fault for not coming to her earlier. That I'd missed obvious signs the person I was living with—the person she'd trusted me to watch out for—was deeply sick.

"I just thought she was eccentric," I said, trying to ignore the heavy sadness bearing down. "How could I ever have guessed something like this? It's completely crazy. I was trying to make things work out okay . . . you know, in the dorm. I didn't know."

The dean nodded, her mouth a solemn straight line. "Okay," she said. "We don't want to come to any premature conclusions, of course. But I'll handle it from here."

"What will you do?"

"Don't worry—I'll do what's best for Celeste. Does David know yet?"

"No," I lied. "Not yet."

We sat for a moment. Her face seemed to sag slightly, as if the conversation had added years to her age. "What happened this semester, Leena?" she said. "I feel like in the past, you would have come to me with this."

I swallowed and tried not to tear up. "I . . . I kept screwing up. You've been so mad at me."

"It's been a rough semester," she said. "That's true. But I would still have been here for you. Always."

"I'm sorry," I said. All her words did was make me feel worse.

The paths crisscrossing the Great Lawn stretched empty; everyone else was in class. I fought against a strong wind as I hurried toward Frost House. Leaves swirled above me like the flocks of ravens in Hitchcock's *The Birds*.

David still hadn't answered my call. I needed to find him. I hadn't told the dean about his part in this whole mess, especially not the fact that he might have been lacing the house with lighter fluid as we spoke, because I wanted to believe that he—*we*—could have a life together here at Barcroft for the rest of the year. A life without Celeste. If the dean knew he was going along with the whole haunted house thing, well, that wouldn't be good. Maybe, just maybe, once he realized his sister was sick, he'd see that I'd actually helped save her. Maybe he'd see that I'd risked my own happiness to make sure she was safe. Maybe he would even realize it now. Maybe I wouldn't have to wait.

My head was killing me. I searched the inside of my jacket pockets, in case I had any of my meds hanging around. Nothing. I'd get some at the dorm. Assuming it was still standing. No—that wasn't really a concern—David hadn't talked about burning down the whole place, and he certainly wouldn't do it without telling me first, letting me get out the things that mattered to me. Still, I couldn't help scanning the distance for any sign of smoke.

Branches swayed in front of the little house when I reached the driveway. My little old lady house. Vulnerable. But not on fire.

I opened the side door. The common room looked the same as ever; clueless as to what was going on around it. Waiting for us to come hang out and watch TV or make microwave popcorn. Or have another Sunday night dorm dinner. All the things I'd envisioned when we moved into Frost House. I automatically straightened the tapestry that covered the couch.

Once in the hallway, I heard the sounds. Objects moving, shifting, in Celeste's room. I moistened my lips. It couldn't be Celeste—she had classes straight through to lunch. And if the dean had called her immediately, she wouldn't have come back here, would she? Would the dean call her? Or send people to pick her up at class in person? A vision of Celeste in a straitjacket flashed in my mind. Being carried out of her class, wrapped up like a lunatic.

Celeste's door was closed. I kept my footsteps soft, so I could make it to my own room first and take at least a little something to help with this headache. The floorboards creaked and groaned.

Click. I stopped. The door to Celeste's room opened. David stood there. His hair leapt out from his head in messy clumps. Circles of sweat darkened his shirt. From the look of the room he had been moving things out of her closet.

"Leen, hey. I'm so glad you're here," he said.

He opened his arms. My body fell into his. I was pulled in two directions. Pulled into his warmth, like I wanted to crawl under his shirt and hide there, as if I could be folded into his body and leave mine behind. But the buzz, the life I felt in his body also gave me strength to remember I'd done the right thing. Energy darted back and forth between us. When I felt the push rather than the pull I separated from him, taking that strength, feeling it in my bones. What I had to do now was a thousand times harder than what I'd already done. A million times harder.

"Did you get my message?" I asked.

"No. You called?" He patted his pockets. "Oh, right. My phone's in my bag. I left it in your room. What'd you say?"

"Did you . . . did you need something in my room?"

"I borrowed a couple of tools." He reached over to Celeste's desk and picked up my hammer. He smiled and raised his eyebrows. "I have a plan. I would've called but I figured you were in class all morning. Shouldn't you be at math?"

"David," I said. "It's too late."

"Too late? For what?"

I filled my lungs as if preparing to be submerged underwater. "I told Dean Shepherd about Celeste."

His head jutted back slightly, his chin pulled into his neck. "You what?"

"If she's not sick, they'll find out. And if she is sick, she needs help."

Now he stepped back completely; I could no longer feel the heat from his body. The hammer dangled from his hand. "You're kidding, right?"

"I knew that you were too close to her to do it yourself. And it had to be done."

"You told the dean *everything*?"

"Most of it. I didn't tell her that you know. I thought . . .

well, I thought it would be better to keep you out of it. Dean Shepherd might find it kind of odd that you believe all the haunted stuff, too."

There were nails in his voice when he spoke. "What were you thinking?"

"We talked about this before, David. You know what I think. Celeste needs help."

"I know she needs help. *I'm* the one helping her. That's why I'm here."

"Please, David. Please don't be mad." I wanted to touch him, but knew it wasn't the right thing to do. I rested my hand on the desk, instead. "This isn't the Dark Ages. They won't just lock her up."

"Shit." He banged the hammer down with a jarring crash, barely missing my fingers. I snatched my hand back.

"This ruins everything," he said. "What the hell do I do now?"

"David—"

"Shut up, Leena. Okay?"

He pushed by me, across the hall, into my bedroom. I leaned against the wall next to Celeste's desk, pressed fingertips against my forehead. What had just happened? My whole body felt cold with dread.

I heard the sound of David putting his coat on, then metal jangling. He stood inside my room, near the door, where I'd hung my keys since the day Celeste gave me his room key. I assumed he was taking it back. *Please don't.*

"I understand what you're feeling," I said, moving into the hall, closer to him.

He came out of my room, hands shoved deep in the pockets of his army jacket. "No you don't. You don't love your family the way I do."

I froze. "What?"

His heavy lids narrowed his eyes into slits. His expression wasn't just anger; it was disgust. "I would die for my sister. You . . . you don't want anything to do with your family. You don't even know what *family* means."

"That's not true," I said, barely able to speak. It felt like he'd taken the hammer and driven a spike straight in my chest. "I love my family. And my . . . my friends are like family." I did. I loved my family and friends—more than anything.

"Who? Viv? Abby? I don't think so. And not me and Celeste, obviously. Unless you show your love through betrayal."

Along with the throbbing pain in my ribs, a fire burned in my head, and coldness penetrated the rest of my body. Anger now. The voice echoed inside my skull. Cubby's voice. The closet's voice. *Tell him,* she said. *Tell him, Leena.*

"What about you?" I said. "You and Celeste are so bonded it's creepy." *Tell him.* "I wouldn't be surprised if you're the one who's been hurting her."

The words sucked the air out of the hallway.

David and I stared at each other. His lips parted, jaw

slack. As shocked as I was that those words had come out of my mouth.

"You think I would hurt Celeste?" he said.

Did I?

Of course you do.

I shook my head to clear her words out. "No. I don't know. I know it wasn't some . . . some ghost."

"How could you be so close to me, and think I would do that?" he said.

"I didn't. I don't." My brain was spinning. Had I ever really thought that? I'd had my suspicions, but did I really believe he was capable of that? "I just don't understand how you can think she's not sick."

"Because she's not!" he said. "How could you be with someone you think might be abusing his sister? God, Leena."

"I don't think that. Really. I shouldn't have said that. I don't know why I did." I wrapped my arms around myself. I was shaking. "David, I told the dean because I'm worried about Celeste. I did it even though I knew it might mean I'd lose you. Doesn't that tell you anything? I love you, but your sister is sick."

David had started walking down the hall, toward the common room. He paused and turned his head slightly, so I was looking at his profile. *Turn,* I willed him. *Meet my eyes. Let me know it will be okay.* He didn't.

"Who's the sick one here, Leena?" he said.

He didn't wait for an answer.

40

A STRANGE CALM SETTLED over the hallway once the side door banged shut behind David. Okay. Okay. It had happened. My limbs tingled on the edge of numbness. I touched my arms. I was still there. I was alive. I touched my face. Dry. I did the same body check I'd done the one time I'd been in a car accident, making sure all of my parts were in their right places. Numb, but intact.

Okay. I was okay. I stumbled into the bedroom. Only, I couldn't feel the floor under my feet.

Once I was back in the closet, physical sensations started to return. First, a sense of the mattress as it held my body, then of the clothes that dangled above and brushed against me. I curled into a fetal position, holding Cubby. As the feeling came back to my skin, though, I realized the numbness had penetrated all the way inside. Where I expected to feel the intensity of sadness, there was nothing.

The worst had happened. I'd lost David, and in a way that meant I'd never have him back. But it didn't seem real. The numbness seemed to be my body refusing to believe what had taken place. I knew this feeling—or lack of it. The moment of divine intervention before all hell breaks loose. "We've grown apart, Leena," my mother had said, the first time my world was demolished. For days I'd been fine after she'd said that. Hadn't told any of my friends, had played the part of the understanding daughter. I'd been fine until the feelings came crashing down, the day I'd emptied my parents' medicine cabinet and lined the pills up on my bed according to size and shape.

This time, I wasn't going to wait until it was too late. I found the plastic baggie of pills, reached inside, fondled the hard bits of betterness. I placed a small oval one in my mouth. Then a round one. The sadness was coming. But I could head it off. Because I knew, I knew what I'd done was right. That was what mattered. The sadness was unnecessary. A stupid, physical reaction. If David had to leave me, well, what was there to do about it?

But why did I say those things to him? Maybe it would have been okay, later.

No, it wouldn't. The words were all around me. *You'd already lost him.*

He might have forgiven me. Understood why I did it.

He never loved you. None of them did.

My family, Viv, Abby. Never loved me? Hearing those words shriveled me inside, as if all my organs were dried and cracked. "No," I protested. "They did. They do."

Another pill or two or three found their way into my mouth, down my throat, leaving a bitter trail. Didn't care what they were. Anything would help.

God, I was tired. The headache I'd had earlier grew and grew so I took something for that, as well. Enough to get rid of this one and the next one. Maybe I could wait it out. The feelings. Just stay in here until it was too late to care anymore.

Shelter. Wait out the storm.

You can. Stay with me. I held Cubby close, almost too exhausted to lift her hollow wood body. These words had nothing to do with her anymore. They were from the walls, the ceiling, the floor. Should this have surprised me? I wondered. Maybe I was just too tired to be surprised.

"I don't understand why this had to happen."

You're safe now, Leena. Admit what you've always known.

"What?" I said. "Admit what?"

Why it's all happened. Why all your pain has happened.

A wave of marrow-deep fatigue swept through me. I needed to sleep—for a week, a month, more—I couldn't imagine I could ever sleep enough.

I drifted off, who knows for how long, but woke when

a steady *beep, beep, beep* filled my ears. I forgot where I was, thought it was my alarm clock. I tried to move, to turn it off, but couldn't. Then I remembered.

Nausea swelled in my stomach. The beeping grew louder. Louder.

The fire alarm?

Had David . . . ?

I reached for the doorknob. My hand could barely stretch that high, my arm was so heavy. I was fighting against more than gravity. I finally felt the knob, turned, and pushed. Nothing. The door wouldn't move. The bolt. Had I locked it? No, I hadn't. The sickness in my gut radiated out.

I lowered my arm.

Your body won't let you leave. It knows what you need. Another pill.

Maybe that would help. Something for energy. This house always knew what I needed, from the beginning. Hadn't it? I slipped another in my mouth. My eyes shut. I lifted my arm again and tried to reach up. Too tired. The alarm blared. He wouldn't really have done that, would he? Why would he do it now? I was so confused.

Footsteps thudded nearby, shook the house.

"Leena?" A voice called from far, far away.

I tried to reach for the door. Gravity's cold nails trapped my arms on the floor. Tried again. Nothing. Now it wasn't just trying to move that was hard, it was trying to breathe. Bricks, walls tumbled on top of me. Pressed me down. Down toward the earth. Squeezing my chest.

A surge ripped through me, vomited through my listless body. The burn. The stink. I had to get out.

Out there are people who don't want you, the walls whispered. *In here is where you belong.*

Was that true? It felt true, inside my bones. My poor, tired bones. Inside my poor, sick gut. But somehow . . .

"Leena?" The door trembled, the knob wiggled back and forth. "Leena, are you in there?" The door wasn't locked; still, they couldn't open it. I knew they wouldn't be able to. Just like David hadn't been able to, that day so many weeks ago.

They don't want you. None of them. Her voice filled the space. Could they hear her, outside the door? *Look what you've let them do to you. There's nowhere for you to go.*

"That's not how it is," I said back. "Things happen. You can't stop things from happening."

Yes, you can. In here.

My arm. Would. Not. Move.

I'll protect you, she cooed. *You can't do it yourself. You're too weak. That's why you came in here. You knew it the first time you saw the house. You knew you needed it.*

"Someone's out there. Looking for me."

You've never been strong enough, she said. *If you were strong, you wouldn't have been with David. Admit it, Leena.*

I'd tried not to be with him, but it hadn't worked. That was true. And now look.

Now you know he never loved you. And you're too weak to take the pain.

"He did love me."

Weak, stupid Leena. I told you not to be with him. But you couldn't resist. You couldn't stop yourself from needing.

"No. I *chose*. I wasn't weak." Shudders rippled through me. Another surge of vomit.

It's okay, Leena. I know. I know you aren't strong enough. But I love you anyway.

"Leena?" More thumping. "Are you okay? Leena, let us know if you're in there. Please. We don't know if it's a fire drill, or what, but we have to get out. Why won't you come out?"

Admit it, she hissed. *You'll never be okay. Not out there. David was right. You're the sick one.*

"No," I whispered.

This voice—Cubby, the closet, the walls—it wasn't me. Wasn't from any place inside of me.

You're the sick one.

Thumping. "Leena, *please!*"

Nothing emerged from my mouth because someone held my tongue, pressed it back into my throat so I couldn't speak, couldn't breathe. I began to gag. I tilted my gaze to the floor, to my arms. Visualized raising them up. But I couldn't. Only one hand. One hand moved. Lifting it was like lifting the whole house. I reached up with my last bit of energy, reached up with that one hand and scratched at the door. My fingernails scraped against the wood. Once, twice.

"Did you hear that?" someone outside said.

Scratched once more. All I had in me.

I couldn't see, couldn't hear, except for the voice. *Stay with me,* she cooed, over and over. *I'm the only one who wants you.* After I reached the heaviest place, so heavy I thought my body was being obliterated, I felt a release, a lightness. Like when you've held your arms against a doorframe and then walk out and they fly up. I flew up. Up and out and high and wide and all over and circling and spreading. And no more containment. Just me, energy, spreading into wood and plaster and brick and floating in the air and filling the space. An angel after all. No more body keeping me tied down. The body was still there, I just wasn't in it.

41

SUN-STREAMS POURED IN from the arched window. Dust particles shimmered in the pathway.

"Would it sound really weird," I asked Viv, my eyes shifting away from the light, "if I told you that part of me . . . part of me didn't come back?"

"Didn't come back?" she said.

"You know, after the paramedics got to me."

Viv reloaded the nail polish brush and stroked the pearly white liquid over my left thumbnail. She'd come down to see me at my dad's condo. "Well, it kind of makes sense," she said. "I mean, we have this life-force energy, right? Who's to say that some of yours wasn't released when your body thought it was the end. Like a leak in an inflatable raft that's then patched up. Right? The air that escapes never comes back."

"Exactly," I said. "I'm not saying it's a bad thing. I just . . . I feel like I left something behind. I never would have believed that, before. I mean, it sounds so stupid. It's the kind of kooky thinking I'd have made fun of."

The springs of the sofa bed creaked as Viv shifted her weight.

"I suppose," she said, "a lot was different before."

Before.

Before, I knew so many things. About David and Celeste. About myself. About real and unreal. I built a fort out of all of these things I knew.

That day in Frost House, the fort collapsed.

Afterward, I searched back through the semester, trying to find new facts to build with. But just as I was ready to nail one down, it would disintegrate in my hands.

Information came to me slowly.

All I grasped at first was that I'd nearly died from a combination of the pills I'd taken and carbon monoxide poisoning. I spent two nights in the hospital: a blur of confusion, the stink of vomit and disinfectant, throat scraped raw, tubes running in and out of my body, fragments of sleep cut short by needles, the claustrophobia of the oxygen chamber, doctors with charts, nurses with implements, and my parents sitting next to me with looks on their faces that said, *How did this happen?* as much as they said, "We love you."

Not that I blamed them for wondering. I was wondering the same thing.

Everyone wanted an explanation. But how could I explain? So I kept most of what happened to myself, only saying enough to assure the hospital psychiatrist I wasn't suicidal and didn't need admission into the psych ward. When I took the pills, my thought process had supposedly been compromised by the carbon monoxide, so they believed I'd just been confused about how many pills I'd taken. I agreed to outpatient therapy.

To my parents' credit, they didn't push. And they tried to do what they could. At one point, I woke to my mother standing next to my bed, a tentative smile on her face, hands behind her back.

"I found something that might make you feel a bit better," she said. She laid Cubby on my pillow. "Your old friend."

"Oh." I swallowed the bile that rose in my throat as I turned my face away. "Thanks. But you can get rid of it."

Viv came for a quick visit the day after I was discharged.

"What's happened since I left?" I said. "I feel like I've been gone for years."

She told me about the chaos of that afternoon. Apparently, a crowd of students gathered outside the dorm and rumors spread across campus the minute the fire department and paramedics arrived, so many trucks that all of Highland Street was blocked off. Dean Shepherd moved them all out of Frost House—Viv and Abby to Dee Hall, Celeste to Revere Hall.

"Celeste is still at school?" I said, shocked. I hadn't dreamed that I'd told the dean about her, had I?

Viv's blank look reminded me she didn't know the whole story. I gave her a condensed version: Celeste's fear that Frost House was haunted, my meeting with the dean, David's anger and his plan to save her—

"Wait," Viv interrupted. "What did David have to do with the carbon monoxide leak?"

"He caused it," I said. "By doing something to the furnace. That was his plan to get Celeste moved out."

Viv shook her head. "That's impossible. The leak had been going on for a long time."

Now it was my turn to look blank.

"The alarm nearest your room was screwed up," she said. "It wasn't calibrated right, or whatever. So it was only when the carbon monoxide reached upstairs that an alarm went off. You guys had been breathing it for . . . well, they don't know how long. Hard to say with windows being opened, stuff like that. Didn't anyone tell you this?"

Did they? "I don't know," I said. "I just remember when they found out the carbon monoxide was from the furnace. The stuff at the hospital is kind of a big blur."

"They still don't really know if it *was* from the furnace," she said. "I don't quite get it, but there was some problem and they couldn't tell. But we all had to get tested for CO poisoning, and Celeste had to get oxygen therapy. David had nothing to do with it."

Until that moment, I'd thought David had left me in the dorm, knowing I would get sick from the carbon monoxide leak he'd caused. I hadn't thought he'd wanted me dead—he wouldn't have known that I'd shut myself up in the closet with my pills. But still . . . I'd used it as an excuse to believe I was better off without him. Better off without a guy who would ever do something like that.

But now?

Before this all happened, I think I would have forced myself to forget about it, to ignore the fact that I wanted to see him. Anything to avoid the risk of further rejection.

Now, though, I realized that reaching out to David or not reaching out—it was going to hurt either way.

I allowed myself to be a bit of a coward and send a message instead of call, so when he agreed to come visit, I couldn't sense his tone of voice.

The day he was coming, my body was so twitchy I felt like I was walking around with my finger stuck in a socket. I tried a deep-breathing technique my therapist taught me. A Valium would have worked better. I knew I shouldn't think that way—didn't want to think that way—but it was a hard habit to break.

Finally, the doorbell buzzed.

We stared at each other, awkward. His face was paler, drawn—more like his sister than ever. After a moment, I stepped forward and hugged him. My cheek pressed into the satiny puff of his down jacket. We stood like that, quiet, for a long time. I loved being this close to him, no matter what had happened.

"I'm sorry," he said. "I'm so sorry, Leena."

"Me too."

A muffled cough came from inside my dad's room. We broke apart.

"He's giving us space," I whispered. "I'll introduce you later."

David nodded. "You look good," he said, running his fingers down my hair. "Are you . . . okay?"

"Pretty much."

"So." He shoved his hands in his pockets. "Celeste is actually . . . She wanted to see you, too. She's at the coffee place, on the corner. I'm supposed to call her when she can come, if that's okay."

"Of course," I said. "Viv told me she's still at school. They let her stay?" I began leading him into the kitchen where I'd set out all our tea choices during my nervous morning.

"Yeah," he said. "Once everything came out, and they realized she was sick, you know, everyone decided she could stay. Thank God."

"Wait, so, she *is* sick?" I said, turning from the electric kettle, confused.

"From the carbon monoxide."

"Right, but . . . that's it? Nothing worse?"

"No!" he said, resting a hand on my shoulder. "I'm sorry, I thought you knew all this. It was the carbon monoxide making her sick. Haven't you read what it can do? Insomnia, delusions, weird physical sensations. Along with Celeste's imagination, and Whip's story about the house. The perfect storm, I guess."

"So, that's why she thought the house was haunted?" I asked.

"The whole thing is pretty crazy. Here we were thinking Frost House was out to get her, and, in a way, it was."

"Wow. I didn't realize she'd been affected so severely." I tried to process this information while pouring hot water into our mugs. "Choose whichever tea you want," I said, and then, after putting chamomile into my own mug, "What about the weird things that happened in our room, though? The vase, the nests . . . Carbon monoxide doesn't explain any of that."

"Probably the cat," he said with a slight shrug.

"Really?"

He stopped dunking his tea bag. "Are you still worried she did those things herself?"

"No. I'm just . . . I don't know. Confused," I said. "I haven't been able to figure any of this out. I mean, I knew that it caused my headaches and probably made me throw up, and made me tired and generally not feel well. But I don't get . . . There's a lot I don't get."

"If I didn't know better," he said, nudging me, "I'd think you were trying to convince me that there *was* something weird going on in that house."

Before, I would have been the first one to buy into David's theory. The first one to say that was what happened to me, too. That my thoughts had been altered, twisted by the unhealthy air I'd been breathing. But then I remember the pull I felt toward the closet, that very first day. And even *before* the first day we moved in, the way I felt the first time I ever saw the house, that intense *need* to live there.

And what had I seen that day last fall? What had I mistaken for smoke, as it drifted from the unusable chimney and danced into the sky?

After sending David away to the coffee shop, Celeste and I sat on my dad's balcony, even though it was cold outside. I think we both wanted as much fresh air as we could get. We sat quiet for a moment.

"So," I finally said. "This is fucked up."

Celeste looked at me and laughed, a real laugh. "Yeah," she said. "It is."

"There are still so many things I don't understand," I

said. "Can I ask you something?"

"What?"

"How did you get the bruises?"

She pulled up the fur-lined collar of her vintage coat. "I'd wake up, find them on me," she said. "And I'd have strange memories of fighting something off. It seemed like I was awake when I did it." She paused. "Who the hell knows? My shrink thinks they happened during my night terrors. That I'd thrash around so much I hurt myself."

"I saw you do that," I said. "I guess it could have happened."

"Maybe." We held eyes, though, and another conversation passed between us. One in which we agreed on the possibility that maybe she *had* been awake when she fought something off all those nights. I knew it then: Celeste was as confused as I was.

"Something else," I said. "Did you ever throw your beetle photo across the room?"

"What?" she said. "No. When did that—?"

"The same night you were burned in the tub. I didn't want to tell you."

"That burn . . ." Celeste rubbed the spot where it had been. "I know which handle I turned that night. The water coming out of the faucet was cold."

"But the faucet was hot enough to burn you?"

She nodded.

"What does your shrink say about that?"

She gave a half smile. "I'm waiting until a later session to break it to her." After a moment she continued. "You know, you were right to tell Dean Shepherd what was happening. Thanks for doing that."

I felt a rush of shame, knowing that the main reason I had done it was that I didn't want to lose Frost House. How could I have thought that I was so weak? How could I have been so convinced that Frost House was the only place I could ever be happy?

I might need a long time to answer those questions. Now, I still had more for Celeste.

"So that night at your parents'," I said, "you had a whole story, about that woman who had lived in Frost House. Didn't you wonder why she hadn't done anything before? To other students? I'm assuming we would have heard if there were other people who had trouble in the dorm."

She tightened her silver-wool-with-sequins scarf around her neck.

"I thought it was because we were the first girls to live there," she said. "It was a woman who died; she'd had a baby girl taken away from her. I thought she wasn't interested in boys." Celeste stared off at a plane in the sky. "I couldn't figure out what she wanted, aside from me leaving, though."

I didn't say anything, just watched our healthy breaths puff white in the cold air and thought about Celeste's theory, thought about my answer to her final question. And while thinking, I realized: I knew everything that had happened

391

to Celeste this semester, but she didn't know anything that had happened to me. Somehow, it didn't seem right.

Then I told her my version of the past months, including my theory of what Frost House had wanted:

She had wanted Celeste to leave. But she had wanted me to stay.

Forever.

42

I DROVE OUT TO BARCROFT this morning. Later today I have a series of meetings with my teachers and Dean Shepherd. I've fallen too far behind to finish the semester in some classes, but we're going to try and figure out if I can still get enough credits to graduate on time.

I'm also having dinner with David. I don't think either of us is sure what's going on with our relationship—things have changed, obviously. But we're taking slow steps, at least toward staying friends. Celeste and I still haven't talked to him about what might have really happened in the dorm. We will, though. It's too big a secret to keep from someone I want to be close to. I told Viv everything, and she immediately knew which possible story she wanted to believe. "I'm so sorry, Leen," she said, giving me a hug. "I should have made us listen to Orin."

When I made plans to come out here today, I was explicitly told—by my therapist, my father, the dean—to stay away from Frost House. Right. Like that was going to happen.

I parked in the gym lot and pushed my way through the bushes and tree branches, into the backyard. I didn't want to walk in off the road, in case someone happened to see me. I'd heard from Viv that the whole Frost House thing had completely overshadowed any other campus gossip. And to think, all they knew was that we'd had carbon monoxide poisoning.

I paused for a moment before going inside. The house appeared just as cozy and welcoming as the first time I saw it. Now, though, I knew what I was seeing was just the architecture, the outer shell; it didn't mean anything about the type of house it was inside. If I could see the house as it really was, it would be dark and windowless. Uninhabitable.

My heart jumped when I entered the common room. The light was dim and, at first glance, it seemed as if a tall figure stood there, waiting for me. But I quickly saw what it was. The couch had been moved into the middle of the room. The other furniture was stacked precariously on top of it—table on top of armchair. Maybe they were painting the walls again? Although I'd heard a rumor that they were talking about tearing the house down, so that didn't make sense.

I worked my way around the odd sculpture and down

the hall. I ran my hand over the plaster wall, listened to the conversation between floorboards. Celeste's door stood open. I pushed it farther with my index finger, but stayed in the hall as I looked in. Shadowy. Empty. Very empty, if that's possible.

I turned my back and crossed the hall. Bright sun filled my room, bright enough so that it obliterated the room's faults—bumpy walls, gaps in the floorboards—instead of illuminating them. The mattress had been removed from my bed. Otherwise, all the furniture was still there.

The door to the closet stood open a crack, the wood on the edge split and splintered where it had been broken when they got me out. I turned away and studied the bare tree branches outside.

The heat wasn't on in the house; a chill breeze leaked through the windowpanes. I could feel it even in my down coat. I pulled my hat over my ears and took a seat in the corner, as far out of the cold drafts as I could get without going in the closet. I spent the morning sitting there, going over the story in my mind, from start to finish. Trying again to piece together the truth of it. Knowing I probably never would have answers for some things, like a tattoo of a stained-glass window—the memory of my childhood and a house that I loved—that's now almost invisible, as if someone wanted it erased.

There is one thing I know to be true, though. No matter what voice said those horrible things to me, that last time in the closet—the voice of my own, darkest insecurities, or . . . something else—in the end, I didn't listen. I wouldn't still be here if I had.

It was almost time for my meeting with Dean Shepherd. I hadn't seen her since a short, confused visit at the hospital. I took a moment to breathe away the rush of nerves, then stood and stretched my chilled, stiff bones.

Took a last look at this beautiful room.

A breeze shivered across my face; I sensed movement. The closet door had blown open wider. I walked in slow, measured steps until I was close enough to run a fingertip along the splintered edge of the door, daring it to bite. Then, closing my eyes, I drew a deep, deep breath. The feeling flooded me. The same pull penetrated my body. It wrapped around me, strong as an undertow; it wanted me to come in. I wanted to go in. I wanted to go inside and shut the door behind me.

But I didn't.

Part of me is still there, I believe. In that way, Frost House will always be my home. But not the rest of me. I shut the closet door. And walked out.

ACKNOWLEDGMENTS

Exuberant and heartfelt thanks:

To my agent, Sara Crowe: for her enthusiasm and hard work, and for placing *Frost* in such good hands. To my editor, Kristin Daly Rens: for her insight, positivity, and patience, and for believing in me. To Sarah Hoy and Alison Donalty: for designing the most stunning cover imaginable. And to the rest of the team at Balzer + Bray: for caring about my book.

To the Vermont College of Fine Arts faculty, especially my wise, witty, and deeply admired advisors—Cynthia Leitich Smith, Brent Hartinger, Sharon Darrow, and Tim Wynne-Jones: for their generous help in building Frost House. It's a much creepier place, thanks to them, and I mean that in the best way. To the students at VCFA, especially my wonderful classmates, the Cliff-Hangers: for their friendship and loyal support. To Galen Longstreth: for her warmth and encouragement. To Jill Santopolo: for all the advice and cheerleading, and for nudging *Frost* in the right direction. And to Jandy Nelson: for making me laugh, keeping me sane, and leading the way.

To all of my amazing friends, especially those who helped me muddle through story issues while writing *Frost*—Stephanie Knowles, Signy Peck, and Samera Nasereddin. To Annie and Robert Del Principe, Julie and Chris Cummings, and Rachel, Bob (and Ava!) Prince: for making sure I have a life outside of the fictional one in my apartment. To Louise Williams: for astute critiques and invaluable guidance when I was starting out. To Sandra Gering: for being a fan of everything I've ever written, down to the last email. To Robin Spigel: for having way more faith in me than I have in myself. To Brandon Russell: for his spoons. And to the real girls of Frost House—Kate Donchi, Christina Henry De Tessan, Marlene Laro Joel, Amanda Lydon, and Christina Weaver Vest: for letting me sully the name of a place that held only good memories.

To Tim Sultan: for taking care of me in so many ways; for inspiring me to be a better writer; and for loving me even though I have two legs, not four.

To Alexandra Bageris: for listening to me read *Frost* aloud and gasping at all the right places; and for over thirty years of being my best friend and encouraging me (sometimes forcefully!) to take risks. I don't know if I'd ever have been brave enough to write a book without her standing next to me.

Finally, to my family: for raising me to be an avid reader; for being so proud, supportive, and loving; for everything.